810

D1241281

Swallowing words before
you say them is so much
better than having to
eat them afterward.

—An Amish Proverb

Sugarcreek Amish Mysteries

A Tempting
TASTE OF MYSTERY

SUGARCREEK
Amish
MYSTERIES

ELIZABETH LUDWIG

Guideposts

New York

Published by Guideposts Books & Inspirational Media
110 William Street
New York, NY 10038
Guideposts.org

Cover and interior design by Müllerhaus
Cover illustration by Bill Bruning, represented by Deborah Wolfe, LTD.
Typeset by Aptara, Inc.

Printed and bound in the United States of America
10 9 8 7 6 5 4

To Mom:
I still remember waking up to the sounds and smells of
you in the kitchen making breakfast every morning.
Thank you for loving your family so well, and
for teaching me to do the same.
I love you!

CHAPTER ONE

And finally, my dearest Cheryl, I encourage you not to forget to give thanks for the many blessings God has bestowed upon you. Though you've endured hardships in your young life, count it all joy, for it is through these very trials that God has brought you to the place you now stand. You have proven yourself a willing vessel, ready to be filled by God and poured out for His purpose. It is a lesson I have learned while serving here in Papua New Guinea. None of us are perfect or by any means qualified, but when we are willing, God promises to equip us for the task. Hold on to this, my darling, and trust in the One who loves you and who gave Himself for you.

Cheryl reread the last line slowly, her aunt Mitzi's voice a soothing whisper in her ear. God had indeed brought her through trials, but she'd never felt overwhelmed, and she'd sensed His loving presence at her side the entire time. That was true when He'd brought her from Columbus to care for Aunt Mitzi's cottage and to run the Swiss Miss, though she really hadn't been so certain at the time. It was true now, on a lazy Saturday afternoon, as she sat on an old wooden porch swing. He was with her, no matter where she wandered.

As if to echo this sentiment, a light breeze ruffled a corner of Aunt Mitzi's letter then swirled up to tickle Cheryl's neck and farther up to stir the leaves in the trees above her head.

Truly, she had much to be thankful for.

Her lips parted in a sigh as Cheryl folded back the flap on the envelope and replaced the letter inside. It amazed Cheryl how her aunt Mitzi's letters always seemed to arrive at just the proper moment, but words on a page couldn't replace the weathered lines of a loved one's face.

"That is a heavy sigh I hear. Is everything all right?"

The sound of Levi's voice instantly made her smile. Cheryl tipped her head back, her heart doing a happy pitter-patter at the sight of his grin and sparkling blue eyes beneath the wide brim of his hat.

He reached for the back of her swing and gave it a gentle push.

"I'm better now," she whispered, just loud enough for him to hear. "I didn't know you were planning to stop by."

He leaned forward and lowered his voice. "I had not intended to, but then I could not stop thinking about you. I figured my time would be better served spending a few minutes with you than being distracted by thoughts of you all day."

The tender look he gave filled her heart near to bursting. How was it possible that this man—so different from any she'd known—turned out to be the one God intended for her to marry? She closed her eyes and lingered in the motion of the swing, the sweet warmth of her future husband's love, and . . .

Cheryl jerked upright, nearly upending herself and Levi when he reached out both arms to catch her.

"Cheryl, what on earth…?"

"I'm so s-sorry," she stammered in the same moment. She reached her feet to the porch and dragged the swing to a stop. "It's just…all of a sudden…"

Heat flooded her cheeks. How exactly did one explain to her fiancé that the thought of becoming his wife suddenly inspired both exhilaration *and* terror?

She sank back into the swing and let her feet dangle just above the painted gray slats of her porch. "We still haven't come to a decision about how we're going to tell your parents about our engagement. It doesn't feel right keeping it from them, Levi. It's just…" Her grip on the chains tightened, the links biting into her palms. "I'm so worried about how they will react once they learn that you will be leaving the church."

Levi ran his hands down the chains of the swing and covered hers, squeezing briefly before he circled to stand in front of her. "We will find a way, *ja*? When the time is right, *Gott* will give us the words to speak. We must believe this."

Cheryl ducked her head. Levi was a godly man, and she trusted him to lead, but the thought of hurting Naomi and Seth filled her with dread.

He tucked his finger under her chin and lifted her face. "We will seek counsel on the best way to approach them. Do not worry, Cheryl."

"Counsel? From who?"

"Your Pastor Lory is a kind man, *ain't so?* And full of wisdom. Perhaps it would be wise if we sat down with him. I can make time next week."

Peace and contentment nudged out the unease rolling in Cheryl's stomach. Life hadn't exactly been easy since moving to Sugarcreek, but she was learning to trust God through the challenges. And now He was giving her a husband to walk alongside her through life, one who would encourage her to seek Him and draw her closer to God. What greater blessing could one receive?

Levi's blue eyes darkened. His hand lingered against her cheek for one brief moment before he sat down next to her. Cheryl's breath caught. For now, their wedding plans remained between the two of them, but soon everyone would know…and possibly sooner than either of them wanted.

She scanned the street outside her aunt Mitzi's cottage. People were busy tending to business—sweeping the sidewalks, pruning flowers, washing windows—but that didn't mean they couldn't spy them out with one quick glance.

Her fidgeting pushed the swing into motion. "Are you sure you should sit here beside me? What if word gets back to Naomi?"

Levi gave a low chuckle. "Then our task of telling her would be made much easier."

"Levi Miller," she scolded playfully and jabbed him lightly in the ribs with her elbow.

He chuckled again and then pushed up from the swing. "Fine, but soon enough I will not be content to admire my future *fraa* from across the room." Her heart thumped as he bent closer. "After all, even the young ones have the Singings during which to do their courting."

His smile faded, and his gaze locked on hers. "I will court you as you deserve, Cheryl Cooper," he said, his voice low.

Cheryl froze, afraid to move lest she break the wonder of the moment. "Levi..."

The skin on the back of her neck prickled, and a feeling of being watched swept over her. Drawing back, she scoured the street once more.

Levi seemed to sense her discomfort. He straightened, and his gaze followed hers. "What is it?"

"Nothing, I guess." After a moment, Cheryl shook her head. "I just thought...for a second I thought...it felt like someone was watching us."

She stood and wiped the dust from her jeans. "I'm sure it's nothing."

His eyes twinkled with humor, stealing her breath in a different way. Oh, but she could hardly wait to get to know everything about this man!

Levi gestured toward the sidewalk. "Join me for an ice cream?"

Cheryl stifled a groan. After two weeks of walking and dieting, she'd finally managed to shed a few pounds and wasn't at all anxious to pack it back on with an ill-advised splurge of chocolate and caramel. "No ice cream, but I'll gladly sip on a Diet Coke while you enjoy some."

"Deal." He pushed open the gate and let Cheryl pass through then walked alongside her toward Yoder's Corner. "Did I tell you that Ranger seems to be doing better?"

"You mentioned it." Happiness stirred her heart. "I think it's safe to say he's over his abduction." Ranger had been stolen not long ago. Thankfully he was returned unharmed, but he had been a bit skittish for a while.

Levi nodded and pushed his hands into his pockets. "It truly is amazing to see how well he gets on with Methuselah and Obadiah. I expected him to be anxious around such big workhorses, but ever since we started corralling them together, he seems to have settled down. It just goes to prove that with enough time and patience, any animal can be acclimated to a new environment."

Cheryl shielded her eyes against the bright sun reflecting on the sidewalk. "That's good news. I need to get out to the farm and spend some more time with him soon."

"I agree," Levi said, but the gleam in his eye made her think he wasn't referring to Ranger.

They reached Yoder's, the conditioned air inside a welcome relief from the outdoor heat. Levi led her to a quiet table away from the noise and bustle of the kitchen. As promised, Cheryl ordered a diet soda while Levi devoured a chocolate sundae.

"It really isn't fair, you know." Cheryl grimaced as she gazed at his tanned arms, broad shoulders, and trim waist.

Levi wiped a spot of chocolate off his chin. "What is not?"

She shoved her soda aside and gestured to the ice cream. "If I ate even half that, I'd blow up like a balloon."

He pushed his empty bowl away and patted his flat stomach. "Come help me in the fields. You will work it off in no time."

She shrugged. "No thanks. I'll stick to my exercise bike."

"*Hmm.*" He feigned a disappointed grimace. "That is too bad. I think I would enjoy working alongside you."

"Maybe...until I spooked the horses or upended a wagon or..." She waited, but Levi's grin only got bigger. She grabbed a menu from a bracket on the edge of the table and slapped him on the arm. "You could at least pretend to disagree."

Honestly, she couldn't be angry. Her occasional lack of grace was a well-known fact. She replaced the menu and laced her fingers on the tabletop. "Anyway...tell me about Caleb. How are things going between him and Alice?"

Like so many other people his age, Levi's younger brother had taken more than a casual interest in seeking a wife. He and Alice Plank were dating, but neither appeared ready to move toward the more meaningful courtship stage.

Levi frowned and propped both elbows on the table. "That Caleb...a steel trap is easier to get things out of than my brother."

He went on, but Cheryl was once again distracted by the feeling of being watched. Her gaze swept the restaurant. At the counter, August Yoder was in deep conversation with Jacob Hoffman, who ran Hoffman's Furniture. Neither of them paid her any attention. There were also several couples seated at the tables scattered about the restaurant, but none of them appeared interested in her and Levi. Near the window, she caught the eye of an older gentleman over a copy of the *Budget*, a local Amish newspaper. He gave a polite nod and went back to reading.

Cheryl blew out a confused sigh. So if no one in the restaurant was watching them, why couldn't she shake the uneasy feeling settling between her shoulders?

The answer was eerily obvious. Whoever watched them *wanted* to remain out of sight. The only remaining question was...why?

CHAPTER TWO

The question of how she and Levi would break the news of their engagement with Seth and Naomi was still on Cheryl's mind the following Sunday morning as she drove to church. In fact, she'd felt so guilt-ridden over keeping a secret from her friend that she'd taken to avoiding Naomi when she came into the Swiss Miss. She and Levi would have to settle on a course of action soon. She missed her friend, and it was obvious by her concerned frown that Naomi knew something was up.

All through Sunday school and the beginning of the worship service, Cheryl fought to keep her distracted mind from wandering to her problems. If Seth and Naomi could not be convinced to support her marriage to Levi...

She shuddered and clipped the thought short before it could take root. Levi was the man God intended for her, of that much she was certain. And as he'd said, the words they needed to convince Seth and Naomi of such would come. She just had to trust God to provide.

"...and we're trusting God to provide during this very difficult time."

Startled by the words, Cheryl sat up straight and focused her attention on what Pastor Lory was saying.

He held up a sheet of colored paper. "Inside your bulletin is a copy of the things the family has requested. Right now they are in desperate need of shoes and clothing, since almost everything they owned was lost in the fire. If you have some things you can donate, please talk to me immediately following the service, and I will be happy to provide you with a list of sizes."

He paused and slid the paper back inside his bulletin.

"Anyone else wishing to contribute can pick up a list of donation sites on the table outside the office. Or, if you'd rather make a cash donation, please place it in the envelopes located in the pew racks in front of you and mark it Carmichael Family. We'll gather all the donations together Monday afternoon and take it all to the family later in the week."

Brad, the youth ministry leader, held up his hand, and Pastor Lory acknowledged him with a wave. "Yes, Brad?"

"Do we know where the family is living? Are they in need of a place to stay?"

The pastor shook his head. "At the moment, the family is living in an RV they borrowed from the Willets." He gave a nod to an elderly couple who were known to travel south in the winter. "Thank you, Andrew and Harriet, for the use of that vehicle."

The couple nodded humbly.

"Of course, this is only a temporary residence until the family can figure out what to do about their home." Pastor Lory paused to pull off his glasses and lay them on the lectern. "I've spoken with the Carmichaels, and they have given me permission to share this next request with you. As many of you are already aware, Mr. Carmichael was laid off last month. What you don't know is that the family was forced to let their homeowners insurance lapse."

There was a collective gasp of dismay at the news.

Pastor Lory held up his hand. "Several people have already come to me to volunteer their time helping with the rebuilding. I have also told the family that I will put them in contact with some local ministry organizations who can help with the rebuilding effort. Unfortunately, while this will take care of the labor, I'm pretty certain the biggest challenge will be covering the cost of the building materials. We will take up a collection at the end of the service, but I do ask that you consider what else we might do to help this family during this very difficult time. I welcome any and all of your suggestions."

Finished, he turned to the music minister and signaled for him to take over. Afterward, Pastor Lory moved smoothly into his sermon, a message that fittingly focused on sacrificial love for others. Cheryl felt her heart pricked as she listened, and she pondered the message all the way home.

The next day, Cheryl found the Carmichaels' dilemma still weighed heavily on her heart while she moved through the chores at the Swiss Miss. As lunchtime neared, she wondered what the family was doing for food. Maybe she could run by the grocery store after work and pick up a few essentials. It saddened her to think of the additional grief and stress the family was experiencing on top of the worry from Mr. Carmichael's lack of a job. She mentally ran through the business owners she knew and vowed to speak with them—see if any of them were in need of full-time help. Then she would make a list she could present to Mr. Carmichael.

"*Guder mariye,* Cheryl."

Naomi watched her from a spot next to the store counter. On her arm was a basket covered with a plain white cloth. She offered it with a smile. "Have you eaten yet? I brought lunch. If you are not too busy, I thought we could sit down together for a nice little chat."

A blush heated Cheryl's cheeks as she straightened. "That was so thoughtful, Naomi. Thank you so much. I would love to have lunch with you."

A relieved look crossed her face, and Cheryl was instantly saddened to think she may have caused Naomi to doubt their friendship. Why, oh, why hadn't God provided an answer for the dilemma she and Levi were facing with his parents?

Forcing a bright smile, Cheryl bent to take a whiff of the food inside the basket. Savory basil and a hint of rosemary tickled her nose. She straightened and sighed in appreciation. "Oh my goodness…is that your pot roast I smell?"

Naomi's eyes twinkled merrily. "It is. I know it is one of your favorites."

"You are so sweet. Go ahead and head on back to my office." She motioned toward one of the coolers. "I'll grab us something to drink. Do you have a preference?"

Naomi nodded and slipped the basket back on to her arm. "A bottled lemonade for me, please."

"Lemonade, coming up."

Cheryl crossed to the cooler, opened the door, and paused to let the blast of cool air waft over her face. Surely Naomi intended to ask what was bothering her. What would she say? Reaching into the cooler, she whispered a fragile prayer for wisdom.

The bottled drinks in hand, she stopped to let Esther know that she was breaking for lunch and then slipped into her office. Naomi already had the basket unpacked and was smoothing the edges of the napkins she'd set next to their plates. Cheryl set one of the bottles next to her and carried the other with her as she circled the desk and sat.

"I'm so glad you stopped by," Cheryl said before Naomi could speak. She twisted the cap off her lemonade and took a small sip. "How is everything at the farm?"

She shrugged as she reached into the basket for forks. "The farm is *goot*. The crops are coming in nicely, and Seth thinks we will have a plentiful harvest thanks to the generous rain this past spring."

"That's wonderful news."

They paused to ask a silent blessing over the food. When they finished, Cheryl picked up her fork and took a bite, sighing with pleasure as the comforting taste of Naomi's pot roast slid over her tongue.

"One of these days you're going to have to teach me your secret. No matter what I try, my pot roast always turns out dry."

Naomi laughed and then took a sip of her lemonade. "*Ach*, it is goot to see you, Cheryl. I have missed our talks."

Cheryl could honestly say the same. She dropped her gaze and murmured her agreement but did not add more for fear of letting something slip.

"Things have been busy at the store?"

Now the pot roast felt like a lump in her throat. Cheryl swallowed with difficulty and took a sip of her lemonade.

"Things *have* been busy but...to be honest, I've just had a lot on my mind."

To her surprise, Naomi didn't ask what. Her smile spoke understanding as she handed Cheryl a slice of homemade bread. "Did I tell you that Sarah will be coming to visit soon? I think she has news she wishes to share face-to-face."

"That's rather unexpected, isn't it?" Cheryl paused with her fork halfway to her mouth. Seth and his oldest daughter had finally reconciled after months of misunderstanding and hurt, but she was surprised by how easily and often she communicated with the family now. "It's good news, I hope."

Enthusiasm lit Naomi's eyes. "I think so. She sounded very happy, which is a very welcome change after so many troubles."

"That's wonderful, Naomi. So I take it the problems between Sarah and her husband have all been worked out?"

She nodded cheerfully as she wiped her mouth with a napkin. "I cannot tell you how glad I am to hear that things are finally better between them." She paused and tilted her head, thinking. "I heard a saying once that a mother is only as happy as her unhappiest child. It is true, Cheryl."

Naomi's gaze returned to Cheryl, and a wave of warmth and affection washed over her at the look on her friend's face. Naomi loved all her children—biological and step—with complete and unselfish abandon. She prayed tirelessly for each of them, and it was inspiring to Cheryl to witness how willingly she welcomed Sarah into her home and her heart.

She gave Naomi's fingers a squeeze. "Let me know what she says."

"Of course."

For the next thirty minutes, she and Naomi chatted about everything and nothing so that by the time they'd finished with their lunch and cleaned up the dishes, Cheryl felt silly for ever having avoided her. Levi was right; God would provide the means and opportunity for talking openly about their plans. Until then, Naomi would be too tactful to impose on their friendship, even if she sensed there was something Cheryl wasn't telling her.

She pressed one last grateful touch to Naomi's shoulder as they rejoined Esther in the store. Business had picked up with the arrival of one of the tour buses, so she thanked Naomi again for lunch before hurrying over to assist a woman reaching for items on an uppermost shelf. When she finished with that customer, she busied herself restocking until a prickling at the back of her neck warned her that she was once again being watched.

Cheryl paused with an apron in her hand and looked around. Near the checkerboard at the front window stood two women, one younger with an earnest look about her, the other older and quite attractive. Both looked away when she spied them watching and bent their heads close enough to whisper.

Were these the same women who had been watching her earlier? Why? Neither of them looked familiar.

Cheryl set the apron neatly on a stack and crossed to join them. "Good afternoon, ladies. Welcome to the Swiss Miss. Is there something I can help you find?"

The women shook their heads, and then the younger gave her companion a nudge. "Go ahead and ask her."

Cheryl smiled encouragingly while the older woman fidgeted with the buttons on her expensive jacket. She was obviously trying to muster the courage to speak her mind. Cheryl crossed her arms and waited.

Finally the woman smoothed a lock of blonde hair behind her ear and then gestured to her head, as if pointing to a prayer *kapp*. "It's just... we saw you talking to that Amish woman."

Cheryl thought for a second. "You mean, Naomi?"

"Is that her name?" The younger woman cast a glance toward the cash register, where Esther was assisting another customer. "And you have an Amish girl working for you."

"Yes, that's Naomi's daughter." Made a bit apprehensive by their questioning, Cheryl frowned uneasily. "Is something wrong?"

"No, no... not at all. It's just..." The older woman shot a glance at her companion, who spoke up, her eyes flashing with excitement.

"We were just wondering if maybe you could tell us a little about them."

"Or possibly introduce us to them," the older woman added.

"You see, we've always been so curious about the Amish people," the younger one continued. "I'm always online learning what I can about them."

"Their lifestyle is just so fascinating."

"And their beliefs are so down-to-earth."

"Traditional."

She put her hand on her friend's arm. "Right, traditional. Like things used to be."

"Exactly."

Both turned their gazes back to Cheryl.

"Which is why we wanted to come to Sugarcreek in the first place."

"To see what it would be like to live like the Amish."

By now Cheryl had begun to feel a little dizzy by the conversation bouncing back and forth between the two women. She sucked in a breath as the younger woman suddenly stopped, her hands braced firmly on her hips.

"So will you? Introduce us, I mean?"

"Um…" Struck by inspiration, Cheryl pointed toward a display next to the counter. "Have you checked out our book display? Many of them are written by actual Amish authors and deal specifically with questions about their lifestyle, dress, manner of worship, and so on. I really think you'll find some of them very interesting, and they are all very reasonably priced."

"*Ohh*," they exclaimed at once and hurried over together to examine the books.

Thankfully, it was also nearing quitting time for Esther. While she got ready to go, Cheryl kept the women occupied showing them every kind of handcrafted Amish product in her store. They were disappointed when they realized that Esther had left for the day, but they were delighted with their finds and left the Swiss Miss with their arms full of purchases. Cheryl was glad when the door closed behind them, and the peace inside the store was restored.

A short time later, Levi arrived. Though it was only June, the sun had already begun streaking his blond hair, adding golden highlights that looked especially striking against his blue eyes. He had his sleeves rolled to his elbows, and his arms looked muscled and tanned. No telling what the two women from earlier would have made of *him*.

Her heart fluttered as she rounded the counter to meet him. "Well, hello there."

"Hi."

It was only one word, but the look that accompanied it made her want to melt into her shoes.

He held his wide-brim hat in his hands and graced her with a gentle smile. "Are you hungry? I thought maybe I'd help you close up the store and then take you to dinner."

Cheryl threw a quick glance around the nearly empty store. "I would love that. Can you wait a few minutes?"

The ringing of the small metal bell above the door interrupted him before he could reply. Cheryl stifled a frustrated growl. "Sorry. I'll be right back."

"No hurry. I will wait as long as it takes."

Sensing his deeper meaning, Cheryl felt her mood brighten. She turned to help her customer with a smile on her lips. To her surprise, it was Pastor Lory who browsed the aisles. His wife often frequented the store, but she couldn't remember the last he'd been in, and never alone.

Levi's suggestion that they seek his counsel played through her thoughts as she approached him curiously. "Pastor Lory?"

He set down the bundle of kitchen towels he'd been examining and smiled. "Hello, Cheryl."

She motioned toward the towels. "Can I help you find something?"

He shook his head. "Actually, I was hoping to speak with you, but I saw you were busy." He gestured toward Levi. "I can come back if this isn't a good time."

Cheryl shot a glance at Levi and then ran her hand through her spiky hair. "No... right now is fine. Would you like to come back to my office?"

He shrugged and slid one hand into the pocket of his blue jeans. "There's really no need, and I promise this won't take long."

"Okay." Cheryl motioned for him to continue.

"You heard about the troubles the Carmichael family is facing?"

"Yes, I did. You spoke about their situation from the pulpit on Sunday."

He nodded. "Well, unfortunately, I haven't been able to secure as much help for the family as I'd like, and I was wondering if you might have a few connections we could try. You've been pretty involved with the community lately—the Swiss Festival and such—and I thought you might be able to share a few ideas."

Instantly, Cheryl's mind began whirling with possibilities. "I could probably think of a few things."

"That's wonderful." He raised his eyebrows hopefully. "Any chance I could get you to stop by the church office later this week so we can talk?"

"Of course," she said quickly. "I would be glad to do that."

"Great. Thank you so much, Cheryl."

The creases along his forehead softened, and the lines around his mouth eased. Pastor Lory wasn't an old man, but she tended to forget that when she looked at his stooped shoulders and graying hair. Suddenly, Cheryl got a glimpse of the burden he carried, not only for his own congregation, but for their entire community.

"I'll start working on putting a list together of people who might be willing to help," she said gently. "Let's see...tomorrow is Tuesday. Would late afternoon work for you, say around five fifteen? That will give me time to close up the store."

His eyes widened in surprise. "Really? So soon? I didn't expect..."

She shook her head. "It's no trouble, Pastor."

"Well then...tomorrow would be perfect. Thank you so much, Cheryl. I'll see you then."

He gave her one last smile before he left. Cheryl quickly finished closing up the store, but even with the promise of a shared meal with Levi, her heart was heavy.

What were the Carmichaels doing while she was out enjoying herself? And why didn't she share the same concern for their welfare as Pastor Lory?

She locked the door and then stepped out on to the sidewalk where Levi was waiting. Suddenly she felt a little guilty for having spent so much time fretting over what she would say to Seth and Naomi. She had a job she loved and a home to go to. She had good friends and a bed to sleep in at night. When compared to the Carmichaels, her problems seemed very small indeed.

"Was that Pastor Lory I saw you talking to?"

Cheryl startled from her reverie. Levi was looking at her curiously, a small smile on his lips. She nodded. "Yes it was. He asked about meeting with me to talk about the situation with the Carmichaels. He thought I might have some ideas for ways we can help."

"And do you?"

She shrugged and motioned toward Yoder's Corner. "Do you want to go there for supper, or would you rather head to my house so we can pick up the car?"

To her surprise, he didn't answer immediately but stood eyeing her inquisitively.

Her hand rose to her mouth. "What? Do I have something in my teeth?"

A low chuckle rose from his throat. "Not at all. I was just thinking...you now call it *your* house instead of your aunt Mitzi's."

She stopped to think. The cottage had long seemed hers in her thoughts, but perhaps she had not voiced it.

The look on his face changed, became more earnest. "You will have a hard time giving it up when we are wed?"

"Well I . . . I guess I haven't really considered it," she said. "In all honesty, I haven't thought much about how it would feel to leave the cottage."

The answer seemed to satisfy him. He turned and swung toward the cottage.

"So no Yoder's tonight?"

He shook his head. "I was thinking more along the lines of the Dutch Valley restaurant."

Cheryl's mouth instantly began to water. She patted her waistline. "You sure know the way to this girl's heart!"

Another thought occurred to her as they covered the short distance to the cottage. Perhaps she could purchase a few gift cards for the Carmichaels while she was there. It wouldn't be much, but it would give them a night away from their troubles. And anyway, it was a start. Maybe she'd have a stroke of inspiration and more ideas would come once she'd had time to think. At least . . . she hoped so.

Chapter Three

The door to Friendship Mennonite Church opened with a whoosh. Cheryl stepped out of the bright summer sun into the cool, carpeted interior. Pulling off her sunglasses, she slipped them into her purse and then walked down the hallway toward the church offices. Kelly, the church secretary, greeted her with a pleasant smile.

"Hi, Cheryl. Pastor Lory is expecting you."

"Hi, Kelly." Cheryl glanced at her watch. "You're here late, huh?"

Kelly shrugged and pushed up from behind a large oak desk. "Just following up on a few contacts who might be able to help with the Carmichaels." She put her hand on the door to a mini refrigerator. "Can I get you something to drink before you go in? I keep bottled waters and canned drinks in here."

Cheryl shook her head. "No, thank you."

Retaking her seat, she waved toward the office adjoining hers. "Go on in then. Like I said, he's expecting you."

"Great. Thank you, Kelly."

Cheryl crossed to a glass door with Pastor Lory's name fixed to it. He saw her before she knocked and waved her in.

"Cheryl, thank you so much for coming. I can't tell you what a relief it will be to have your input." He stood and shook her hand before inviting her to sit in one of the chairs opposite his desk.

"It's my pleasure." Cheryl set her purse down and made herself comfortable. "I haven't been able to get the Carmichaels out of my mind since last Sunday, so I'm glad to do anything I can to help. Oh, and before I forget…"

She took several gift cards out of her purse and slid them across the desk to Pastor Lory. One was for dinner at the Dutch Valley restaurant, and the other two were for the local cinema. "They're for the Carmichaels. I realize it's not much, but I thought maybe a night out would do the family some good."

Pastor Lory's eyes shone. "I appreciate this, Cheryl. Truly. I'll get them to the family tomorrow." He laid the cards in his desk drawer and then opened a dark blue folder and removed a sheet of paper with several names typed on the front. "This is a list of businesses who have agreed to help. Some of them have offered to donate food and clothing, and I've got a lead on some appliances and used furniture, but of course, none of that does the family any good until we can do something about getting their house rebuilt."

Cheryl nodded and perused the list silently. "This looks really good. You've been busy."

He gave a self-conscious shrug, as though it made him uncomfortable to hear himself praised. "Kelly has been a big help tracking down leads. The problem is, as much as I appreciate the information we've been able to gather so far, it's not really what the family needs."

She grimaced and folded her hands in her lap. "Money?"

He gave a curt nod. "And building supplies. Now, workers I think we can get."

"We've got a lot of talented men in the church."

He nodded and pulled out a church directory. A number of pages had been tabbed and names circled. "Several of them have said they can get friends to help once the materials are lined up. I even have a contractor who has agreed to head up the project and an architect who will draw up the plans as soon as we are ready."

Cheryl drew in a deep breath and handed back the list. "But therein lies our problem. Without the money to purchase the materials, we're pretty much at a standstill."

He laid the list on his desk and sank back in his chair. "Exactly."

She rubbed her hands against the arms of her chair and frowned. "Well, I can honestly say this is one time I wish I still lived in Columbus."

Pastor Lory's eyebrows rose, and Cheryl realized how her words had sounded. She shook her head and held up her hand. "I only mean that there were so many ministerial organizations there to help in situations like this one—not that I would ever want to move back."

They both laughed, and then he gave a grudging nod.

"I have to agree with you there, I'm afraid. While I'm grateful for our close-knit community, we are somewhat limited in what we can do in situations like this one." He grabbed a pencil and began tapping the end against his desktop. "There just aren't the organizations in Sugarcreek like what you would find in a larger city. I could contact some old friends from my seminary days, I suppose. An old buddy of mine pastors a large church in Cleveland and another friend..."

Cheryl sat forward as a seed of an idea sprouted. "Hold on a minute, Pastor. I like the idea of contacting your friends, but...what if we reached out to other churches right here in Sugarcreek?"

He stopped tapping, and his brows drew together in consternation. "You mean...like an alliance?"

She blinked. "A charitable alliance...I like it!"

"I do too, but..." A bit of the excitement on his face faded. "How would that work?"

She scooted to the edge of her chair and crossed her legs at her ankles. "We'd need someone in charge of coordinating the effort, for sure. And that person would need to contact all the area churches to see who was interested in participating."

Pastor Lory held up his hand. "All this sounds like a great idea, Cheryl, and I don't mean to throw a damper over it, but..."

Her enthusiasm gusted out of her in a whoosh. "You're not sure how any of it will help the Carmichaels with their most urgent needs?"

He shook his head. "Not really. Not in the short-term."

"Well..." She pinched her lip, thinking of ways to help that would be more immediate. "What if we held some kind of fund-raiser?"

He grabbed a notepad and flipped open to the first page. "All right, so what are you thinking? Like a car wash...or maybe a meal?"

"Among other things." Cheryl drummed the arm of her chair then snapped her fingers as an idea struck. "I've got it!"

From the corner of her eye, she saw Kelly lean around her desk to peer at them through the glass door. Cheryl laughed and lowered her voice.

"Okay, so if there's one thing I've learned since coming to Sugarcreek, it's that people love to cook. They're really proud of their homemade jams, cheese, and...pies." Too excited to sit still, she stood and began pacing. "What if we held a combination bake-off-slash-fund-raiser? I'm thinking like a carnival kind of thing, with the main attraction being a pie contest."

Pastor Lory dropped his pencil with a clatter and rose to pace with her. "I like it. I can get with Brad. He's always raising money for the youth. I'm sure he'll have some ideas for activities we can put together quickly."

Cheryl stopped pacing to point at the bulletin board in the hall outside his office. Visible through the glass door was a poster announcing their upcoming VBS, a flyer with the details for the Women's Ministry Tea, and a cupcake decorating class a lady from a local bakery was hosting.

"And if we create some flyers, I'm sure we'll be able to pique enough interest for a pie contest," Cheryl said. "We can start by charging an entry fee."

"And auction off the pies afterward," Pastor Lory said, his words coming faster as his enthusiasm for her idea grew. "Maybe even get the entrants to donate a few extra pies."

"I'll get some of the local businesses to help us advertise," Cheryl said. "I'm sure most of them will be glad to display posters and such."

His smile broadened, and he rounded the desk to pat her on the shoulder. "I love this idea. Thank you so much, Cheryl. I just knew you'd be the person to ask about putting something together."

"Really?" She stood straighter, filled with happiness and a tiny bit of pride at his confidence in her. "Thank you, Pastor. I'm just glad to be of help." She reached down to grab her purse and slid the strap over her shoulder. "I'll get right to work putting together the details. We'll meet again soon?"

He nodded. "Okay. And in the meantime I'll call Brad so we can create a list of fund-raisers we can do in conjunction with the pie contest. We've got plenty of games and stuff in storage. Won't cost us a thing, so any money we make will go directly to the Carmichaels."

"Sounds good." Struck by another idea, Cheryl stopped at the door. "You know what? While I'm asking around town about putting up the posters, I think I'll see about collecting a few items for a silent auction."

Smiling widely, Pastor Lory shook his finger at her. "You are a godsend, Cheryl Cooper. Thank you so much for your willingness to help."

His praise ringing in her ears, Cheryl fairly skipped to her car. Helping others really did feel good, especially when the people were members of their community.

"Thank you, Lord, for allowing me to be a part of helping this family," she said, buckling herself into her car and starting the engine. She could hardly wait to tell Levi what she and Pastor Lory had planned. But first...

She smiled as she pulled on to the road and turned in the direction of the Millers' farm. First, she intended to talk to Naomi and most likely sign her up to be the pie contest's very first contestant.

CHAPTER FOUR

Cheryl looked around at the people gathered inside the Swiss Miss. She'd spent the afternoon pushing tables against the walls and clearing space for chairs. Even so, a number of people stood gathered in small clusters near the windows and the cash register. She smiled, proud of the number of pastors, community members, and business owners who had shown up at the first meeting of the newly formed Sugarcreek Charitable Alliance. Along with these, she was pleased to see several Amish members of the community in attendance, since many of them operated businesses in town as well. She held up her hand, encouraging everyone to silence so she could open the meeting.

"Good evening, everyone."

When the excited chatter still had not quieted, she cleared her throat and tried again, a little louder.

"Good evening, everyone. I'm so happy to see you all tonight. Thank you so much for coming."

Gradually, the crowd's attention turned to Cheryl. Beginning with Pastor Lory, she introduced the ministerial staff present and then invited each one to tell a little about themselves and their church. While they spoke, Cheryl spotted Naomi and Levi sliding into seats near the back of the store. Levi craned his neck to see around those who'd chosen to stand, and Cheryl knew he was hoping for a glimpse of her. She flashed a quick smile.

On their heels, Doris and Rex Carmichael entered. Both looked haggard but hopeful as they leaned into each other while they looked for a chair. Cheryl offered them a shy smile and pointed to some seats in the corner before turning her attention to Pastor Lory. As they had discussed at their follow-up meeting, she invited him to state the reasons for establishing the alliance, as well as address the needs of the Carmichael family.

Pastor Lory stood. He was well liked by the community and respected by the other pastors present. Cheryl saw many heads bobbing while he explained the need for an alliance. She took notes as he went on to clarify why they'd chosen to meet at a business rather than one of the local churches. Most people understood the desire to establish the alliance as a cooperative effort—one that belonged to the community instead of any one church or denomination, while another suggested they move future meetings to the community center or Village Hall. Hearing this, Mayor Weller, who had shown enthusiastic support when Cheryl spoke to him regarding the alliance, agreed to look into reserving a meeting room. He promised to get back with Cheryl with a date.

Finished with the business of introductions and explanations, Pastor Lory moved on to the Carmichaels' situation. He read through a lengthy list of needs then directed a glance toward the back of the room. "Doris? Rex? Is there anything you'd like to add or that I forgot to mention?"

The Carmichaels looked at each other and then back at him and shook their heads.

"I think you've covered everything, Pastor," Rex Carmichael said. "But I would like to add that we are very grateful for the support our community has shown." He took his wife's hand. "It means a great deal to us both. Thank you all."

There was quiet murmuring across the room when he finished, and several people reached out to pat Rex on the shoulder or to wrap Doris in a hug. Cheryl felt her eyes well with tears as she watched.

Pastor Lory folded the list in half and laid it alongside his phone on the table. "As you can see," he concluded, "the family's circumstances are quite dire, which is why we are thinking of coordinating some kind of fund-raiser to kick off the work of the Sugarcreek Charitable Alliance."

Questions followed, most of which Cheryl answered. She went into some detail with the pie contest and was pleasantly surprised by the amount of excitement her ideas generated.

August Yoder raised his hand. "Who will we get to judge the contest?"

"Are you volunteering?" Cheryl teased.

Laughter followed, which increased when August blushed and muttered, "I would be glad to, except I think my wife might be better qualified. She is the baker in our family." He straightened and pointed a finger at her. "But you, on the other hand, Miss Cooper, would make a fine judge."

"Me? Oh, I don't think…"

"I think that's a wonderful idea," Gail Murray interrupted. She cleared her throat self-consciously when attention swung toward her. "Sorry, Cheryl. I wasn't trying to volunteer you or anybody else for that matter. What I meant is we should get all the restaurant owners and vendors who sell food to judge." She turned to scout out Kathy Kimble, the owner of the Honey Bee Café. "I just think that you really would be the most qualified, wouldn't you agree?"

There was general assent as several people echoed Gail's opinion.

She raised her hand. "And I'm not trying to get out of helping. The rest of us could pitch in with the legwork...like making the posters and stuff, or helping with the registration."

"I can make the posters." Heads turned in the direction of Roxanna Velandria, owner of the local art gallery, Artistic License, who piped up from one side of the room. "We have all the supplies at the art studio, and designing them would be fun."

"And I will be glad to help distribute them," Jacob Hoffman added. "I can even donate a few of the clearance items from the furniture store...maybe for a silent auction?"

He looked around and smiled widely when people nodded in agreement and appreciation.

A mixture of excitement and panic rose in Cheryl's chest. She wanted to hold the pie contest, and still thought it a good idea, but never expected to judge. She glanced toward the back of the room, where Levi watched her with an amused smile. Catching her eye, Naomi just shrugged. Obviously, she wasn't surprised to see that

Cheryl had landed in the middle of all the action. It was getting to be a habit.

Cheryl held up her hand. "I'm so glad you are all excited about this endeavor, and I'm sure we all have lots of ideas to share. In fact, I've already done some checking into a silent auction, so if you'll get with me after the meeting, Jacob, I'll give you the information I've already collected."

He nodded, and Cheryl picked up her notepad. "Okay, so back to the pie contest…before we decide on judges, I think we all need to understand that they will most likely know some of the contestants. Is everyone okay letting someone who is friends with one or more of the contestants be a judge?"

"This is a small town," Jacob said with a shrug. "Just about everyone here knows everyone else, ain't so? Besides, it is for a good cause. I do not think anyone will be too worried about the judges being biased."

A murmur of agreement rippled across those gathered, and several heads bobbed along with Jacob's.

Cheryl picked up her pen. "Well then, let's go ahead and start making some lists of people who can help and start assigning duties. We'll also need to keep a list of the activities and who will be responsible for coordinating them." She glanced at Jacob. "Since we already talked about the silent auction, would you be interested in coordinating it? You would be responsible for securing the donations and handling the setup. Once the auction is over, you would also be responsible for getting the items to the winners and tallying up the proceeds."

He grinned and gave her a hearty thumbs-up.

"Awesome. Thank you, Jacob." Cheryl jotted his name on her notepad and then dove into assigning tasks to the other events she and Pastor Lory had already discussed. While she worked, she added several other ideas offered by those in attendance to the list. Along with the pie contest and silent auction, they would sell drinks and BBQ, seek donations for a raffle, and sell tickets to area attractions, the proceeds of which all the business owners cheerfully agreed to donate to the Carmichaels. There would also be a bake sale and a yard sale.

Cheryl was quite satisfied by the time she had finished putting the finishing touches on her list, and she was confident that they would put a hefty-size dent in the amount the Carmichaels needed to rebuild their home. She read through all the information they'd collected so far and then suggested they conduct another meeting the following week just to make sure each committee was up and running. When they finished, Pastor Lory closed the meeting with prayer and dismissed everyone with wishes for safe travel home.

Pastor Lory rubbed his hands together and leaned toward Cheryl in order to be heard above the excited chatter that erupted the moment the meeting was adjourned. "So what do you think, Cheryl? The meeting went well, wouldn't you say? I am very happy with the number of people who turned out, considering it was such short notice."

Cheryl scraped together the rest of her papers and dropped them all into her bag. "I agree. It's all very exciting." She tossed a quick glance toward the back of the room. "Have the Carmichaels gone? I was hoping to speak with them."

Pastor Lory scanned the room. "Last I saw, they were talking to Jacob Hoffman, probably about the silent auction." He rubbed the back of his neck. "I sure am glad they came tonight. I hope you don't mind that I invited them. I figured they should be involved since this is all to benefit them. Doris really liked the idea of doing the pie contest. And she said something about helping out with the silent auction."

"No, it was a good idea to invite them. I'm glad they came," Cheryl said. "Only, they didn't mind us sharing their needs this way?"

Again, he shook his head. "I talked to them before I said anything. It's hard for them, Rex especially. He's a proud man, but I think he realizes this is bigger than the two of them. Right now their whole family is learning to rely on their Christian brothers and sisters. It's a lesson for us all, I think."

"You're right," she said, thankful for a man with as much wisdom and foresight as Pastor Lory.

She thought about her move from Columbus and how quickly the town of Sugarcreek welcomed her as one of their own. She picked up her bag and hung it on her shoulder.

"You know, Pastor, this may sound a little silly, but I remember being surprised when I first moved here. The family of God is so big…so alive. Not that I didn't realize that there were Christians in Sugarcreek. I guess it just surprised me to realize that God's people are *everywhere*. Does that make sense?"

He nodded and opened his mouth to answer, but he was interrupted.

"Cheryl?"

Hearing Levi's voice, she stepped back to include him and Naomi in their conversation. While Naomi chatted with Pastor Lory about the pie contest, Cheryl turned to Levi.

"So? What did you think?" she whispered.

Levi's eyes crinkled as he smiled. "You did very goot. I am proud of you. This is a wonderful thing you are doing for the Carmichaels and the community."

Of course the alliance was for a good cause, but hearing the approval in her future husband's voice brought grateful tears to her eyes.

"You really think so?" she whispered.

Levi closed the distance between them, shifting so that his broad back screened them from the people who still remained in the room. "I do," he whispered back. "You have a very tender heart, Cheryl Cooper. It is one of the things I..."

"Levi? I *thought* that was you and Naomi I spied sitting in the back. It is goot to see you."

Levi's lips thinned as he cut off what he'd been about to say and stepped aside to include a young Amish woman named Ellen Lengacher. Cheryl had met her last year when Levi was speaking to her father regarding the purchase of some land. Cheryl had mistakenly assumed the relationship was far different, and though it wasn't the young woman's fault, she still felt a tiny bristle of irritation every time she saw Ellen.

Determined not to give in to such petty feelings, Cheryl forced a bright smile. "Hello, Ellen. Thank you so much for coming tonight. Is your father with you?"

Her father owned a local tack and leather goods store, so Cheryl had felt obliged to invite him. She had not, however, expected his daughter to be with him—his very attractive... very skinny... very vivacious daughter. Cheryl bit down on her bottom lip.

"He was, but he had to leave a little early. We have several mares ready to foal, and he wanted to check on them. I was hoping I could ride home with the Millers since our farm is right next to theirs." Her gaze darted to Levi. "You would not mind, would you?"

Cheryl gritted her teeth. There it was... the reason for her dislike. Ellen seemed like a nice girl, but she did little to hide her regard for Levi—and so, nice or not, that made her a thorn in Cheryl's side.

Levi shifted with discomfort and looked at Cheryl. "Uh... *ne*. We do not mind."

"Ellen, how nice to see you." Naomi had finished with Pastor Lory and now turned to welcome the young woman with a smile.

"*Danki*, Naomi. It is nice to see you too."

Ellen continued with something in Pennsylvania Dutch, and Naomi responded in kind. Though they weren't talking to her, Cheryl couldn't help but feel excluded. No doubt the woman had done it on purpose.

Cheryl pushed the uncharitable thought away as Naomi gestured to her. It was not fair to assume something about a person simply because she'd shown interest in Levi. After all, she and Levi had not announced their engagement and so Ellen had every right to suppose he was eligible.

Realizing that Naomi was waiting on an answer, Cheryl blinked and cleared her throat. "I'm sorry, I didn't catch your question."

Naomi's eyes sparkled with humor. "I said I think you are the person in charge of the pie contest, ain't so? Ellen is interested in entering."

Cheryl bit back an inner groan. "Well, I'm not exactly sure who will be in charge, but I would be happy to get you the details, of course."

Ellen gave an unconcerned shrug. "Oh, do not bother. I would not want to cause any extra trouble. I will just stop by the farm and get the details from Naomi. That is"—she turned her bright gaze to Naomi—"if it is all right with you."

Cheryl clenched her hands into fists, her fingernails pinching painfully into her palms. Of course Ellen wouldn't mind stopping by the farm. That was exactly what Cheryl was afraid of... that she would find a reason, any reason, to put herself in Levi's path.

The problem was, so long as she and Levi kept their engagement a secret, there was nothing she could do to stop her.

Cheryl lifted her chin in feigned confidence. "That will be fine, Ellen, and thank you so much for your interest in our cause."

There. She'd managed the words with just the right balance of poise and politeness, all of which went out the window when Cheryl looked up and caught a hint of a smile on Levi's lips.

So maybe she *hadn't* fooled everyone. Then again, she thought as she offered a shy smile back, maybe she didn't want to. And she could wait for the right time to let the world in on her and Levi's secret. That is...

She shot another worried glance at Ellen.

As long as they didn't have to wait too long.

CHAPTER FIVE

The Wednesday morning of the start of the fund-raiser dawned clear and bright. Cheryl was thankful as she packed note-pads, pencils, and score sheets into her trunk alongside two large boxes stuffed with napkins, plates, and just about every utensil she owned. Sugarcreek had seen more than its share of rain the past two weeks, and there had been talk of postponing many of the outdoor activities the charitable alliance had planned. Fortunately, the pie contest wasn't one of them since it was being held indoors. Besides, the freshly baked pies couldn't wait and neither could the Carmichaels.

Slamming the trunk closed, Cheryl hurried to climb into the driver's side. She hated being late, but Beau had been especially difficult the entire morning. Today of all days, he'd chosen to squeeze himself through the door she'd propped ajar and then perched in the lowest limbs of the large oak tree in the backyard and stared, unblinking, at her. Every time she'd tried to fetch him, he'd yowled and climbed another branch.

Sliding the key into the ignition, Cheryl scowled and reached down to rub her scraped knees. She hadn't climbed a tree in years and would rather not have done so today.

Beau peered innocently at her from the kitchen windowsill. Cheryl wagged her finger at him as she backed out of the driveway and turned for Village Hall.

"Stubborn cat. Lucky for him, I didn't fall out of that tree and break my leg," she muttered to herself, although really it was probably lucky for *her* that the neighbor's kids hadn't come out and scared Beau farther up into the branches. She'd likely never have gotten him down.

She giggled as another thought struck. Then again, she hadn't seen many cat skeletons in the trees outside her house, so he probably would have found his own way down...eventually.

Village Hall wasn't far, just a straight shot across town, and she made it there without any further interruptions. To her surprise, the parking lot was already quite full when she arrived, and she had to circle around twice before she found a spot to slip into. It was farther from the door than she would have liked, since she had several items to carry inside and she would have to make at least two trips to haul everything out of her trunk. She had just wrestled the first box out of her trunk when Levi's welcome voice called to her from across the parking lot.

"Cheryl, wait up. Let me help you with those."

Cheryl sighed with relief as he jogged over and took the box from her. "Thank you, Levi."

"Is there anything else?"

"Yes, but I think I can get it." She stacked the notepads and pencils inside the smaller box filled with tablecloths and cardstock they would use to write down the entrants' numbers. She locked up her car and then fell into step alongside Levi as they made their way toward the entrance.

"Looks like we'll have a good turnout," Levi said. "Did you notice all the cars in the parking lot? A lot of people are already here, although most of them are just helping set up."

"I know," Cheryl said. She grimaced at the throbbing in her knees. "I meant to be here an hour ago, but Beau..."

"Cheryl, thank goodness you're here." Gail Murray ran over to clasp Cheryl's arm. Her face was red, and sweat dotted her temples. "Where do you want us to set up the tables for the pie contest?"

"Um..."

Gail threw open the door, and Cheryl glanced down the long hall off the main entrance. "I think Mayor Weller said the main meeting room would be open. Let's display the pies there where everybody can pass by to see them. It's large enough to conduct the judging too."

Gail nodded and scurried to open the door to a large room that opened off the main hall on Cheryl's right. Thankfully, someone had the foresight to stack tables against the wall, so all they would have to do is line them up and cover them with the paper tablecloths Cheryl had brought.

Since both her hands were full, Cheryl indicated the tables with a nod. "Levi, do you think you could get a couple of the men in here to help you with those?"

"Ja, of course. Where would you like me to set this?" He hoisted the box high. Cheryl pointed to a spot near the wall, and he set it down then went to fetch help with the tables.

Meanwhile, Cheryl took the cardstock out of the box in her arms and handed it to Gail. "Here you go. Do you think you could get started assigning numbers to each of the contestants?"

"Sure." Gail slid the cardstock under her arm and pulled a small notebook from her purse. "Here is the latest list. Want me to check them in as they arrive?"

"Would you?" Cheryl nearly crowed with relief. "That would be a huge help, Gail."

"No problem." She patted Cheryl's shoulder and then jabbed her thumb toward her own chest. "You leave the registration to me. I'll look around and get someone to help. I think Martha Glick said she would do it."

"*Ohh*...yes. Martha will do great." The room was quite large, with tall windows on two sides and pale butter-colored walls. Cheryl pointed to a spot near the door. "Maybe we should set up an actual registration table?"

Gail's head bobbed. "Good idea. That way everyone will see they need to register when they arrive."

Cheryl checked her box and then crossed to the one Levi had set down. "I know I have a poster for that in here somewhere." Spotting it, she slid it out along with a roll of tape and handed both items to Gail.

Gail eyed the poster in appreciation. "This will be perfect. Did Roxanna make it?"

"She did. Isn't it pretty?"

"Gorgeous." She tucked the poster under her arm. "All right, thanks, Cheryl. I'll take it from here."

Gail smiled and set off with a wave. Grateful to have been relieved of at least one responsibility, Cheryl set about sorting through the tablecloths. In the meantime, Levi returned with Jacob Hoffman and two others. They had the tables erected in no time with seating for the judges and were working on arranging chairs for spectators. By the time the first contestants began arriving with their pie entries, Cheryl felt she had things well in hand, thanks to a number of willing volunteers. She had just finished putting name placards and other finishing touches on the judges' table when Naomi appeared bearing a beautiful coconut custard pie for the first round of competition.

"Guder mariye, Cheryl."

"Good morning." Cheryl eyed the pie with its mountains of frothy meringue and toasted coconut. "Naomi, that pie is gorgeous. However did you get the meringue so high?"

Naomi smiled shyly and thanked her with a slight dip of her head. "It is an old family recipe."

"Well, I for one can hardly wait for the judging to start. I skipped breakfast so I would have plenty of room for pie." She patted her stomach for emphasis and then pointed toward one of the display tables. "Let's set it down over there. Have you picked up your registration number?"

She nodded and held her folded piece of cardstock high. "Right here."

"Good, but don't let me see the number." She shielded her eyes. "The first two rounds are going to be blind judging. We aren't supposed to know whose pie is whose."

She led her to the table where Naomi carefully placed her pie upon a stand then stood back to eye her work critically. "*Hmm*...maybe I should have added more coconut. Do you think I should have added more coconut?"

Cheryl laughed and patted her friend on the shoulder. She had certainly learned one thing by moving to Sugarcreek: the Amish were competitive when it came to their baked goods.

"It's perfect just the way it is," she whispered, "and don't forget, it's for a good cause."

She straightened and waved to the Carmichaels, who had arrived to help with the cleanup. Today Doris actually looked hopeful instead of weary. There was color in her cheeks, and her brown eyes sparkled. Her long brown hair was pulled back into a ponytail, but a few stray tendrils framed her face. She fairly bounced as she waved back to Cheryl and then spread her hands wide in amazement at the number of people crowding into Village Hall.

"You are right." Naomi smiled at Doris and then rubbed her hands together and reached down to straighten her apron. "Well, I suppose I should go and check on the *kinder*. Elizabeth is helping them set up a few things for the silent auction."

"You brought things for the auction?" Surprised, Cheryl set down another pie stand and then braced her hands on her hips. "You didn't have to do that."

"It was not me." She nodded toward her stepson. "Levi donated several of his Bible covers."

Cheryl's heart warmed as she let her gaze drift to him. "Really?"

"And Esther and Elizabeth brought a basket filled with things they stitched. Elizabeth is especially pleased with a set of hand towels she finished last week. And Esther added some pillowcases covered in violets."

"I'll have to be sure to take a peek." Cheryl smiled, her heart filled almost to bursting at the love and support her friends had shown. She gave Naomi's hand a squeeze and then turned to welcome the next contestant with their entry.

By early afternoon, three long tables groaned beneath the weight of so many fresh coconut pies. Rather than allow a random sampling, the pie committee had voted to conduct the contest in stages, with a preliminary round ordered to cut the entries to a manageable number before the first round, which would be done in public. A different flavor of pie was requested for each round of judging. Tomorrow's round would consist of apple pies, and the final round remained a secret to everyone since the pie of choice would be drawn from a hat.

Cheryl wiped her arm across her brow as she examined the many entries. All the pies looked delicious, not just Naomi's. If looks were anything to go by, she and the other judges would have a hard time deciding which of the entries would be going on to the second and third rounds. Speaking of which...

She glanced at her watch. It was only a quarter after one, which meant she still had almost forty-five minutes before the preliminary round of judging began. Maybe now would be a good time to grab a peek at the other activities going on outside.

Weaving through the people packed inside the meeting room, she offered several smiles and multiple "thank you for coming" greetings before she reached the door where Gail Murray and Martha Glick sat registering contestants.

Gail looked up from her chart with a smile. "Hey, Cheryl."

"Hi, Gail. Hi, Martha."

"Hello, Cheryl," Martha said.

"How's everything going?"

Gail's smile widened. "Great. So far we have twenty-seven entries checked in. Can you believe that? The entry fees alone are going to net us just under seven hundred dollars."

"Really? That's fantastic."

Gail held up her clipboard. "And everybody has a number that corresponds with their pie."

"Awesome. I'm glad we decided to use numbers instead of names on the entries. I really think that will make the judging fair for everyone."

Both women nodded in unison.

"I agree," Gail said. "I'm glad you thought of it."

"Not me. Pastor Lory suggested it." Cheryl poked her thumb toward the door. "Okay, well, I'm going outside for a minute. Think you ladies can handle everything in here?"

Martha nodded, and Gail tapped her pencil against her notepad. "Sure. But first…where do you want me to send the judges once they get here?"

"There's a long table with a red-and-white checkered tablecloth toward the front of the meeting room. Just ask them to take a seat behind their names. I won't be long," Cheryl promised and then turned to squeeze past a large group of people lingering near the door.

Outside, an equally large number crowded around the silent auction tables. Cheryl was pleased to see that many of the bid sheets already contained bids, probably due to boisterous encouragement from Jacob Hoffman. He worked the crowd like a peanut salesman, directing people to the various items on display easily and with lots of laughter on both sides.

Rows upon rows of items packed the tables—everything from fishing gear to homemade arts and crafts. There was even a beautiful handcrafted turquoise necklace that Cheryl couldn't resist placing a bid on. Onyx beads were interspersed among the turquoise, and on either side of the center beads, two filigree silver beads set off the piece to perfection. The description card said the necklace had been donated by one of the local jewelry store owners, and Cheryl made a note to visit even if she didn't win the necklace.

Across the parking lot, a large yard sale had been set up with families from all over Sugarcreek donating the proceeds, or a portion of them, to the Carmichaels. Like the silent auction, a great number of people browsed the tables, and Cheryl smiled, pleased that they had been able to coordinate the sale with the pie contest on such short notice. It certainly provided the draw they were hoping for from the public.

"Cheryl!"

She turned to see Esther waving so wildly she nearly knocked the prayer kapp from her head.

"Look." Esther pointed to the bid sheet pinned to the basket she and Elizabeth donated as Cheryl approached. "We have so many bids already. People are really interested in Elizabeth's things."

Her face beamed with happiness and pride for her sister as she spoke.

"That's wonderful, Esther." Cheryl gave the girl's arm a squeeze. "Where *is* Elizabeth?"

"She went to pick up some things for *Maam*. She should be back soon."

Cheryl grimaced. "Well, sugar and grits. I was hoping to thank you both for supporting the silent auction. Will you let her know I stopped by? Just in case I don't get a chance to see her later this afternoon."

Esther nodded. "I will, but more than likely you will see us both at the pie judging."

"You're coming?"

"Of course. Maam spent almost two hours fussing over her pie this morning. I have never seen her so nervous. I thought we should be there just for moral support."

Cheryl laughed. "That's probably a good idea. I know she'll appreciate you being there."

"And look at Levi's bid sheet."

Esther held up the specified paper. Cheryl's eyes widened. Several of the Bible covers already had bids well above what she sold them for at the store. "Wow. Maybe we need to ask more for them at the Swiss Miss."

Esther laughed and clapped her hands together enthusiastically. "This is more fun than the county fair last September." She frowned as though second-guessing herself. "The animal exhibits were fun, I suppose, and the truck and tractor pulls were interesting to watch, but this is for a much better cause."

"Thank you, Esther," Cheryl said with a smile. "I'll look for you later."

"What is this? No fair outbidding me."

Levi's voice came from directly behind her, and Cheryl resisted the urge to melt against his strong chest.

"You bid on your own sisters' basket?" she said instead.

"Someone had to." Humor and teasing sparkled in his blue eyes as he looked at Esther. "I wouldn't want to risk ruining the family reputation by having this sad little basket sit here without any bids."

"*Humph*. So much you know." Esther held up the bid sheet proudly for him to see. "We already have several people signed up."

"Really?" He squinted and pretended to peruse the list, which Esther quickly jerked away.

"Shoo now, before I tell Maam on you." To add emphasis, she wagged her finger under his nose and then propped both hands on her hips.

Cheryl couldn't help but laugh as she watched the exchange between brother and sister. Though she frowned, Esther probably enjoyed his teasing as much as Levi did.

"All right, I'd better get back for the judging." Cheryl motioned toward the building. "I think I just saw Kathy and Greta go inside."

She waved good-bye to Esther but was pleasantly surprised when Levi fell into step alongside her.

"So who else is judging the pie contest?" he asked. "Is it just you, Kathy, and Greta?"

Cheryl shook her head. "No, we also have Laura Early and . . ." Burning started in the pit of her stomach. "Richard Wellaby."

"Uh-oh. Is he not the grouchy old curmudgeon who used to own a gift shop down the street from yours?"

She cut him short with a nod. "I know, but he volunteered."

"I thought the judges were going to be local business owners, mostly cooks and bakers?"

"Well, we couldn't exactly tell him no, and there really wasn't a rule or anything prohibiting him from judging so . . . you know."

He frowned. "Surely he realizes what all this is for. I hope he does not intend to stir up trouble."

"Me too," Cheryl whispered as they ducked into the building.

The preliminary round of judging proved far easier than Cheryl had anticipated. Though all the pies looked good, only a few stood out in consistency and appearance, and the judges were in surprising agreement as to which eleven entries should move forward, even with Richard on the panel.

After a short break to give the judges a chance to stretch their legs, Cheryl made her way around the chairs that had been set up for the public to the table where Kathy, Laura, and Greta sat. Richard had not yet returned, but it was still almost fifteen minutes before the first-round judging was to start. Cheryl gave last-minute instructions to Pastor Lory, who would be emceeing the contest, before going to join the others. A couple of minutes later, Richard strode back into the building, his usual scowl firmly in place. Sweat dampened his forehead, and he looked a bit peaked as he slid back into the seat next to Cheryl's.

"Hi, Richard," she whispered, bending toward him and offering a smile in an attempt at friendliness. "Everything okay?"

"Yep. Let's get this show started," he replied without actually looking at her.

"We've actually got a few minutes still." She motioned toward the crowd. "This is fun, right?"

Richard merely grunted. Honestly, why had the man even bothered signing up? She resisted the urge to ask and turned her attention to the pastor, who had picked up a handheld microphone. He tapped it once, then twice. Satisfied it was on and working, he began the introductions starting with Cheryl. One by one, he made his way down the table. Each judge acknowledged the pastor's remarks with a nod or a wave, except for Richard, who merely scowled.

"And now for the rules." Pastor Lory pulled a long scroll from his pocket and let it roll to the floor with a flourish. When the laughter subsided, he said, "All the contestants have received a copy."

Cheryl felt her own smile widen. She had been right asking him to emcee. He was perfect.

He held up his hand. "In all seriousness, folks, our judges will be assigning scores to each remaining entry based on the following criteria." He lifted one finger as he cited each item. "First, visual appeal. I'm sure we can all agree that these pies look delicious. My mouth is watering."

General agreement erupted, and he rubbed his stomach.

"The second criteria is flavor, and the third, originality. Each judge will cast their vote for their favorite entry, but in the event of a tie, Mayor Weller has graciously agreed to step in and cast the deciding vote. Mayor Weller, where are you?"

From the back of the room, Mayor Weller raised his hand and waved to the crowd.

"Thank you, Mayor. And now..." Pastor Lory rubbed his hands together and then motioned to the pies lining the tables. "I'm sure the judges are just as ready to move on with this contest as I am."

Laughter rippled across the room, and Cheryl took a moment to enjoy the overall atmosphere of cheer and goodwill that usually accompanied only Christmas. This was a good thing they were doing here in Sugarcreek...caring for one another, being neighborly, getting to know each other...

A sharp crack cut through Cheryl's musings. Like everyone else in the room, she jerked her head sideways just in time to see one of the pie tables give way.

CHAPTER SIX

T he pies!"

The words had no more than left Cheryl's lips than people sprang into action. Cries of "catch them" and "look out" blended to create several moments of scrambling and confusion. Next to her, Greta Yoder leaped to her feet, almost upending the judges' table when her hip collided with the corner.

"Oh for heaven's sake," Richard growled, grabbing the edge and setting the table back on all four legs. "This is a fine mess. Who's in charge here?"

"Please everyone…if you wouldn't mind returning to your seats…" Still clutching the microphone, Pastor Lory urged everyone to sit down before turning toward the collapsed table and the ruined pies. A flush colored his face as he motioned a couple of people forward. "Do we know whose entries these are?"

"I can find out." Cheryl crossed to the mess on the floor and squatted down to look. "Actually, Pastor, only two of these pies are ruined." She pointed to a third pie that had somehow escaped destruction. Having been farthest from the collapsed end, it had slid down the length of the table and settled atop the two on the floor.

Cheryl handed the still-intact pie to Kathy. "Can you hold this please?"

Her hands now free, Cheryl poked through the layers of coconut cream and meringue until she found the number cards assigned to each entry. Holding one up by the corner, she shook it free of most of the remnants of pie.

"Number seven?"

"That's my pie!" From the back of the room, Tillie Gleason waved a jeweled hand. Heels clattering, she wove through the standing crowd until she reached Cheryl. "I'm entry number seven."

Cheryl shook her head sympathetically. "Oh, Tillie, I'm so sorry. Are you sure one of these is yours?"

Tillie frowned and bent down to retrieve the empty pie dish. Flipping it over, she shrugged and pointed to a soggy strip of masking tape. "It's mine, all right. I put my name on the bottom of the pan this morning."

Which sort of defeated the purpose of having blind entries, but considering the circumstances, Cheryl elected to keep the thought to herself and retrieved the second card. "Number four?"

A groan accompanied the reading of the number. There was more rustling, and this time Rhoda Hershberger raised her hand. "That is my number."

Cheryl's heart sank. Rhoda was fun-loving and sweet and the last person who deserved to have her entry smashed on to the floor. As she approached, Cheryl pointed to the surviving pie hopefully.

"Any chance that one is yours?"

Rhoda dashed that hope with a pert shake of her head. "No, Cheryl. I am afraid not. I did not use a glass dish." She pointed to the overturned metal pie dish on the floor. "That one is mine, I am sure of it."

Cheryl sighed and held up the last card. "Well, that only leaves entry six."

"I'm number six." A plump woman in her mid-to-late forties rose and walked to the front of the room where she handed Cheryl her matching number card. "I made that pie. Good thing I used heavy cream in my recipe. That's probably the only thing that kept it from sliding all the way off the table with the other two."

A round of laughter followed her remark. She blushed and thrust out her hand. "I'm Bertie Ford."

"Pleasure to meet you, Ms. Ford," Cheryl replied.

"Just Bertie," she said and then jammed her hands on to her hips. "Well, this is a fine mess. What happens now?"

Cheryl looked helplessly at the other judges, who merely shrugged, except for Richard. He raised his eyes to the ceiling and blew out a frustrated sigh.

"Looks like this is going to be a long afternoon," he muttered.

"To be honest, we really didn't plan for something like this happening," Cheryl said quickly, hoping to nip Richard's tirade. She glanced at Pastor Lory, who thankfully stepped up to take things in hand.

"Folks, obviously our panel of judges is going to need a little time to figure out what to do next. Why don't we give them a few minutes to confer"—he turned his wrist and glanced at his watch—"and then we'll resume the contest in, say, thirty minutes."

There was muffled conversation and scraping of chairs. Before everyone could leave, Pastor Lory raised his hand. "Folks, if I could have your attention for just a moment. Could I get a handful of men to help me with this mess?"

A couple of men, including Levi, started toward the tables. Pastor Lory turned to Cheryl and lowered his voice. "Why don't you and the other judges step into one of the smaller meeting rooms to talk about what we should do from here? We'll stay and clean things up while you all figure it out."

There was nodding by the judges all around. Pastor Lory conferred with Mayor Weller a moment and then returned and pointed to a door across the hall. "According to the mayor, that one should be open. I'll come and fetch you once we get order restored in here."

"Thanks, Pastor," Cheryl said. Turning to the other judges, she said, "Let's go ahead and pick up our stuff while we talk. Make sure you have your folder with all the information I gave you and the contest rules."

Once everyone had gathered up their things, Cheryl led the way across the hall to the room the pastor had indicated.

"So now what?" Richard demanded, rubbing his knuckles across his scalp as Cheryl closed the door. He hooked his thumbs into his suspenders and then hunched his shoulders and glowered. "We've barely even started this contest, and it's already a mess."

"Now, Richard," Cheryl began, "this isn't a disaster. I'm sure we can…"

"How are we supposed to judge the ruined entries?" Laura Early asked. She shot a worried glance at the other judges and then wrung her hands. "It's such a shame. It doesn't seem right to disqualify the two that fell."

"What else can we do?" Greta Yoder said. "It's not like we can sample them now." She directed a questioning look toward Kathy and Cheryl. "Either of you got any ideas?"

"We could pick two others from the preliminary round," Kathy suggested.

"Hold on a minute…" Cheryl held up her hand, effectively nipping the conversation on replacing the entries before it could take off. "Before we make any hasty decisions, why don't we go ahead and have a seat?" She pointed and then moved toward the conference table at the center of the room. "We can look through our folders better here. I'm sure there is something in the contest rules that will guide us, so why don't we get them out and go over them together?"

Once everyone was seated, Cheryl opened her folder and took out her copy of the rules. "Okay, so everybody should have a copy of these, right?" She gave a wry shrug. "I'm ashamed to admit I only read over them once, so I'm not exactly sure what they say about handling disqualifications or in this case, ruined entries."

Richard gave a disgusted grunt and shoved his folder away. "Well, that's kind of ridiculous, isn't it? I mean, who came up with these rules anyway?"

"I borrowed them from the organizers of the Swiss Festival," Cheryl said calmly, trying hard not to let irritation over Richard's negative attitude get the best of her. "They hold different food contests every year, so I figured the rules they use are pretty much tried and true."

"That was clever thinking, Cheryl." Laura cast a dark glance at Richard. "We all appreciate the amount of time and effort you've put into this, right, Richard?"

"Humph." He pulled the folder back and flipped open the cover. "Where are those rules anyway?"

"They should be right on top." Cheryl held hers up. "They look like this." She waited while the others riffled through their folders. "Okay, so everybody got theirs?" There were nods, and then Cheryl set hers down and took out a pen. "So why don't we start by taking a moment to read through them silently to ourselves? When we're done, we'll go back over them as a group and see what we come up with."

Richard sighed, but everyone else nodded, so Cheryl ignored him and set to work. Cheryl, Kathy, Greta, and Laura all marked places on their rules sheets as they read. Laura's pencil scratched the sheet several times. When they were done, Cheryl looked up and asked for their input.

"All right, so what did you all find?"

"I think it's pretty clear." Greta looked up from her pages. Her mouth curved down, and she shrugged almost apologetically. "Did you all see rule number six about ruined or damaged entries?"

"Rule number six refers to entries damaged by the contestant," Laura protested. Her pages rustled as she flipped to the rule in question. "It's referring to entries that are dropped or damaged when the contestant is presenting to the judges."

"And we weren't going to have the contestants present," Kathy added. Her head swiveled as she looked from one end of the table to the other. "We are using blind entries, right?"

"But it still says entries damaged before judging takes place are disqualified," Greta pointed out. Her jaw firmed, and she raised both hands. "Look, I agree this situation seems a bit unfair, but what are we really talking about here? It's not like the contestants are vying for some great prize. This is a charity event, after all."

There was a pause following her remark, and Cheryl shrugged. "Greta is right...this is a charity fund-raiser."

"Whoa, whoa." Richard held up his hand. The legs on his chair scraped the floor as he shoved backward. "Hold on a minute now. You mean to tell me that because this is a charity event, we aren't going to take the judging seriously? Why even have judges if it's going to be a complete waste of our time?"

"No one said we wouldn't take it seriously," Greta said with a scowl to match his.

Richard seemed taken aback by Greta's show of bravado. His eyebrows rose, and his mouth dropped open at her words.

"That's right, Richard," Cheryl said, a little less forcefully than Greta had. She turned to the other judges. "I suggest we talk to Rhoda and Tillie, inform them of the stipulation regarding damaged entries in the rules, and see what they recommend." She waited a moment, and when no one offered another suggestion, she said, "So we're agreed then?"

There were murmured agreements around the table, and even Richard eventually gave a grudging nod.

Greta's lips turned in a wry smile. "Disqualifying the two that fell would definitely make the first round a whole lot easier. We would only have to cut one more pie from the competition since we vote for eight to go on to round two."

"That's true." Laura's shoulders relaxed, and she pushed a lock of her graying hair behind her ear and laughed. "I tell you what, I thought I wouldn't mind judging, but having to narrow down the entries is going to be harder than I thought. I know almost everyone who entered, and I hate the idea of hurting someone's feelings."

"But we don't know who baked which pie," Cheryl said. "That should make narrowing the field easier."

"Thank goodness for that. I'd like to be able to look my friends in the eye come Monday," Laura said, chuckling. "And it's probably good that we familiarized ourselves with the rules again. I mean, I read through them last night"—she directed a pointed look at Richard—"but now they are fresh on our minds."

"Okay then," Cheryl said quickly before Richard could reply with something biting. "I'll bring Rhoda and Tillie in so we can discuss where to go from here."

She pushed up from her chair and made for the door. As she walked, she cast a quick glance at her watch. They still had ten minutes left before Pastor Lory said they should reconvene. Rhoda and Tillie were no doubt nearby. Maybe outside…

Levi stopped her just as she exited the room. "Cheryl, do you have a moment?"

She hesitated and shot a quick glance toward the main meeting room. "Actually, I was just going to fetch Rhoda and

Tillie. Have you seen them? We have a little problem with the contest rules."

"Ne, I have not, but Cheryl…"

"Okay, well, I'm just going to take a quick look around and see if I can find them. The judges would like to speak with them. But if you see them, grab them for me, will you?"

"Cheryl, wait."

There was a tightness to the muscles in Levi's face that arrested Cheryl in her tracks. She stopped, giving him her full attention as she met his gaze. "What is it? Is something wrong?"

Levi looked around, and Cheryl had the distinct impression that whatever he needed to say, he did not want to be overheard. Her stomach fluttered uneasily, and she reached out to lay her hand lightly on his arm.

"Levi, what's wrong?"

His blue eyes fastened on hers. "I was helping the others clean up. We picked up the table that fell, and I happened to get a look underneath."

"And?"

His hands fell to his sides helplessly. "Cheryl, I think someone intentionally tampered with the table."

Chapter Seven

Cheryl stared at Levi in silence, feeling slightly sick to her stomach.

"Cheryl, did you hear me?" Levi grasped her elbow firmly, and his touch had the odd effect of jerking her from her frozen stupor.

She blinked rapidly. "Wait. You can't mean that someone intentionally destroyed those pies...right? Why would anyone do that?"

Levi scratched his temple. "Whether their intention was to destroy the pies or not, I cannot say. I only know that it appears as though the bolts that hold the table legs erect were deliberately loosened."

"But that's..." Cheryl dragged her gaze to the table in question, as though by staring at it she might somehow glean the truth. "How can you tell?"

Levi led her over to where the table leaned against the wall. Squatting down, he pointed to the bolts and the surrounding scratch marks. "See here? These look like someone used the wrong size wrench or possibly a pair of pliers to loosen the bolts."

Cheryl squinted. The marks just looked like scratches in the metal. "What do you mean?"

"An ill-fitting wrench would have slipped and caused the damage. Pliers might have done the same if the person using them was in a hurry or..."

"Or what?"

He shrugged. "They were not very strong. At least not strong enough to clamp down hard on the bolt."

"But it still doesn't make any sense, Levi. Why would anyone want to hurt the Carmichaels after all they've been through?" she asked. The sick feeling in her stomach intensified.

"Are we certain it was the Carmichaels they wanted to harm?"

She thought a moment and then shook her head. "No, I guess not." She glanced uneasily at the other tables and back at Levi. "Have you checked to see if any of the other tables show signs of tampering?"

He shook his head. "There was not time."

She lowered her voice. "Maybe we should take a look. Discreetly."

He pointed to the one nearest her. "You check that one. I will look under the other. If you see anything suspicious, call me."

She nodded and tried to appear nonchalant as she rose and meandered toward the table. When she was close enough, she reached into her pocket and took out her car keys. No one appeared to notice as she pretended to fumble with them. She let them slip from her fingers. They hit the floor, and Cheryl nudged them under the table with her foot. A second later, she ducked under the tablecloth for a quick peek.

Unlike the first table, this one appeared solid and secure. No scratches sullied the bolts, and a gentle tug barely managed to move the legs. Cheryl grabbed her keys and pushed out to stand.

"Nothing under my table," Levi said quietly, coming to stand next to her.

"Mine either," Cheryl said. "Thank goodness."

His eyebrows bunched. "So you think it was just an accident and not tied to the contest at all?"

Cheryl pinched her bottom lip as she thought. "I don't know. I mean, I suppose it could have been an accident. A lot of people go in and out of here in a month. Maybe somebody damaged the table the last time it was used and forgot to say anything to the staff."

Furrows lined his brow as he frowned. "Ja, that *could* be it, I suppose."

She peered into his face, wishing she could read his thoughts. "But you don't think so?"

He jammed his hands into his pockets. "Let us just say I think we should keep our eyes open for any other strange occurrences."

"Okay."

His quiet reservation spoke more than if he'd just come right out and said he was worried. Cheryl glanced around the meeting room. The men had just about finished cleaning everything up and were now putting away the mops and buckets and rearranging the tables.

She motioned toward the exit. "I suppose I had better go and find Rhoda and Tillie."

"Should I help you?"

She hesitated and then shook her head. "I would rather you checked on Naomi. I haven't even had a chance to talk to her since this morning. I'd like to know what she thinks about all this, especially the scratch marks. Maybe she can come up with another explanation for what happened."

"I will find her." He gave her a reassuring smile before he opened the door for her to walk through.

Fortunately, Cheryl spotted Rhoda and Tillie straight off. They were standing together under a large oak and appeared to be deep in conversation. Now *there* was something Cheryl had never thought to see. Rhoda and Tillie were about as far apart in their lifestyles and beliefs as could be, and yet they smiled and chatted as easily as old friends.

Cheryl approached them timidly. "Excuse me, ladies?"

Both turned to look at her. Tillie spoke first, the rings on her fingers flashing as she waved toward Village Hall. "Are we ready? Have the judges come to a decision?"

"Actually, they asked if you wouldn't mind coming inside for a minute. There is something we would like to discuss with the two of you."

"Of course," Rhoda said and held out her hand. "After you, Tillie."

"Thank you." She eyed Rhoda and scratched her temple. "Say, I don't think I told you, but I sure am sorry about your pie. It really looked good. A lot better than mine. I'm sure you worked really hard on it, and it was a shame to see it ruined."

"Thank you, Tille. I am sorry about yours too," Rhoda said.

So they hadn't been discussing the contest? What on earth had they found to talk about? Cheryl frowned. Granted, she and Naomi were friends, but that was because they'd discovered over time how much they had in common. Knowing Tillie and Rhoda, Cheryl found it hard to believe the two had much in common...

Cheryl pushed the thought from her mind as they reentered the cool interior of the building. She led the way to the room where the other judges waited and then held the door for them to step inside. After a brief explanation of the rules, Cheryl spread her hands in appeal.

"So you see, ladies, we find ourselves in an unfortunate conundrum. Some of us feel that we can't exactly disqualify your entries because according to the rules, you weren't presenting your pie. And yet..."

"To delay would mean putting off the Carmichaels another day." Rhoda folded her hands in her lap calmly and shook her head. "This we cannot do. The whole purpose of this fund-raiser is to get them the money they need for their home, ain't so?" She turned a questioning look to Tillie. "What do you think?"

"Rhoda's right," Tillie said firmly. "And I hardly think putting off the contest another day for me to bake another pie is worth the effort." She chuckled and gave a wave of her jeweled fingers. "I mean, it ain't likely that I was going to win this bash anyhow. I'm surprised I even made it past the preliminary round. I say we just call forfeit and get on with it, except..." Her face softened with compassion. "You had a better chance of winning. What do you think, Rhod?"

Rhod?

Cheryl ducked her head and somehow managed to hide her surprise. Exactly how long had these women known each other? And why did Tillie seem so completely at ease with someone she barely knew when Cheryl still felt like an outsider at times, with everyone except the Millers?

"I agree. The pie contest is for a good cause. We will just forfeit our entries."

"But what about your entry fee?" A worried frown creased Laura's brow. "It hardly seems right to let you forfeit your entry fee when you hardly even got the chance to compete."

The two women looked at each other and shrugged.

"Just put it in the kitty for the Carmichaels," Tillie said. She offered her elbow to Rhoda. "What say we sit back and enjoy the rest of this shindig from the audience?"

Rhoda smoothed the fabric of her plain dress and then rose with Tillie. "It will be nice to just observe for once and not have to worry about baking any more pies. At least, not for the contest," she corrected. She turned to look at Cheryl. "I will still be happy to donate a couple for the bake sale after the contest is over."

"Hey, that's a good idea." Tillie elbowed her friend jovially then turned her smile to Cheryl. "Count on me for a couple too. They won't be as good as Rhoda's, of course, but maybe if you stick with the blind entries, they'll fetch a good price." She threw her head back and gave a laugh that seemed to rise from her belly.

"That would be perfect," Cheryl said gratefully. "Thank you so much, Rhoda. You too, Tillie. I know I speak for all of us when I say we are truly sorry for what happened."

Tillie dismissed her apology with an unconcerned shrug. "Nothing to be sorry about. Just an unfortunate accident, that's all. Could have happened to anybody."

But was it an unfortunate accident?

Cheryl fidgeted in her chair. "Okay, well, thank you both so much for your understanding. I'll be sure to let the Carmichaels know about your generosity so they can thank you in person. And now…"

She grasped the edge of the table and looked around at the other judges. "If everyone is in agreement, I say we go back and finish the first round of judging."

There was an almost tangible sense of relief as the judges reentered the meeting room. Cheryl took a moment to explain to Pastor Lory and the Carmichaels what the judges had decided before turning to address the audience. No one seemed to mind that the two entries would simply be forfeited, especially when Cheryl explained it was the women's idea. In fact, they applauded until Rhoda and Tillie rose to accept their appreciation.

"Are you sure you all weren't just looking for an excuse not to sample Tillie Gleason's pie?" Dan Dekker teased from the back of the room when the applause faded. "I hear it was likely to eat a hole clean through the plates."

There were several guffaws from the men and loud shushes from the women, but Tillie took the teasing in good-natured stride. She wagged her finger at Dan and then draped her arm around her husband's neck.

"Bob, here, has eaten my cooking for years, and he ain't any worse for wear." She slanted a glance at him coyly. "Ain't that right, sweetheart?"

Bob patted his round belly. "Darlin, I haven't complained in twenty years, and I'm not about to start now."

To Cheryl's relief, laughter followed. With the cheerful atmosphere restored, she gave a nod to Pastor Lory so that he might resume the contest.

Next to her, Greta leaned over to whisper, "Well, I for one am sorry I won't get to taste Rhoda Hershberger's pie. I hear that woman can cook."

"For sure and for certain," Cheryl whispered back and then inwardly smiled at the use of the colloquialism. Apparently, spending time with the Millers was rubbing off.

She tossed a quick glance toward the back of the room where Levi sat alongside Naomi. Of course, adopting some of the Amish ways wasn't necessarily a bad thing, especially if she and Levi intended to make them all family.

Smiling at the warm thought, Cheryl hardly noticed when Pastor Lory set a slice of creamy coconut pie topped with frothy meringue in front of her. Only when Richard snorted did she think to pick up her fork and take a bite.

Warm custard and sweet vanilla melted over her tongue. This wasn't such a hard gig, she thought as she picked up a napkin and smoothed it over her mouth. She just might enjoy judging what remained of the contest.

Movement from the back of the room caught her eye. While Pastor Lory turned to fetch another slice of pie from a different entry, Cheryl looked to see what was going on. It was Levi. His head was bowed, and his shoulders were hunched. Apparently he was looking at something...something that appeared to have fascinated him.

Suddenly, he straightened, and his gaze locked immediately on Cheryl. Very slowly, as though he were trying to avoid drawing attention, he lifted up a rusty pair of pliers.

CHAPTER EIGHT

Knowing Levi had found the pliers that might possibly have been used to loosen the table legs made focusing on the pie contest difficult. Though they were all delicious, Cheryl had to force herself to concentrate on the remaining entries, and even had to ask for a second bite on one of them when she realized the first one had slid untasted down her throat.

What did the pliers mean? Were they right to assume that someone had damaged the table intentionally? If so, why?

Each judge had been given an equal number of scorecards. For this first round, they would indicate their preferences from highest to lowest using the numbers assigned to each entry. Fortunately, this first round was easy since the entry Cheryl ranked lowest lacked height to its meringue. She scored each entry quickly and then gave her card to Pastor Lory, who had agreed to tabulate them.

"All right, folks." Pastor Lory held up all of the judges' scorecards. "We have our first-round results." He waited until the applause subsided before continuing. "My staff and I will take just a few minutes to look these over…"

Laughter rose from the audience since his "staff" consisted of himself.

"...after which we will announce the names of the people moving on to the second round. While you are waiting, please take a moment to visit the silent auction or the BBQ sale going on outside. We will reconvene in thirty minutes."

He'd barely finished before Cheryl scraped her chair back and hurried over to where Levi and Naomi stood. "What did you find?"

Naomi placed her finger to her lips and gave a slight shake to her head. "Perhaps we should step outside."

Cheryl cast a quick glance around. Though no one seemed to be watching, Naomi was right...it wouldn't be good to draw undue attention.

Levi opened the door, and the three of them slipped outside into the warm sunshine.

"So?" Cheryl asked once the door shut behind them. "Are they the pliers used to sabotage the table?"

Levi took the pliers from his pocket and handed them to her. "We found them in a box near one of the tables. I thought the box belonged to Maam, otherwise I might never have looked inside."

"But I am afraid showing them to you during the judging may have distracted you." Naomi frowned in concern. "Perhaps we should have waited to let you know."

"No, I don't think so." Cheryl tapped the pliers with her fingernail. "But are we even sure these are the pliers the person used?" She looked at Levi. "Remember, we said the table could easily have been damaged before today."

"Except..." Levi took the pliers from Cheryl and spread them wide. "Look at the teeth on these pliers. What do you see?"

Cheryl squinted to peer at them. Finally she shrugged. "Are they dirty?"

"We do not think so," Naomi said. "The legs on the tables are all painted brown. The bolts and hinges as well."

"We think these pliers have dried paint chips on them from the scratches," Levi said.

"Which would prove they were used on the table that collapsed." Cheryl gave a firm nod. "I think we should show them to the other judges. What do you think?"

"Cheryl, wait." Naomi restrained her with a gentle touch to her arm. "Did not the judges already decide to forfeit the two entries that were destroyed?"

"Well, yes, but..."

"And Rhoda and Tillie agreed, ain't so?"

Her shoulders drooped. "Sugar and grits. I see what you mean."

"Plus, we cannot prove who tampered with the tables or even if it was done intentionally," Levi said. "It could in truth have been a very unfortunate accident."

"So unless we can come up with more proof, there is hardly any sense telling the judges about the pliers now, is there?" Naomi asked. "It might only put a cloud over the competition when there should be none."

"Except that if it *was* intentional, we still don't have a clue as to why the person tampered with the table," Cheryl said.

Levi bumped the pliers lightly against the palm of his other hand. "You are right. We should at least find out who they belong to so we can keep an eye on them."

"How do we do that?" Cheryl motioned toward the parking lot. "Half the people here could have brought them. I carry a set of tools in my trunk myself, just in case of an emergency." She grimaced. "Not that they would do me much good. Everything I know about cars I could squeeze into a thimble."

"We could always ask." A breeze ruffled the strings on Naomi's prayer kapp. She caught them in one hand and held them under her chin.

Levi agreed. "Honesty is best. I will say I found them in a box and ask if anyone knows who they belong to. Maybe the owner will just step forward."

The door opened, and Pastor Lory poked his head out. "Cheryl? The scores are tabulated. We're ready now."

She straightened. "Coming, Pastor." When he retreated inside, she turned to Levi. "Okay, so you and Naomi will see if you can find out who left the pliers?"

He nodded and gave her a teasing smile. "It looks like this time I might be a little more involved in solving one of your mysteries, ain't so?"

She laughed. "I believe you might be right."

Turning, she went back inside and rejoined the judges at the table. In her haste to retake her seat, she knocked over her name card. She fumbled a bit before finally setting it upright.

"Is everything all right?" Kathy whispered as she passed Cheryl a cold bottle of water.

"Fine," Cheryl whispered back and accepted the water gratefully. The heat had definitely turned up outside. She was glad the same wasn't true inside, at least not yet.

It was all she had time for because at that moment, Pastor Lory stepped back to the microphone. In his fingers he gripped a small white card.

"All right, folks, I have here the names of our second-round contestants. Is everybody ready?"

Cheerful hooting erupted, followed by light applause led by the Carmichaels. Cheryl couldn't help noticing the smile on Doris's face and was glad to have had a part in putting it there. Still, a tiny seed of doubt rooted in her heart. Was it possible that not everyone here felt the same way?

"All righty then, here are your semifinalists. Now remember, folks..." He paused for dramatic emphasis, and a groan rumbled across the room. He held up his hands with a smile. "The names are not in any particular order. Okay? Now, without further ado, the first person moving on to the second round is...Agatha Hilty!"

He paused to let the applause quiet down before reading on. "Our next semifinalist is...Ellen Lengacher."

Cheryl groaned silently as Ellen stepped forward, a delicate blush coloring her cheeks. It would have been nice not to have to worry about hiding her feelings where this pretty young woman was concerned.

"Also moving on…Bella Sweetin. And joining her is Bertie Ford!"

Obviously, the pastor was playing to the crowd, and Cheryl couldn't fault his enthusiasm. Still, she wished he would hurry through the list so Levi could ask about the pliers.

"Joining them are"—he looked up from the card and smiled—"actually, these two women tied in the rankings so I will read their names together…Clarice Shumacher and Tory Landry."

Clarice shrieked with excitement, which caused several members of the audience to jump.

"Sorry! Sorry," she said. "I'm just so happy. Thank you all very much."

Kathy leaned over toward Cheryl. "I'd like to thank the Academy, my parents, my…"

"Shush," Cheryl said, hiding a grin.

Pastor Lory's smile broadened as he reached the next name on the list. "Now, here is something different. Representing the men…"

That was all Cheryl could hear. Harvey Ackerman was the only male to enter the contest, and the room nearly exploded with enthusiastic applause when his name was called. Harvey stood near the back of the room. He swiped the baseball cap from his head and took a bow.

"And now…" Pastor Lory eyed the two remaining contestants, one of which was Naomi.

Cheryl's heart beat harder inside her chest. Of course, she had no way of knowing if Naomi's entry was one she had ranked highly, but she certainly hoped so. Naomi was an outstanding cook.

Sandra Remis stood next to Naomi, shuffling her weight nervously from foot to foot. Though Cheryl hoped it would be Naomi who moved on, she couldn't help but feel a bit of Sandra's excitement.

Pastor Lory studied the two remaining contestants. "One of you ladies will be moving on. The other will be going home."

His overly dramatic flair invited laughter.

He held up the card. "Are you ready, ladies?"

The two nodded, and Pastor Lory cleared his throat. "The person moving on to the next round is...Naomi Miller."

Which left only Sandra. Cheryl couldn't help but feel a little sorry for her as Sandra's face registered her disappointment. From the opposite end of the line, Agatha hid a snort behind her hand.

"Remember, folks," Pastor Lory continued quickly, disrupting Cheryl's contemplation of Agatha's odd reaction, "all of today's events are for a good cause, so be sure to come back out and support us tomorrow, all right? Judging for round two will begin promptly at two o'clock, assuming we don't have any more catastrophes before then."

Cheryl's face warmed at the round of guffaws that followed.

"Pastor Lory, if I may?" Levi approached the stage and handed the pliers to the pastor. "These were found in a box earlier today. Would you mind asking who they belong to?"

"Of course." He held up the pliers. "Folks, before you leave, would you mind taking a look at these? Does anybody here know who they belong to?"

"I do." Harvey Ackerman pushed forward through the crowd and extended his hand. "Those are my pliers, Pastor. I recognize them because of the red handles. Where on earth did you find them?"

CHAPTER NINE

Harvey owned the pliers? He chatted with Pastor Lory a moment then took the pliers and ambled off.

Cheryl cast a startled glance at Levi and Naomi. Granted, she didn't know Harvey well, but what she did know of him made it hard for her to believe him capable of intentionally tampering with the tables.

As the crowd thinned, she stood and moved over to him. "Say, Harvey, have you got a minute?"

He nodded as he shoved the pliers into his shirt pocket. "Sure thing. What can I do for you, Cheryl?"

She gestured toward his pocket. "I was just wondering about those pliers. You didn't by any chance happen to use them here for something, did you?"

He scratched his temple and frowned. "I sure didn't, which is why it's so odd that they showed up here. I usually carry them in the toolbox in my truck. Can't imagine how they got into that box, unless someone borrowed them, which could happen, I suppose. People are always taking things out of my toolbox." He shrugged. "Who knows? Not a big deal I suppose."

Cheryl bit her lip. "But you are sure they're yours?"

He patted his pocket. "Absolutely. My wife gave them to me years ago as an anniversary present. They're part of a set. Sure am glad to have them back. I would have hated having to explain to her how I lost them, although honestly..." He spread his hands wide. "There's really no telling. I could have just as easily dropped them in the parking lot or something, and somebody picked them up and brought them inside."

His answer was reasonable, she supposed, but Cheryl still wasn't quite certain there wasn't more to the pliers showing up when they did.

Harvey jerked his thumb over his shoulder. "Well, I'd better get going. I've got to get me some apples if I'm going to have my pie ready for tomorrow." He tipped his head and lowered his voice conspiratorially. "My mother always used Honeycrisps. I like to mix them with a nice Granny Smith. Gives the pie a little snap."

Cheryl stared at him in amazement. "Wow, Harvey. I didn't realize you were such a chef."

He winked. "I like to keep that tidbit under my hat. My *chef's* hat."

He laughed, and Cheryl thanked him then watched as he sauntered away.

As soon as he was gone, Levi approached with Naomi.

"Well?" they asked in unison.

Naomi shushed Levi with a pat to his arm and then turned to Cheryl. "What did he say?"

She shoved her hands into her pockets. "He claims he doesn't know how he lost them. He said he might have dropped them or somebody may have borrowed them, which could be true, I suppose, but I get the feeling we should keep an eye on him."

Sighing heavily, she turned from the door. "Anyway, we're no closer to knowing anything, and I'm hungry. Anyone care to join me for some BBQ?"

"I will," Naomi said.

"I will too." Levi patted his stomach. "Watching you sample all those pies made me hungry. Do you suppose Jacob will have some coconut pie to go with his hot dogs?"

They laughed, and Cheryl immediately felt her mood lighten. "Maybe. Let's go see how the Carmichaels are doing too. I heard somebody say they are helping with the yard sale."

"Ja, that is correct." Naomi pointed across the parking lot. "I saw Mrs. Carmichael heading that way after the contest finished."

Levi laid his hand over his stepmother's shoulder. "But first, food, ja?"

His stomach growled as if on cue, and all three of them laughed before setting off toward the BBQ tent. A healthy crowd was gathered around, even though lunch was long past. Cheryl wandered over to August Yoder, who was handling the grill like a master.

"Hello, Cheryl." His booming voice filled the large tent. "I wondered when you would be by. Would you like something to eat?"

"If there's anything still left." She eyed the crowd again. "Did you have a good turnout?"

"Very good." He lowered his voice and tipped his head closer. "I think the Carmichaels will be pleased."

Cheryl gave his arm a squeeze. "Thank you, August."

He nodded and handed her a plate loaded with chicken and ribs. "There you are. And one for our friends as well, ja?" He pointed to Levi and Naomi with the tongs. "What can I get for you?"

"The same," Levi said. He took a long whiff and smiled appreciatively. "If it is half as good as it smells, it will be delicious."

August chuckled and handed them both a plate then gestured toward a row of tables. "Don't forget to check out the potato salad and rolls. They are from our restaurant. Greta baked them fresh this morning."

Cheryl couldn't help but smile as the three of them made their way toward the tables. She had no idea Greta did so much baking on top of agreeing to judge. So many people...so willing to chip in and help one of their own. She loved Sugarcreek. She loved feeling like a member of the community.

She sighed as she sank into a chair across from Naomi and Levi.

"That is a tired sound," Naomi said, passing Cheryl a napkin and keeping another for herself.

"Tired but happy too." Cheryl unfolded the napkin and laid it over her lap. "I just can't believe how many people have jumped on board with all this. It really is wonderful being part of such a caring community."

She paused as a sudden idea struck.

A caring community... like the one the Amish belonged to. It was something they were known for, and one of the reasons so many people—Englishers—found them fascinating. No wonder so many people traveled to places like this one. They wanted a glimpse inside the lifestyle they read about in books.

Levi's low voice plucked her from her thoughts. "Are you all right, Cheryl?"

"Oh yes. I'm fine." Realizing they were both watching her curiously, she shook her head and gave a wave of her hand. "I was just thinking." She inched closer to the table and bent over her plate for a deep whiff. "Anyway, this smells delicious."

Levi took her cue and bowed his head for a silent blessing of their meal. Naomi and Cheryl did the same. When Levi signaled the prayer was finished by raising his head, Cheryl reached for her drink.

"So what did you two think about Harvey's story?" She took a sip of her soda then set her cup aside. "Assuming Harvey really did drop his pliers, do you think the paint on them was just a fluke?"

"It is a strange coincidence," Naomi said, tapping her fork against her plate thoughtfully, "but I do not think there is any way we can prove anything one way or the other."

"I suppose you're right." Cheryl chewed a bite of her chicken slowly. "I don't know...maybe I'm making too much of this."

They ate in silence for a while, and then Naomi took a bite of her potato salad. She nodded in approval. "This is goot. I will have to ask Greta for her recipe. I think she added something more than just dill relish."

"Ah, there you are, Naomi. I have been looking all over for you." Ellen Lengacher plopped into the chair next to Levi's, a bright smile on her face. "I wanted to congratulate you on making it to the second round of the pie contest."

Naomi offered a polite smile. "Danki, Ellen. Congratulations to you as well. Your pie was beautiful."

"Danki."

"You will have to tell me your secret for getting your meringue so high," Naomi continued. "Did you add vanilla to your egg whites?"

"Just a bit." As she leaned closer, her arm brushed Levi's. She brought her hand to her mouth and continued in a loud whisper as though she didn't notice. "But the secret is in the vanilla. I use pure vanilla, not the extract. Instead of being brown in color, it is clear, so I get all the flavor but my meringue keeps its pristine white."

"That is interesting."

"We all have our little baking secrets, ain't so?" Ellen's gaze drifted to Cheryl. "It was very kind of you to work so hard putting all this together. I am sure the Carmichaels are very appreciative."

Cheryl swallowed a suddenly dry bite of her lunch. "Thank you, Ellen."

She nodded and then turned her bright smile to Levi. "I saw you and some of the other men helping as well. This has certainly pulled our community together, ain't so? Amish and *Englisch* alike have been pitching in. It is quite amazing to see."

"There is not so big a difference between us," Levi said, looking a bit uncomfortable as he fidgeted in his seat. He dropped his gaze, refusing to meet Cheryl's eyes or Naomi's. "Those of us who love Gott will show it by loving one another."

Ellen's sharp laugh splintered the air. "You are being kind, Levi, but I think we all know there are many differences between Englisch and Amish. Is that not right, Cheryl?"

Cheryl lifted her chin, certain Ellen was baiting her but not exactly sure why. "The Amish lifestyle is very different from the English one, that is true, but I happen to agree with Levi. God doesn't look on the outward. He looks on the heart. In that way, I do think we are more alike than we realize."

Ellen's lips spread in a slow, satisfied smile that made Cheryl wonder what she'd said that could possibly be so pleasing. She didn't have time to ask, however. Naomi gathered their plates and stood.

"Ach, I should fetch Esther and Elizabeth. It is already later than I expected. Your *daed* will be wondering where we are." She turned to Levi. "You will fetch the buggy?"

"Ja, Maam. I will have it ready."

"Danki."

Ellen stopped her before she could leave. "Naomi, please tell our Elizabeth hello for me. I have not seen her in so long. I miss our talks. Of course, we have both been busy adding to our hope chests. I should ask her if she has any good patterns for my linens."

"I didn't realize you and Elizabeth were close," Cheryl said. She uttered the words before she could think and then wished she could pull them back. There was a smugness about the way Ellen looked at her that set her teeth on edge.

"Oh, I am close to all the Millers. Our families have long been friends. In fact"—she rose and crossed to stand next to

Naomi—"I think I will walk with you and say hello to Elizabeth myself."

"That will be fine," Naomi said. "I am sure Elizabeth would very much enjoy a visit from you." Her eyebrows lifted as she looked at Levi. "Are you coming, Son?"

"Ja, Maam. I will just be a moment."

He waited until Naomi and Ellen had gone before turning to look at Cheryl. "I am sorry about the things Ellen said."

Though she tried not to let it show, Cheryl had a knot in her throat the size of a baseball. She swallowed hard and forced a casual shrug. "Oh well, that's just Ellen, I suppose. She sees things as black-and-white. She is right though," she added, her voice dropping to a bruised whisper. "There are a lot of differences between English and Amish."

"We already know this, and we have talked about it." Levi took a step closer. "Cheryl, I do not want you to let any of the things Ellen said bother you. Regardless of what she says, it is not how my family feels. It is not how *I* feel."

The urgency in his voice did much to soothe her hurt feelings. She smiled up at him gratefully.

"What are you doing tomorrow after the pie contest?" he asked. "Do you have any plans?"

"None. Why? Are you thinking of coming by the store?"

He lowered his head, hiding a small smile. "I have something in mind."

He'd piqued her curiosity. Cheryl forgot all about Ellen as she bent to peer into his face. "Oh, really. What?"

He looked at her then, his eyes sparkling with the joy of a secret. "I said I would court you, remember?"

"I remember," she said, her breath hitching in her throat.

She watched, fascinated as he leaned toward her ever so slowly. "Then prepare to be..."

"Cheryl?"

Laura Early's voice carried a note of urgency that froze both Cheryl and Levi. Together, they turned to see her approaching at a pace just under a jog. Her face was flushed, her graying hair looked slightly disheveled, and in her hand she clutched a small slip of paper. She waved it at them as she skittered to a stop. "Thank goodness I found you. I was afraid you'd left."

Cheryl reached out to touch her arm. "Laura, are you all right?"

Laura pressed her hand to her chest, huffing as she struggled to catch her breath. "No," she managed at last. "I'm not all right, and you probably won't be either. I think we have a very big problem."

CHAPTER TEN

Cheryl took a deep breath, hoping the extra oxygen would combat the feeling of foreboding creeping over her. It did but not much. She stepped forward to clutch Laura's arm. "What is it, Laura? What's going on?"

Laura jabbed out her other hand. "Take a look at this. Bella Sweetin just gave it to me."

Cheryl took the slip of paper and frowned. "A grocery receipt?"

She shook her head so hard she knocked her glasses sideways. She jabbed them straight with her index finger. "Not just any grocery receipt. Look at the items listed and then look at the back."

She hopped from foot to foot as Cheryl scanned the receipt. Nothing unusual. It was a standard sales receipt from a local grocery store called Chester's. Cheryl shopped there herself from time to time.

"I don't get it, Laura. What am I looking for?" Halfway down the list, she stopped.

"What is it, Cheryl?" Levi pressed closer to her side.

"Piecrust?" Cheryl whispered. She glanced at Levi and back at Laura.

Laura waved her finger in a circle over the receipt. "Now look at the back."

Cheryl flipped it over. On the back someone had scrawled, *One of your semifinalists is a cheater.*

She lowered the receipt slowly. "Who does it belong to?"

"Bella says it belongs to Tory Landry."

"Tory!" Cheryl swallowed nervously and lowered her voice. "How does she know it's hers?"

"She says she found it next to her bag."

"Did she see it fall out?"

"I don't know. I didn't ask her." Laura chewed her fingernail nervously. "Should I have?"

"It's all right." Cheryl raked her fingers through her hair. If Tory bought a piecrust for her entry...

Levi ducked into her line of sight. "I do not understand. What is the problem?"

Cheryl ran her tongue over her dry lips. "Buying a piecrust is in violation of the rules, Levi. They specifically state that all of the ingredients must be homemade."

Levi frowned and jammed his hands into his pockets. "Did Tory know this?"

"All the contestants received a copy of the rules," Laura said. "I printed them out and put them in each person's contest packet myself." Desperation darkened her gaze as she turned to stare at Cheryl. "What are we going to do?"

"Well, first, I think we should go and talk to Tory," Cheryl said. "There is a slim chance that this is just a silly coincidence. She could have bought the crust anytime, right? I don't see a date on the receipt. And she could easily have used it for something else."

Laura blew out a breath. "Right. You're right. That's a good point." She cast a glance side to side. "Have you seen her?"

Though the crowd had thinned some, there were still plenty of people milling about the parking lot and among the tables.

Cheryl shook her head. "Do you think maybe she went home?"

Levi hitched his thumb toward the building. "There were still some people inside packing up their things. I will go and check."

She gave his arm a squeeze. "Thank you, Levi. Laura and I will look around out here."

He set off toward Village Hall, and Laura and Cheryl hurried toward the silent auction tables.

Halfway there, Laura blew a wisp of hair from her forehead. "I don't get it, Cheryl. What is with this contest anyway? It's like we're jinxed or something. Why not bring the receipt to the judges? And why write a cryptic message on the back? That seems a little bizarre to me."

If only she knew! Cheryl stifled a wry smile. In her book, Sugarcreek was the birthplace for cryptic messages. "Maybe the person who found the receipt didn't want anyone to know they were the one turning Tory in."

Laura seemed relieved by her answer. "You think so? You think maybe they just wanted to be anonymous?"

"It's possible. Anyway, I'm sure it's nothing," Cheryl said, trying to sound confident when inside she wondered if Laura was right. Three possible disqualifications in one day? At this rate, there wouldn't be any entries left to judge.

"There she is!" Laura patted Cheryl's arm excitedly. "Over by the yard sale. Let's go catch her."

Laura was half a head shorter than Cheryl, but it was still all she could do to keep up. As they neared the tables, she grabbed Laura's arm to stop her from peppering Tory with questions.

"Laura, slow down. We should take Tory aside, somewhere private."

Understanding crept over Laura's face, and she nodded. "You're right. We don't want to embarrass her."

"Or ourselves, if all this proves to be a giant mistake."

Laura sucked in a breath. "You're right. Sorry."

Cheryl released her arm, and they walked the rest of the way to the tables. Tory was examining a child's plastic picnic table and chairs, but she looked up when she saw Cheryl and Laura approaching.

"Good afternoon, ladies."

"Hi, Tory." Cheryl swallowed a sudden knot and glanced at Laura, who seemed all of a sudden to have forgotten why they came.

"Uh, Tory, are you busy? Can we speak to you a minute?" Cheryl asked.

Tory set the chair down and straightened. "No, I'm not busy. What can I do for you?" Her gaze bounced from Laura to Cheryl. "Is this about the contest?"

"It is actually." Cheryl directed a pointed glance at Laura. When she didn't move, Cheryl looked back at Tory. "Would you mind stepping inside with us a moment? We'd like to ask you about something."

"Sure." Tory smiled brightly as she turned toward the building. "This really has been a lot of fun, Cheryl. I'm so excited about making it to the next round. There were so many good-looking pies to choose from. I'm sure that was thanks to all your hard work advertising the event. It really was sweet of you putting it all together."

Cheryl hid a grimace. Several people had told her that today, but she sure didn't feel sweet.

Inside, Village Hall was quiet and cool. Cheryl motioned toward the smaller room where she and the judges had met earlier that day. "Let's step in here, shall we?"

"So what's this about?" Tory said as Cheryl closed the door behind them. She winked and lowered her voice. "Am I in some kind of trouble?"

She certainly wasn't acting like someone who'd broken the rules. Maybe all this really was just an unhappy coincidence. Cheryl gestured to Laura. "Show her the receipt."

Finally, Laura seemed to snap from her stupor. She handed the receipt to Tory and then stepped back. "Someone found this by your things earlier today. By any chance, is it yours?"

Tory's brow furrowed in confusion as she glanced over the receipt. "Yeah, this is mine. I bought a few things in town yesterday, but it's no big deal. I never keep my receipts. This one probably just fell out of my purse."

Cheryl shook her head in frustration. "No, Tory, it's not the receipt we're concerned about. It's the piecrust."

"Huh?" Tory scratched her head. "What about it?"

"Did you use it for the coconut pie entry you submitted to the contest today?" Laura blurted.

Tory looked from one to the other. "Well...yeah...but...I don't understand. Is that a problem?"

"Actually, it is," Cheryl replied sadly. "The rules specifically state that all of the pie has to be homemade."

"What?" Tory's brown eyes rounded. "You're kidding me."

"Look at the back of the receipt," Cheryl prompted softly.

The confusion on Tory's face changed to horror when she flipped the receipt over and read the back. Her fingers shook as she scooped a lock of her long brown hair behind her ear. "I don't get it...W-what does this mean?"

"Didn't you read the rules, Tory?" Laura asked as she took the receipt back. "They were in your information packet along with the schedule of events and a few other things."

She grabbed the fringed string dangling from the collar of her blouse and began running it through her fingers. "Sort of...I mean, I skimmed through them, but I didn't see anything about not using store-bought crusts."

"They don't exactly use those words," Cheryl explained. "They just state all of the pie has to be homemade."

"But the rest of the pie *was* homemade." Tory held up her hand. "Honest."

"We believe you." Cheryl sighed and began to pace. "Unfortunately, the rules are very clear on this one."

"So...I'm disqualified?" Her face flushed, and her shoulders dropped. "I mean, it's not like I was *trying* to cheat."

"Of course not." Laura laid her hand on Tory's shoulder.

Cheryl stopped pacing and crossed to stand next to her. "We will have to talk to the other judges about it, but, unfortunately, since you have admitted to using a store-bought crust, I'm afraid we aren't going to have much of a choice but to disqualify your entry. I'm really sorry, Tory."

Tory hung her head. "Don't be. I understand. I really do. It's just..." She pressed her hands to her cheeks. "Oh, I'm so embarrassed. You don't think people are going to believe I did it on purpose, do you?"

"We'll make sure to say it was an oversight," Cheryl assured her quickly. "In fact, if you would rather make the announcement yourself..."

Tory cut her off before she could finish. "No." Her cheeks reddened, and she started again. "I mean, thank you, but no. I already feel like such an idiot. Getting up there in front of everybody and admitting that I...that I..."

"Made a mistake," Laura finished gently. "It was a mistake, and I think you are being entirely too hard on yourself."

She wrapped Tory in a hug. Catching her eye over Tory's shoulder, Cheryl gave her an appreciative smile. Laura was a very kind person, and she was glad she was getting the chance to know her better thanks to the pie contest.

After a moment, Tory thanked them and left, and Cheryl pointed toward the parking lot. "Well, there aren't many cars left. I don't think there's much chance that we will catch anyone still here. Should we try calling everyone and set a time to get together this evening?"

Laura nodded and pulled out her cell phone. "I think that's a good idea. I know I have Greta and Kathy in my contacts. Not so sure about Richard."

"I can find his number. We could meet at the Swiss Miss. Say around six?"

"Yep. That should give us enough time to reach a decision."

Cheryl snapped her fingers. "Oh, but wait. If the judges vote to disqualify Tory's entry, we'll need to get ahold of Sandra Remis and tell her she's moving on to the next round. She'll need time to get her entry ready."

"You're right. Move the meeting up to five thirty?"

Cheryl agreed with a quick nod. "Okay, you call Greta. In fact, she might even still be here since August is running the BBQ."

"I'll check."

"Great. I'll call Kathy and Richard."

"All right." Laura grabbed her hand and gave it a squeeze. "This is such an awful coincidence, isn't it? I mean, who would have thought that three entries would be disqualified? True, the first two were an accident, but still."

Her words echoed Cheryl's thoughts. She gave a wave as Laura moved off and then pulled her phone from her purse. This task wouldn't be pleasant but best to get it over with. Heaving a sigh, she dialed Kathy's number.

CHAPTER ELEVEN

Cheryl woke to loud purring somewhere in the vicinity of her right ear. Peeling open her eyelids, she saw Beau staring lazily at her, the end of his tail flicking gently against her chin.

"Beau?" She sat up in the bed and scratched the fur between his ears. "What time is it?"

The clock next to her bed read six thirty. She still had thirty minutes before she had to hit the shower and head over to the Swiss Miss. Esther and Lydia were running the store today, but she wanted to be there to help them open. Afterward, she'd go by Village Hall to oversee the setup for the second day of fund-raising. Groaning, she slid her legs over the edge of the bed and slipped into the bathroom to brush her teeth. After the events of yesterday, today *had* to be better. At least, she hoped so.

Shuffling to the kitchen, she pondered the meeting with the judges last night. Of course, Greta and Kathy had been sympathetic, but Richard's words haunted her.

"A mixed-up, thrown-together mess ... that's what we've got. We'll all end up with pie on our faces before it's through. Literally."

Cheryl sighed. He hadn't come right out and blamed her for the turn of events, but the implication was clear. And to be honest, she had to agree with him ... at least in part. They had put things together quickly. Maybe too quickly, even if it was for a good cause.

Beau meowed at her feet and began rubbing lightly against her legs while he waited for her to fetch his breakfast.

"Honestly, you're worse than a kid when it comes to patience," Cheryl said, setting a can of his favorite cat food on the floor and moving to the coffee maker.

At least one person was pleased with the way things had turned out. Sandra Remis had been happy to hear she'd be moving on but saddened to hear that it was due to Tory's disqualification. In fact, all the judges had tended toward sympathy where Tory was concerned, except for Richard, whose comment that he wasn't so certain it had been a mistake had ignited a firestorm of discussion that lasted for almost an hour.

A few minutes later the smell of freshly brewed coffee filled the air. Cheryl paired a cup of it with toast and a slice of cantaloupe then moved to the table to sit and enjoy her breakfast. Sunlight streamed through her kitchen window, and Cheryl found herself lingering over her coffee. How nice it was to have a comfortable home, a job she loved, and friends around her, all things she took for granted most days. Certainly that wasn't true for the Carmichaels. Maybe she could offer Mrs. Carmichael a position at the Swiss Miss. It would have to be part-time, of course, just a few hours a week to start, but it was summer, and with business picking up, she could use the extra help.

Finished with her breakfast, Cheryl carried her empty plate and cup to the sink and then readied herself for the day. In no time, she was out the door. She spent a little over an hour at the Swiss Miss before meandering down Main Street toward Village Hall. August Yoder was already setting up the smoker in the parking lot. After all this was over, she'd have to remember to extend him a special thank-you. Jacob Hoffman was there too, getting the tables set up again for the silent auction. Cheryl gave them both a wave before making her way inside. There wasn't nearly as much to do today, but she still wanted to make sure things were tidy and the judges had everything they needed at their seat.

A short while later, people began arriving with their entries for the second round. Cheryl watched for Naomi and was glad when she spotted her among the earliest to arrive. She set down her notepad and hurried over to say hello.

After a quick hug, Cheryl stepped back to peer earnestly at Naomi. "You heard what happened?"

Naomi set down her pie and then brushed some crumbs from her fingers. "I am happy for Sandra, but what a shame for poor Tory. Was she very disappointed?"

Cheryl nodded sympathetically. "She was and worried that people would think she'd done it on purpose."

"Surely not. Anyone who knows her knows she is too sweet and kind to consider such a thing." She frowned and pinched her bottom lip. "Levi said someone found the receipt next to her things?"

Cheryl nodded and gripped Naomi's arm. "I'm glad you're here. I've been dying to ask you about something."

Her eyes widened. "Of course. What is it?"

Cheryl looked over her shoulder. Though more people had begun arriving, no one appeared to be paying them any mind. Quickly, she filled Naomi in on the details of the receipt, including the mysterious message scribbled on the back.

"Obviously, someone besides Tory knew about the piecrust," she finished. "Why do you suppose they didn't just come to us—or ask Tory about it, for that matter?"

A frown troubled Naomi's lips. "Perhaps they were afraid it would be considered tattling, or maybe they just wanted..."

She trailed off and put her fingers to her mouth.

"What?" Cheryl knew that look. Naomi had an idea in mind. "What did you think of?"

She smoothed the fabric of her plain dress as she fumbled for words. "It is just that...well...Sandra Remis did have the most to gain from Tory's disqualification."

"But it wasn't Sandra who found the receipt. It was Bella."

"Ja...but she could have planted the receipt there for Bella to find."

Cheryl gaped, started to speak, but then lowered her voice and started again. "You think Sandra turned Tory in on purpose? But why? There's no prize at the end of it. I mean, it's a charity event, not *Cake Boss*."

"Cake...what?" Naomi fluttered her hand dismissively. "It does not matter. If it *was* Sandra, and we cannot be sure it was, she did not do wrong by turning Tory in."

Cheryl frowned disapprovingly. "Maybe not, but turning someone in behind their back? That doesn't sit well with me. It feels underhanded... and a bit unscrupulous."

"I agree," Naomi said slowly. "Whoever did this must have had their reasons. Even if we do not approve of their methods, it is goot that you found out about the rule violation now instead of later in the contest. Imagine the humiliation it would have caused to discover the mistake if she had won, for example."

A shudder traveled down Cheryl's spine. "I'd rather not, if you don't mind." She tapped the tip of her finger against her chin, thinking. "Okay, assuming Sandra did have a motive, what about the two entries that were disqualified when the table fell? She didn't have anything to do with those entries."

"None that we know of."

"But you think it's worth investigating?"

Naomi lifted one shoulder in a half-shrug. "It would not hurt to check. Rhoda and I are close. I can check with her to see if she has any connection with Sandra."

"And I can speak to Tillie."

Cheryl pointed to a couple of contestants who were just arriving with their entries. "Hopefully, there will be no more strange disqualifications today, or people will start to wonder what in the world is going on."

Herself included. Before she could ponder it further, Agatha stomped toward them, lips set in a grim line.

"Is it true?" She balanced her pie in one hand. The other, she propped on her hip. "About Sandra Remis…is it true she's back in the contest?"

"Um…" Cheryl shot a quick glance over at Naomi, who lifted her eyebrows and turned from them discreetly. Cheryl directed her gaze back to Agatha, who had begun tapping her foot rather impatiently.

"Yes, Agatha, Sandra is back in. Unfortunately, Tory was unaware of the rule stating that all of her pie had to be homemade. She purchased her piecrust, which resulted in a disqualification. Sandra, of course, was the next contestant in line, and therefore she was the one selected to compete in the second round."

The words came out a bit more stilted than she had intended, but having been caught off guard, it was the best Cheryl could manage. Agatha's mouth opened and closed for a moment, and then she spun and stomped off with her pie held high.

Cheryl stared after her incredulously. "What on earth was that about?"

"I have no idea," Naomi said, turning back around, "but perhaps the situation bears investigating." Her lips curled in a conspiratorial smile. "Want me to see what I can find out?"

"Now, how did you know?" Cheryl said, returning her friend's smile. "And let me know if you uncover anything."

She told Naomi good-bye and then left to go in search of the other judges. Today's competition was a little different, and she wanted to make sure everyone was prepared before the judging actually started. In addition to taste-testing the entries, the judges would be reviewing each recipe for originality, but they still wouldn't know whose pie was whose. That wouldn't happen until the final round, when the contestants would be required to give a verbal *and* visual presentation of their pies before the judges tasted them.

She glanced at her watch. It was just after one. Still plenty of time before the contest was to begin. She spotted Greta and Laura talking together and crossed to meet them. A short while later, Kathy and Richard joined them.

Kathy motioned toward the pies lined up neatly near the front of the room. "There sure are some beautiful entries up there."

Laura smoothed a lock of hair behind her ear. "I agree. Judging will definitely be a little harder this time around."

"Maybe studying the recipes will help," Greta said. She moved her hands as though weighing something on a scale. "Give us something to differentiate in case of a tie."

Richard had mostly ignored their conversation, but now he frowned. "Aren't we missing one?"

"What?" Cheryl turned to count the pies. "Sure enough, there's only seven." She glanced at her watch again. "It's only one fifteen, though, and the contest doesn't start until two. There's still plenty of time. Who are we missing? Maybe it's someone who will be coming from work."

Greta pointed out the window. "There's Gail. She's handling the registration again today. Let's go ask her."

"You hens go ahead," Richard grumbled. "I'm going to get me a cup of coffee." He hunched his shoulders and set off in the opposite direction without another word.

"Did he just call us 'hens'?" Greta snorted in disgust and jammed her hands on to her hips. "One of these days, that old *rooster* is going to get what for."

"Try and be back by quarter till." Cheryl cupped her hand to her mouth, but whether Richard heard or not she couldn't tell. He ambled along as though she hadn't spoken. She let her hand fall.

"Sure we can't just disqualify him from judging?" Greta said wryly, quirking an eyebrow.

"Ugh. Let's just go see what Gail has to say," Cheryl replied.

Kathy pointed toward the judges' table. "If you don't mind, I'm going to stay here and start getting the cards ready for scoring."

"I'll stay and help too, if you don't mind." Laura pulled a tissue out of her pocket then lifted her glasses to dab at her eyes. "The farther I stay from the smoke from the BBQ pit, the better. My allergies are going haywire."

"That's probably a good idea, Laura." Cheryl reached into her purse and took out several new pens. "Here, just in case we need a few more. I noticed we were short some yesterday afternoon. Probably walked off with some of the kids."

"It happens at the Honey Bee all the time," Kathy said, slipping the pens into her pocket.

Cheryl turned to Greta. "Okay, let's go."

A sunny smile matched the pretty yellow shirt Gail wore. Matched with a pair of dark blue jeans and white canvas tennis shoes, she looked like the subject of a Norman Rockwell painting. As they approached, a breeze lifted the tips of Gail's hair. She smoothed the loose ends from her forehead and then waved cheerfully. "Good afternoon, ladies. All set for another day of judging?"

"I think so," Cheryl said, returning her smile.

"Hopefully the competition will go a little smoother from here on out, huh?" She jabbed the pencil in her hand toward Village Hall. "Just so you know, I asked Mayor Weller and a couple of the boys to inspect the tables before setting up." She patted Cheryl's arm. "Don't you worry, honey. There won't be any mishaps today!"

"That's great, Gail. Thank you," Cheryl managed, feeling a little awkward in the face of her concern. She was trying to be kind but... surely she didn't blame her for the events of yesterday?

"Um, Gail? Greta and I noticed there is one pie missing from the competition. Did someone not check in?"

"*Hmm.*" Gail put her pencil between her teeth and began flipping through the pages on her clipboard. When she found the page she wanted, she took the pencil out and pointed. "Let's see... Bella is here. So are Agatha and Bertie. Ellen Lengacher checked in. Harvey and Sandra are here, oh, and Naomi Miller. That just leaves..." She flipped through several more pages. "Huh. Looks like the only person we're missing is Clarice Shumacher. I could've sworn I saw her earlier. I must have been mistaken."

"That's odd." Greta frowned and looked at her watch. "Clarice is never late for anything. In fact, August and I tease her about always being twenty minutes early."

"Maybe she got stuck in traffic?" Cheryl suggested, which sounded weak even in her ears since traffic only backed up in Sugarcreek when the Swiss Festival was in full swing.

Gail slid her clipboard under her arm. "Want me to give her a call?"

"Would you?" Cheryl glanced back toward Village Hall. "Greta and I need to get inside and help Kathy finish setting up."

"No problem." Gail pulled her cell phone out of her pocket. "I'll find out where she is and let you know."

"Thanks, Gail."

Waving good-bye, Cheryl and Greta hurried back inside. Not only did Kathy have pens and paper at each judge's place, she was busily setting bottled waters next to the notepads.

"Hey, Kathy, we're back. Where's Laura?"

She looked up with a smile. "In the restroom freshening up her makeup. She'll be right back." She indicated the water bottles. "Hope you don't mind. I thought it might help us to have something to rinse our taste buds with between each entry."

Cheryl gave her a hearty thumbs-up. "Hey, that's good thinking. Thanks, Kathy."

Greta's lips turned up wryly. "Except that today's entries are apple. Maybe we should brew a quick pot of coffee instead."

"Or order a tall glass of milk," Kathy said.

They laughed, and Cheryl looked around for Richard. She spotted him standing next to Harvey, his head bent and his hand angled to hide his mouth.

She grabbed her water, unscrewed the cap, and took a sip. "Wonder what they're talking about," she said as she replaced the cap.

"Richard and Harvey? Who knows. Could be anything from politics to cotton farming." Greta shrugged and then hitched her thumb over her shoulder. "Hey, I really am going to go and fetch a cup of coffee. I think they're selling some over at the bake sale. Do you want anything?"

Cheryl thought about it and then shook her head. "No thanks. I had a cup this morning. Any more, and I'll be jittery all afternoon."

"Okay. I'll be right back." She winked. "Save a seat for me."

Her hips swayed as she hastened through the people lining up to get inside. Cheryl glanced at Richard. He was still talking to Harvey, only now his hands swung up and down in agitation. What *were* they talking about?

Whatever it was, it was none of her business, Cheryl reminded herself. She scanned the room for Levi. He would probably be arriving soon if he hadn't come with Naomi. More than likely he would try to get all his chores done before heading into town...

Spying him near the back, Cheryl lifted her hand to wave, only to freeze when she saw Ellen sidle over to him, a coquettish smile pasted on her lips. Cheryl lowered her gaze. Levi was trustworthy and his intentions were always honorable, even if Ellen's were not.

Her dark thoughts made her glad once again that the entries were numbered instead of labeled. She really didn't think she could be fair otherwise. It would be too tempting just to disqualify Ellen's entry and send the girl on home.

"*Psst...*Cheryl."

Having been caught brooding, Cheryl jumped and then craned her neck, looking for the source of the loud stage whisper.

"Over here." Gail motioned to her from the side of the room away from the pie entries. Strangely, she seemed to be hiding behind a rolling chalkboard. In her hand, she clutched her cell phone.

Cheryl crossed over to her and pointed to it. "Did you get ahold of Clarice?"

Gail's eyes were wide and round in her pert face. She grabbed Cheryl by the arm and pulled her behind the chalkboard. "I sure did. But Cheryl...you are never going to believe this."

CHAPTER TWELVE

Cheryl's stomach clenched with Gail's words. Instinctively, she cast a glance around to make sure no one was watching and then inched farther behind the chalkboard, out of sight of prying eyes.

She ran her tongue over her lips. "Believe what, Gail? What did Clarice say? Is she on her way?"

Dismay washed over Gail's face as she shook her head. "Afraid not, Cheryl. Clarice said she's too sick to compete."

"What? What's wrong with her? Did she say?"

Gail clutched her phone so tightly her hands shook. "Clarice said it was the strangest thing. She felt fine yesterday *and* this morning. She even went into town to grab a bite to eat for breakfast. Remember when I said I thought I'd seen her?"

Cheryl nodded.

"Well, that's when it happened."

Cheryl crossed her arms over her chest. Gail was right…she was hardly able to believe what she was hearing. "I think you'd better explain, Gail. What exactly did Clarice say happened?"

Gail waved her phone frantically. "Clarice said she's never had anything come over her so quickly. One minute she was fine. The next, she was rushing to the bathroom. Right now she's sick as a dog and terrified of bringing her pie up here in case she makes anyone else sick."

Needing to do something to relieve the tension building inside, Cheryl began pacing—which actually proved rather difficult since the chalkboard was only four feet wide. She strode two paces, turned, and strode back. "So...apparently she thinks it's some kind of bug, right?"

"Beats me." She lifted her hands in the air helplessly. "Regardless, Clarice said there is no way she is going to make it in time for the judging. She said to give you her regrets and tell you to go on without her."

A knock sounded, and then Levi poked his head around the chalkboard. "Everything okay over here?"

"Levi." Cheryl quit pacing to stare at him.

Levi hooked his thumbs into the pockets of his trousers. "You two looked like you were having a pretty serious conversation. I came over to make sure everything is all right."

So he had noticed, even with Ellen doing her best to distract him. Cheryl immediately felt a surge of love and satisfaction sweep over her.

"So?" His eyebrows rose. "Is everything okay?"

"Yes, everything is...well actually..." Her shoulders slumped. "The truth is we've had a disqualification."

"Another one?" His eyes rounded in disbelief. "Who?"

"Clarice Shumacher. Apparently she's come down with some kind of bug and won't be able to compete."

Relief flooded his face. "Oh. Is that all? I thought you meant..." He cut his gaze to Gail and stopped short.

Cheryl shot him a grateful glance. The last thing she needed was for rumors regarding a possible saboteur to start circulating, especially if there wasn't one—which was beginning to seem more and more unlikely.

She fluttered her hand toward the judges' table. "If you both will excuse me, I better go find the other judges and let them know what is going on."

She drew a deep breath and ducked out from behind the chalkboard then hurried toward the judges, her thoughts in a muddle. Surely someone wasn't intentionally trying to make another person sick. Cheryl had a fleeting thought of the recent incident of Naomi's poisoned jam but dismissed the idea as too absurd to happen under these circumstances. But was it any less probable that all the disqualifications were a coincidence? Just what was going on?

In short order, Cheryl gathered the other four judges into a corner and explained what Clarice had said.

"So we're down to just seven entries?" Laura whispered, glancing from one face to another.

"I don't know about you all, but I think this is starting to get a little ridiculous," Richard said, a smidge too loudly. He turned to glare at Cheryl. "Shouldn't you be doing something about this?"

"What *can* she do?" Greta demanded in a harsh stage whisper. "It's not like she has any control over who gets sick."

"We're all concerned," Cheryl said, trying hard to sound calm. "I'm sure there is a reasonable explanation, but for now…"

"Reasonable explanation for what?" Sandra Remis stood staring at the judges. She waited until they broke huddle and then let her gaze bounce from one to the other. "Is something wrong with the pie contest?"

"Something is wrong with the contest?" Pastor Lory chimed in.

Unfortunately, he stood a tad too close to the microphone. At the sound of his amplified voice, a sudden hush fell over the crowd. Cheryl felt nearly a hundred pairs of eyes swing to fasten on her.

"Um..."

No choice now. Her legs felt weighted as she made her way over to Pastor Lory. He half-turned his back to the audience and covered the microphone with one hand. "Cheryl, is everything okay?"

"The contest is fine, Pastor," she said with more confidence than she actually felt. "I'll explain everything."

His brows bunched doubtfully as he stepped aside to make room for her. The phrase "could have heard a pin drop" ran through Cheryl's head as she stared out at the curious faces. Delores Delgado's was among them, and she clapped her gaze on her friend from the Sugarcreek Police Department desperately. She cleared her throat, which of course the microphone intensified into something akin to a hacking plague.

She took a small step back and sucked in a breath. "Folks, I have just informed the judges that one of the contestants, Clarice Shumacher, has taken ill. Now as far as I know, it's not serious, but she will not be able to compete this afternoon."

People in the audience exchanged glances. Any other time, Cheryl would have thought nothing of it, but even she could see the speculation on their faces.

She forced a bright smile. "That is, of course, good news for one lucky contestant, right?"

Delores's mouth dropped open. Heat suffused Cheryl's face. That came out all wrong!

"W-what I mean is," she stammered, "we will proceed with the judging for the remaining seven entries and hope that Clarice gets to feeling better soon."

Cheryl handed the mic back to Pastor Lory. Her ears burned so hot she barely heard as he skillfully restored enthusiasm to the crowd. She slunk back to her chair and sat down without looking up. Next to her, Laura reached over to give her hand a squeeze.

Thankfully, the next part of the competition went without a hitch. There were *oohs* and *ahhs* from each of the judges as the pies were sampled and exclamations of delight when the corresponding recipe cards were passed around. One in particular caught Cheryl's eye. It called for a half cup of homemade apple butter.

Cheryl scanned the audience until she spotted Naomi. This one had to be hers. She took a bite of the pie and was delighted when the warm, cinnamony flavor melted over her tongue.

After a few minutes, Pastor Lory stepped up to the microphone. "All right, judges, you've had a chance to sample each of the seven remaining entries. Does anyone need a second sample?"

Richard raised his hand. "If I could, I'd like to sample number four again, please."

Pastor Lory smiled and made a big show of dishing up a second helping of the requested entry. He set it before Richard with a flourish and then stepped back as Richard took a nibble, then another, and finally, a healthy forkful.

"Well, if that doesn't tell you what you need to know, I'm not sure what will," the pastor said.

There was brief laughter, and then Pastor Lory looked over at the judges again. "Anyone else?"

He waited a moment, but when there was no comment, he looked out upon the audience. "All right then, folks. Since they will also be comparing recipes, let's give these fine judges one hour to make their decision. That should be just enough time for you to check out the silent auction or stop by and see August Yoder for some good old-fashioned BBQ."

Murmured conversation swelled as people filed out of the meeting room.

One hour. Cheryl quickly ranked each of the entries on her scorecard while the other judges did the same. After that, it was a simple process to compare the recipes and create a final ranking for all contestants. When they finished, they still had just under half an hour.

"Restroom break," Greta said. Her chair scraped the floor as she stood and stretched her back. "See you folks back here in twenty minutes."

"Wait for me, Greta." Kathy rose quickly and walked with her toward the restrooms.

Laura picked up her phone and motioned toward a quiet corner. "While we're waiting, I'm going to make a quick call. Frank wasn't feeling well when I left this morning. I'm going to check on him. I sure hope he doesn't have the same bug Clarice has." She hurried off, already dialing.

That left Cheryl and Richard. He scowled at her from the opposite end of the table, his shaggy brows bunched.

"I think I'm going to step outside for a bit of fresh air," Cheryl said, rising hastily. She looked toward the doors and then reluctantly back at Richard. "Would you care to come along?"

For a split second, she feared he'd say yes. Instead, he grimaced and put his hand on his belly. "Too hot out. Plus, all that smoke from Yoder's grill is making my eyes water. I wish he'd move that thing a little farther from the door."

He did indeed look peaked, but Cheryl doubted it was due to the smoke. "I'll see what he can do. Be right back."

She scurried toward the exit, glad to make her escape. Richard hadn't been all that bad, except for his complaining. Still, spending time in his company tended to sour her mood, and she was worried enough over all the disqualifications without adding anything else.

Cheryl pushed open the door. A blast of sultry air stole her breath, and she immediately made for the shade of a large maple. Richard was right about one thing—it was warm, and likely to get warmer as the day progressed.

As she neared the tree, several low voices caught Cheryl's attention. At first she only meant to cool off, but when the subject of their conversation became clear, she couldn't help but eavesdrop.

"C'mon. Don't tell me you actually believe that table collapsing was an accident. Think about it. What are the odds?"

"It could have happened. I mean, you heard the judges. And Pastor Lory said…"

"Seriously? You're being naive, Jennifer."

A third voice joined the conversation. "Becca, be nice."

Cheryl couldn't help it. She peeked around the trunk of the large tree and spied three young girls, all probably in their late teens, huddled together talking, their backs toward her. The tallest of the three, with smooth blonde hair and a perfectly golden tan, spoke.

"What? I'm just repeating what Ellen said… I think it's entirely possible that somebody might not be playing nice."

What Ellen said? Cheryl felt her cheeks warm.

Becca leaned in and lowered her voice. "Not everyone is who they appear, you know. I heard it was that Miller woman."

"The Amish one?" Cheryl recognized her voice as the one who'd cautioned Becca about being nice, so that meant the shorter girl with dark hair was Jennifer.

"I thought they were supposed to be above that kind of stuff," Jennifer said. She waved her hand. "Like 'holier than thou' and all that."

"They're human, aren't they?" Becca smirked. "I bet they're not even all that religious." In her hand, she held a large Icee. She took a bite and then swirled her spoon around the cup. "They're probably just acting like that to try and prove…"

Becca glimpsed over her shoulder, caught sight of Cheryl, and grabbed her friend's arm and nodded in her direction. All three girls gaped at her guiltily before moving off.

They actually thought Naomi was responsible for the disqualifications? Ridiculous. Cheryl felt indignant that anyone would even say such a thing. She hurried her steps to catch up with the three girls.

"Excuse me."

The brown-haired girl, Jennifer, looked over at her and then pulled the other two to a halt. Cheryl willed the racing of her heart to slow. It wasn't these girls' fault that Ellen had been spreading rumors about Naomi. Still, she felt it was up to her to see that they didn't repeat it.

"I...uh...I overheard you saying you'd heard Naomi Miller was responsible for the table collapsing."

The two shorter girls looked away, obviously uncomfortable. Becca's face reddened, but she nodded. "That's right."

"And it was Ellen Lengacher who told you that?" Cheryl fought to keep her tone from sounding accusing.

Becca glanced at her friends and then at Cheryl. "Well, not exactly. I was getting some BBQ when I heard her talking to a few of her Amish friends."

Cheryl was really hot now. She crossed her arms to keep them from shaking. "Do you mind if I ask what else she said?"

Becca pushed a lock of loose hair behind her ear. "Well, she didn't come right out and accuse her of anything. She just said something about the Miller lady being really proud of her title...best pie maker, or something like that." She bit her lip. "I saw you talking to her inside. Sorry if we said something to make you mad."

"No, I..." Cheryl retracted the words she'd been about to say and nodded. "It's just that I know Naomi pretty well. She'd never do anything to hurt another person. And about the Amish?"

Becca's eyebrows rose. "Yeah?"

"They really are just trying to live a life that is pleasing to God. It's not about trying to look religious."

Becca's face slowly changed from skeptical to interested. "Okay. Thanks."

Cheryl gritted her teeth as the girls walked off. Of all the nerve...Ellen accusing Naomi of intentionally sabotaging the fund-raiser and then pretending to be all friendly. Why, if she saw her right now, she'd do more than give her a piece of her mind, she'd—

Suddenly, the wail of an ambulance cut into Cheryl's dark thoughts. At first it was some distance away, but it drew quickly closer the longer she listened. She narrowed her eyes as the emergency vehicle veered into the Village Hall parking lot and rocked to a stop near the door.

Did someone get overheated? Had there been an accident or something? She took a hesitant step toward the ambulance as the doors swung open and two paramedics stepped out. Spying her, one of them waved her over.

"Excuse me, miss. Do you know where we can find Richard Wellaby?"

"Richard? Why...yes...he's one of our judges. Last I saw him, he was inside." She pointed toward Village Hall.

The paramedic's gaze followed where she pointed and then he nodded. "Thank you."

Cheryl stood, mouth agape, watching as the two paramedics rushed past her toward the building.

What on earth happened to Richard?

Chapter Thirteen

It only took about fifteen minutes for the paramedics to check Richard's vitals and then load him into the ambulance. From her vantage point, Cheryl caught a glimpse of him—wide eyes, pasty skin, and hair damp from sweat. He looked positively ghastly. She feared it was his heart and whispered a quick prayer as the ambulance drove away.

Levi and Naomi stood next to the windows along with several other onlookers. Cheryl eased over to them. "What happened? Does anybody know?"

"Ach, Cheryl, there you are." Naomi took her hand and squeezed it tight. "Poor Mr. Wellaby. One minute he was fine, the next he was white as a sheet and complaining of pain in his stomach."

"He said he felt nauseated," Levi added. "He was shaking so badly he could hardly stand, so I offered to help him to the restroom. That is when I noticed how much he was sweating."

"Pain in his stomach, shakes, sweating…" Cheryl frowned. "Do you think maybe he had a heart attack or something?"

"Could be, except for the stomach pains." Naomi cupped her chin, thinking. "Sounds more like the flu."

"He sure came down with it fast. He was fine this morning," Cheryl said and then caught herself. "Which is exactly what Clarice said when Gail talked to her this afternoon."

Both Naomi and Levi turned to look at her.

Cheryl gestured toward the other contestants who stood clustered together near the door. "The lady that dropped out, remember? She said she was fine this morning, but this afternoon she was too sick to enter."

"So then it *must* be some kind of contagious illness," Levi said.

"Maybe." Deep down, Cheryl suspected something far different...something more sinister. She motioned toward the judges' table. "You know, I think I'm just going to take a quick look around. I'll catch up with you both later, okay?"

Naomi's brows rose, but she said nothing as Cheryl gave a wave and headed toward the tables. The pies were still where they had left them. All but one of the pies was missing a piece. The last one, the one that Richard had eaten so much of, sat off by itself. It was a beautiful pie. The crust was flaky and golden, buttery on the tongue. The filling, too, was good, though a little sweet for her taste, the apples thinly sliced and layered almost two inches thick. It certainly looked harmless. Cheryl leaned forward for a closer examination.

"Cheryl?"

"Sugar and grits!"

Cheryl jumped, nearly bumping her head on Ellen's bent form. Both women straightened and stared wide-eyed at each other.

"Sorry, Ellen. You startled me."

Ellen's gaze slid from her to the pie and back. "What are you doing?"

"I was just...I just..."

Ellen tilted her head, waiting, then narrowed her eyes and peered at her suspiciously. "Why were you staring at that pie?"

Cheryl fished for an easy answer then decided it was better to settle on the truth—at least part of it—rather than fabricate a lie.

"Just a hunch." She gestured toward the exit. "I suppose everyone is ready to hear the results of the judging?"

Ellen still looked dubious, but she nodded. "I should join them. Now that the excitement with Mr. Wellaby is over, people are probably anxious to get started."

Her chin rose, and she turned to go. Cheryl took a step forward.

"Ellen, if you have a minute, there's something I'd like to speak with you about if you don't mind."

Ellen looked a bit hesitant as she shifted her weight from foot to foot. "Do we have time? I thought you said we needed to get back?"

"It's important," Cheryl insisted. "And it won't take long."

She pressed her lips together tightly and crossed her arms. "All right. What is it?"

Cheryl pointed toward the door with her thumb. "I was outside a little bit ago, and I overheard a couple of girls talking. One of them mentioned some remarks you made regarding Naomi Miller."

"Naomi?" The disdain disappeared from her face, and Ellen looked over her shoulder guiltily. "What about her?"

Cheryl reminded herself to reserve judgment until she'd heard the explanation from Ellen's own lips. "One of the girls said she heard you saying you thought Naomi might be behind some of the earlier disqualifications. Is that true?"

Color bloomed in Ellen's cheeks. Cheryl waited quietly.

"Well...I never said...that is, I did not..." She reached for the strings of her prayer kapp and nervously smoothed the fabric.

Though the words angered her, Cheryl knew how easy it was to regret something she'd said.

"A gentle answer turns away wrath, but a harsh word stirs up anger."

She took a deep breath. "I realize you had no way of knowing those girls were listening or how they would interpret your words. Of course, they don't know Naomi, or you, or they might have reached another conclusion. But with things as they are, could it be that the things you said led them to assume Naomi was guilty of something really terrible?"

Ellen bit her lip and cast her gaze downward. "I admit, I did sort of get carried away. A couple of my friends and I were talking, and I suppose I just let my imagination get the best of me. I know better than to give rein to my tongue. It was wrong to gossip." She lifted her eyes, her lashes wet. "I should not have said what I did about Naomi. She is a kind woman and does not deserve my cruel words. I am sorry."

Cheryl bristled beneath her smile. Ellen seemed sincere; however, that did little to repair the damage that might have been done to Naomi's reputation. "Perhaps you should apologize to Naomi."

"Of course." She scanned the hall and then brought her gaze back to rest on Cheryl. "I appreciate your speaking to me about this instead of going to Naomi. It is what an Amish person would have done, but I did not expect it from an *Englischer*."

"Actually…"

"And now I should look for Naomi before the contest resumes. I am sure she is here somewhere. Perhaps I will find her with Levi. Danki, Cheryl."

She couldn't exactly take back the suggestion, but Cheryl was forced to grit her teeth as Ellen peered innocently at her. "You're welcome."

She made as though to turn but stopped and laid her finger against her kapp. "Before I go, may I ask *you* something?"

Cheryl hesitated, sensing there might be barbs behind Ellen's benevolent smile. "All right," she said cautiously.

"You are quite close friends with Naomi, ain't so?"

Cheryl narrowed her eyes. Surely Ellen wasn't going to suggest that the judging was unfair? "Yes, we are quite close, but I told everyone that before I agreed to judge."

Ellen's smile was almost condescending. "Ne, Cheryl. I only meant to ask how two people who are so very different in their beliefs can be such goot friends. It is unusual, is it not?"

She crossed her arms protectively. "Unusual? Perhaps, but as Levi pointed out, people who love God…"

Ellen dismissed the reminder with a wave of her hand. "I know what Levi said, but I am wondering how you feel. What do you have to gain by befriending an Amish woman, and one so much older than you?"

"Ten years is not much older," Cheryl began, her defensive hackles rising.

Ellen brought her finger to her lips and tapped lightly. "You know, come to think of it, I have seen many curious Englischers around Sugarcreek. You know the kind I mean? People charmed by our way of life. They take pictures when they think we are not looking and whisper behind our backs."

She gave an exaggerated shake of her head. "They do not realize that to be Amish is more than just plain clothes and buggy rides. Our way of life is hard work too. Maybe they would not be so enamored by us if they had to plow behind a horse or wash their clothes by hand."

Cheryl felt the accusation in her words even if she didn't come right out and speak them. She stiffened her spine and formed her response carefully. "You know, Ellen, when I first moved to Sugarcreek, I saw preconceived ideas and misconceptions on *both* sides. I think the key to overcoming them is not letting those things keep us from learning who a person really is inside, whether it be beneath a bonnet or a baseball cap."

"*Hmm...*" She smiled stiffly. "Clever. I only wonder if..." She shrugged off the unfinished thought. "No matter. I am sure *you* are not like those other people."

It was not intended as a compliment, and they both knew it. Rather than let her anger overtake her, Cheryl smiled and took a step back. "All right then. Thanks for talking with me, Ellen. I suppose I had better get back to judging the contest."

Ellen opened her mouth as though to say more but was cut off by the hurried approach of Pastor Lory. Though he tried to appear calm, it was obvious by the sweat dotting his upper lip and the nervous fluttering of his hands that he was upset.

"Cheryl, could I speak to you a moment?"

"Of course, Pastor." She glanced at Ellen. "If you would excuse us?" She took the pastor's arm and walked with him toward the far wall, away from people. "What can I do for you?"

He removed a handkerchief from his pocket and wiped his brow. "I'm sorry, Cheryl. The hospital just called. It's about Richard."

Cheryl was almost afraid to ask the question simmering on her tongue. "He's all right, isn't he?"

Worried lines creased Pastor Lory's forehead as he nodded. "He will be but… Cheryl, it's not his heart or the flu. They think he has food poisoning."

CHAPTER FOURTEEN

"Food poisoning!" Realizing how loudly she'd spoken, Cheryl leaned closer and lowered her voice. "From what?" She sent a furtive prayer heavenward that it wasn't intentional.

The pastor looked miserable as he hunched his shoulders and whispered, "They're saying it had to have been one of the pies."

"But that's impossible. We all ate the pies."

"They said there was nothing else in his stomach." He spread his palms wide. "I'm sorry, Cheryl, but I think we're going to have to cancel the remainder of the competition."

She held up her hand. "Hold on a minute, let's…let's not do anything hasty." Cheryl bit her lip, thinking. Suddenly, she sucked in a breath and lifted her gaze. "Entry number four."

Pastor Lory frowned. "Excuse me?"

"Richard asked for a second helping of it, remember? What if that was the pie that made Richard sick and all the others were fine?" Spying several curious glances directed their way, she took a breath and lowered her voice to a whisper. "It doesn't seem fair to disqualify everyone, especially when no one else was affected."

He rubbed his knuckle against his scalp. "I don't know, Cheryl…"

"Okay, then let's at least ask the other judges what they want to do. After all, we've already completed this round and the scores have been tabulated."

Cheers erupted from across the room. In the center of a large group of people, Rex Carmichael raised his glass while the people around him began chattering excitedly.

"And what about the Carmichaels?" Cheryl gestured toward Rex. "What will they do if we pull the plug now? It wouldn't be fair to keep all the entry fees. We'd have to return the money, and the Carmichaels would be left with nothing."

Pastor Lory fidgeted nervously, his fingers tugging his collar while he paced. Finally, he blew out a breath.

"All right. I suppose we could talk to them"—he lifted up one finger in warning—"but we need to make sure they understand that we have no way of determining whether it was that particular pie or another that made Richard so sick."

Cheryl nodded eagerly. "Of course."

He rubbed his head again. "Who would have thought a simple pie contest would be this much trouble? Honestly, I haven't been this worried since Ethel Brewbaker suggested we change the carpet in the sanctuary. Anyway, let's gather up those judges."

Like Cheryl, the judges were concerned to hear of Richard's preliminary diagnosis, but no one showed any concern about continuing with the competition. Cheryl breathed a sigh of relief when Greta firmly and loudly declared that she would be glad to continue with the judging alone if need be.

Cheryl looked around at them all. "So we're in agreement then? We move forward with the competition?"

All three heads and Pastor Lory's bobbed in unison.

Slowly, Kathy raised her hand. "I only have one question, Cheryl. What do we do with the pie Richard ate?"

"I think we have to disqualify it," Greta said quickly.

"But what if it wasn't that pie that made Richard sick?"

"Do we take that chance?" she insisted. "None of the rest of us got sick, but I think that's only because we ate such a small amount."

"I agree," Laura said, a trifle reluctantly. "I mean, it's a shame and all, but I certainly don't want to risk food poisoning."

"Shall we take a vote?" Cheryl asked. At their nod, she said, "Okay then...all in favor of cutting entry number four?"

All four of them and Pastor Lory raised their hands.

"We still have to cut one more," Kathy said.

"We could cut the one with the lowest score and bump the second lowest up," Greta suggested. She glanced at Pastor Lory. "You know the ranking of each entry, right?"

His head bobbed in agreement. "Yes. It will be easy to pull out number four and drop the lowest."

Cheryl raised her eyebrows. "Everyone okay with that?"

There was general consent around the table. Though it was by no means a perfect solution, it was certainly the most fair. Cheryl gave a firm nod and rose. "All right then, let's go and inform the contestants of our decision. Once we've spoken to all of them, we'll go ahead and make the announcement public."

Laura nodded her approval. She braced both hands on the table and stood. "That's a good idea, Cheryl. We definitely should talk to the contestants. Why don't the rest of you wait here? I'll call them in."

"Thank you, Laura," Cheryl said, retaking her seat. What a predicament! All she'd wanted to do was help the Carmichaels. Instead, she felt like she'd orchestrated a disaster.

A moment later, the door opened and the seven remaining contestants filed in. Obviously confused by the turn of events, they eyed the judges curiously. Cheryl glanced at Naomi. What if her pie was number four?

She cleared her throat nervously. "I'm sure you're all wondering why we've called you in here."

As succinctly as she could, Cheryl explained Richard's condition and the judges' decision. When she finished, she looked over at the other judges. "Does anyone else have anything they'd like to add?"

They all shook their heads. Cheryl turned to the contestants. "Does anyone have a question?"

Ellen Lengacher raised her hand. "How do you know which pie made Richard sick?"

"Well, that is a little tricky," Cheryl confessed. She grabbed the contestants' number cards and spread them out on the table. "The only thing we can determine is that there was *one* pie that Richard took a second helping from. The rest of us only had a small taste of each pie, so we're assuming we didn't eat enough to be affected."

There were troubled frowns on all the faces, so rather than keep them wondering any longer, Cheryl took her cue from the pastor and stood. Leaning forward, she pulled out a contestant card and held it up. "The entry we are disqualifying is number four."

"But that is my pie!" Ellen stepped forward. A flush colored her cheeks, and her eyes flashed angrily.

Cheryl clasped her hands together tightly. "I'm very sorry, Ellen…"

Her gaze traveled over each of the judges. "This is not fair. I did not make Richard sick."

"Ellen," Naomi began gently.

Ellen shook her head. "They do not even know for sure it was my pie." She glared at Cheryl. "This is because of what I said earlier, ain't so?"

Indignation grew in Cheryl's chest. "Of course not, Ellen. The judges and I felt this was the only fair decision."

Pastor Lory held up his hand. "And remember now, the judges had no way of knowing whose pie was whose."

Thank goodness. Cheryl blew out a sigh, grateful for the bit of saving grace that had kept the entries a secret.

"You see, Ellen?" Naomi patted her shoulder. "There is no bias here."

Even as Naomi said the words, Cheryl read the question in her eyes.

What did you and Ellen talk about?

Cheryl gave a slight shake of her head, indicating they would talk later.

Ellen stomped her foot. "Well, at the very least, I think it is only fair that I be allowed another entry."

This was something they had not considered. Cheryl bit her tongue and looked to the other judges. They swiveled their heads like puppets to look at each other, probably as perplexed as she felt.

Harvey Ackerman stepped forward and held up one hand. "Hold on now, Ellen. Are you sure you want to do that? Remember what this contest is for."

Sandra, Agatha, and Bella all dropped their gazes. Bertie looked on helplessly.

Ellen sputtered a moment as she eyed the other contestants for signs of support. Though everyone appeared sympathetic, they all seemed to agree with Harvey and remained silent.

Finally, Ellen lifted both hands into the air in surrender. "Fine. I do not think it is fair…but neither do I want to hurt the Carmichaels."

A smile of approval bloomed on Naomi's lips. "You are doing the right thing." She reached out to pat Ellen's shoulder, but in doing so, her bag slipped from her arm and fell to the floor with a thud.

Ellen quickly bent to retrieve it. "Let me get that for you…"

She grabbed one handle but failed to secure the other. The bag flopped open, spilling the contents into a heap. Ellen covered her mouth with her free hand and then quickly dropped to her knees and began scraping Naomi's things together. "*Es dutt mir leed!* I am sorry."

"It is all right." Naomi squatted down next to her. "Do not worry."

"Here, let me help too," Cheryl offered. She grabbed a small packet of tissues and a mini notepad and handed them to Naomi. "Here you go."

Naomi took them and stuffed them back into her bag. "I have been meaning to clean out some of these things anyway. I can hardly even remember what I have in here."

Cheryl reached out, intent on grabbing Naomi's wallet. Instead, her fingers curved around a small plastic bottle. Her eyes rounded as she read the label.

Syrup of ipecac?

Stunned, she turned to stare at her friend. "Naomi?"

"Ja?" She paused from gathering her things to look at her. Spying Cheryl's face, she put out her hand and straightened. "Cheryl? What is wrong?"

Cheryl held up the bottle. Dread and disbelief made her stomach cramp. Swallowing hard, she forced the words from her dry throat. "Naomi…what is this, and why do you have it in your purse?"

CHAPTER FIFTEEN

Naomi's brows bunched in confusion. She took the bottle from Cheryl and studied the label. Suddenly, recognition of what she held and what it was used for dawned. She looked at her purse, then the bottle, then at Cheryl, her eyes wide and horrified. "I have never seen that before."

"But we all saw it fall out." Ellen shoved the bag toward Naomi as if she no longer wanted to touch it. "It has to be yours."

"Hold on a moment... What is that?" Agatha demanded. She strode across the room and jabbed her long, narrow finger toward the bottle. "Isn't that stuff supposed to make you sick?"

Bertie's head bobbed, and her eyes widened until she looked like an owl. "It's for triggering vomiting, like when a person accidently ingests poison or something and you need to get it out." She turned her round eyes to stare at Naomi. "I read all about it once when I was volunteering for the Poison Control Center. Why do you have it?"

Suddenly, something inside Cheryl snapped. She didn't know how the ipecac had gotten into Naomi's purse, but if she said it wasn't hers, then it wasn't. *Period.* But that meant someone was trying to set up her friend... again. With memories of poisoned jam swirling in her head, she shot to her feet and crossed to stand in front of Naomi.

"All right, everybody, let's just take a deep breath." She held up her hands, waited until everyone reclaimed their bearings, and then nodded. "Good. Now obviously there has been some sort of mistake."

"Mistake?" Harvey snorted and crossed his arms over his chest. "I should say so."

"Hold on, Harvey," Bella said, raising her palm to halt the flow of words from his mouth. "Cheryl is right. We can't jump to any conclusions here."

Harvey jabbed one of his stubby fingers toward the bottle. "That is ipecac." He swung his finger to point at Naomi. "It came from her bag. That's not a conclusion, that's a fact."

"Bella is right. We don't know how that bottle got there," Pastor Lory said. He turned to Cheryl. "Should we give the two of you a moment to talk?"

She nodded gratefully. "Would you please? I'm sure we can get to the bottom of this."

"Of course." Pastor Lory spread his arms wide and ushered everyone toward the door, including the remaining judges. "C'mon, folks, let's give these women a little privacy while they try and sort this mess out."

As they filed past, Cheryl studied their faces. Harvey looked flustered and a little irritated. Bella looked worried. Agatha, Ellen, and Sandra all looked angry, and Bertie...

Curiously, Bertie showed no expression whatsoever.

Cheryl sighed and closed the door behind them. Naomi hurried over, her hands wringing the white cotton apron around her waist. "Ach, Cheryl...This is just...I have no idea...Not again!"

Cheryl grabbed Naomi and pulled her into a firm hug. Slowly, she felt the tension seep from her friend's shoulders.

Blowing out a breath, she stepped back and stared into Naomi's eyes. "Someone is trying to make it look as though you are sabotaging the other entries."

"But who would do such a thing?" Her face went white, and her chin trembled a bit. "Not Bridget Marshall."

"No, not Bridget," Cheryl agreed hastily. "It can't be her. She is still serving her probation. Plus, she and Carter moved away after that incident with the rat poison last winter."

"Then who?"

"That's what we need to find out."

Her eyebrows rose hopefully. "So...you believe me about the ipecac?"

Cheryl nodded adamantly. "Of course."

In her relief, Naomi let her shoulders sag. "Danki, my friend. That means a lot to me." She shook her head in disbelief. "I just cannot understand it. Why would anyone do this?"

"I think I have an idea," Cheryl said scowling. "Earlier today Ellen admitted that she'd been spreading gossip about you."

Naomi's mouth fell open, and her eyes reflected her hurt. "What? But...why? What did she say?"

Cheryl's scowl softened, and she stepped back toward the table. "She admitted she'd said something about you being proud of your title as one of the best pie makers in Sugarcreek, but to be honest, she did admit she'd been wrong to say the things she did. She said she was going to try and find you so she could apologize personally. Maybe she only said that to try and take the attention away from herself and what she was doing."

Naomi thought for a moment and then frowned. "Ne. Ellen is young and immature, but I do not believe she would do anything so devious. What motive could she have?"

Her response was not unexpected. Naomi always chose to believe the best about a person unless they proved otherwise, which made this whole business and the incident last winter so infuriatingly unfair. So maybe it wasn't Bridget...but it had to be someone who knew what had happened...someone close to either Cheryl...or the Millers.

"All right," Cheryl said slowly. "Then our only recourse is to try and figure out who does have a motive." She paced the room lengthwise, stopped, and paced back. "Now who are the suspects? Obviously, we can't discount any of the contestants. I mean, it has to be one of them."

"Why?"

"Why?" Cheryl stopped pacing to stare at her friend.

Naomi nodded. "Anyone could be tampering with the outcome of the contest. It does not necessarily have to be one of the contestants."

Cheryl bit her lip, thinking. "So...you mean the person isn't necessarily targeting you?"

She wrung her hands helplessly. "Well, it could be the pie contest itself that someone is trying to stop."

"But why would anyone want to sabotage a fund-raiser?"

Neither woman said anything for a moment, and then Cheryl scurried over to the table, ripped a piece of paper from her notepad, and then grabbed a pencil.

"Okay, so either the person has something against you personally, which is why they chose something that had happened to you before…" She wrote down the number one and jotted Naomi's name down next to it. She quirked an eyebrow and bit the eraser on her pencil. "Or possibly it's me they're after. After all, I am the organizer of the event. Maybe the person just wants to make me look bad."

Naomi drew close to the table as Cheryl wrote the number two and her name beside it. Bending low, she pointed to the next line on the paper. "I think you need to add a third option."

"What?"

"There is one thing we have not thought of yet." The creases in her brow deepened. "The Carmichaels."

Cheryl's mouth dropped a bit. "You mean somebody could have a grudge against them?"

"It is possible." Naomi shrugged. "It is sad to think on, but there is always a chance that whoever is doing these things simply doesn't want the Carmichaels to get the money."

Outrage built inside Cheryl's chest. "Naomi, they've lost their home. A person would really have to have something against them to be that cold. What could they possibly have done to inspire that kind of spite?"

"Maybe we should talk to them," Naomi said. "Perhaps they can shed some light on this matter."

Cheryl set her pencil down and pushed back from the table. "Not *we*, Naomi. Much as I'd like your help getting to the bottom of this, I really don't think it would be wise to let you go along. Whoever is responsible for the accidents so far has already tried involving you. The last thing I want is to give anyone more reason to suspect you of any kind of wrongdoing."

Naomi bowed her head. When she looked up, there was resignation, but determination too, in her eyes. "Perhaps that is wise. Still, I do not like you traveling out to see them alone. The Carmichaels live quite a ways out of town."

Though she didn't want to, Cheryl grudgingly agreed. "I probably won't be able to get out there until late this evening. By that time it will most likely be getting dark, and if I remember right, the road to the Carmichaels' farm is pretty treacherous."

"I would feel better if Levi went with you."

"So would I," Cheryl said slowly. So much for Levi's talk of courting. Tonight would have to be about tracking down a culprit. "I'll talk to him after we finish with the judging."

"You still plan to continue?"

"What else can we do?" Cheryl turned and picked up the stack of scorecards. "Ellen's pie has been disqualified, but we still need to cut the finalists down by one."

Naomi's jaw worked, and then she slowly reached out and took the cards. "Ne, Cheryl. You do not. I will step down from the competition."

"What?"

She pressed the cards tightly to her middle. "It is the only way to convince people that I did not have anything to do with the disqualifications."

"But that's not fair. Everyone knows you are innocent."

"Everyone?" Naomi's eyebrows rose.

Cheryl could not meet her eyes. "Okay...so maybe there are a few people who don't know you as well as I do. I still think..."

Naomi cut her off before she could finish. "Better to tamp any suspicion now than to let it grow into something we cannot control." She gave Cheryl's hand a squeeze then pulled her number from the stack of scorecards and held the rest out. "What matters is that we help the Carmichaels, not winning some silly competition. Besides, with me out, I can keep a better eye on things, make sure no one plays anymore dirty tricks, ain't so?"

With some reluctance, Cheryl accepted the scorecards back. "I still don't like it." She lifted her chin defiantly. "I say we get to the bottom of this and expose the real culprit."

Naomi agreed with a faint smile, one that did not quite reach her eyes. Obviously, being framed for something as insidious as sabotage affected her deeply, but to be targeted twice? In response, Cheryl felt herself filled with righteous indignation for her friend. Naomi did not deserve to have something so ugly cast upon her. Unfortunately, only the people close to her knew that. Others would speculate about her character. They would whisper and gossip behind her back or say unkind things about the Amish in general. Worst of all, they would believe her guilty.

Cheryl squared her shoulders. She couldn't let that happen. She had to find the *real* guilty party and bring them to justice before this whole thing got out of hand.

And she had to do it fast.

Chapter Sixteen

The Carmichaels lived outside of Sugarcreek on a stretch of country road called Crooked Run. In the daylight, one did well to travel it with care. At night, with clouds covering the moon...

Cheryl gripped the steering wheel tightly. Next to her, Levi rode in silence, his eyes focused toward the bit of pavement visible through the windshield in the glow of her headlights.

"This is one time I would say a buggy is better," he said, breaking the quiet inside the car.

"This is one time I would probably agree with you." Cheryl risked a quick peek at the navigation system on her phone. "Five more miles." She slowed the car as they rounded yet another sharp curve. "Not even any streetlights out this way."

"Too many Amish farms," he said. "It is actually a very pretty drive in the daytime."

Finally, the Carmichaels' driveway came into view. Though the house was completely gone, the RV they had borrowed still cast a welcoming glow through the windows. Cheryl breathed a sigh of relief as they pulled in and parked.

"Good thing it's summer," she said as she unclipped her seat belt. "Come fall, when the deer are moving to avoid hunters, that road would be twice as scary."

"Or twice as nice." Levi smiled, and his eyes twinkled in the warm circle cast by the dome light. "I kind of enjoy watching wildlife from a buggy seat."

"Is that what I have to look forward to?" she whispered softly, the reason for their coming momentarily forgotten.

"Among other things."

His smile slowly faded, and though he didn't say it, Cheryl knew exactly what he was thinking. Her gaze fell to his mouth.

"We...uh..."

"We should get inside," they said together, both scrambling for the door handles before their emotions could run amok.

Levi joined her at the driver's door, his arm gently brushing hers as they walked up the driveway toward the Carmichaels' RV. Even that slight touch sent shivers coursing over Cheryl's flesh. She sighed in happiness thinking of the joy she would feel twining her fingers with his or experiencing the warmth of his hand on her back after they were married. That day could not come soon enough.

As if sensing her thoughts, he leaned in closer, adding his soothing voice to the chorus of frogs and crickets filling the air. "I cannot wait to make you my wife."

They had arrived at the stairs, and Cheryl nearly stumbled before reaching for the railing.

"Don't do that," she scolded gently, to which Levi only laughed.

Doris Carmichael answered at Cheryl's knock. Her hair was up in a ponytail, and she looked a bit ruffled around the edges with her shirt collar crumpled on one side, but she offered a welcoming smile as she caught sight of Levi and Cheryl standing on the top step.

She opened the door wide and beckoned them in. "Hello, you two. Come on in." Then she called to her husband, "Rex! Cheryl and Levi are here."

Levi swept the broad brim hat from his head and then stepped back to allow Cheryl to enter. From the back of the RV, scuffling sounded, and then a door slid open and Rex appeared. He too looked slightly disheveled. "Sorry about that. I was just putting the kids to sleep."

Doris motioned toward a coffeepot on the counter. "Would either of you like something to drink? We have coffee or water."

"No, thank you. I'm fine." Cheryl shook her head and so did Levi.

Rex gestured toward a light blue couch flanked by two matching captain's chairs. "Please have a seat."

"How did the fund-raiser go today?" Doris asked the moment everyone was settled. She took the chair closest to the door, her fingers drumming nervously on her knees. "Did we have a good turnout?"

"I'm not really sure about the other activities," Cheryl said. "I didn't have a chance to talk to August this afternoon, and Jacob has been busy taking care of the silent auction. This weekend will be the clincher. We've got several more events planned, so we'll know for sure how well we did then."

All of which was true, thanks to the disaster with the pie contest. Cheryl shot a glance at Levi. He turned to look at Rex.

"How is the job hunting coming?"

Rex blew out a heavy sigh. "If I'm honest, I'm starting to get a little worried. I figured I would have something lined up by now. Instead, I'm looking at about another five weeks before my unemployment runs out."

He forced a smile that Cheryl sensed was for his wife's benefit. "But I've heard of a couple possible leads, so we're hoping something turns up before then, right, honey?"

She tossed a troubled glance toward the back of the RV and lowered her voice. "We haven't really told the children everything. We don't want them to worry."

"Of course," Cheryl said. With each word, the knot inside her stomach grew. This family had already faced so much. It hurt to even think that someone might intend them further harm.

She lifted her chin. "Before I forget, I have a bit of good news I've been meaning to talk to you about."

Doris's eyes lit hopefully. "Oh?"

Cheryl nodded. "It's about the Swiss Miss. I've been meaning to take on a little part-time help, and I was wondering if you might be available."

"I would love to," Doris said without even asking about the hours.

"It'll only be a few days a week to start," Cheryl continued slowly, "and I can't pay all that much."

Doris shook her head. "Doesn't matter. Whatever you've got is fine."

"Great. Stop by next week, and we'll work out the details."

Cheryl was instantly reminded of an Amish proverb she'd seen displayed on a plaque at one of the local gift stores: You can tell a man's character by what he turns up when offered a job— his nose or his sleeves. Her heart warmed for this family, which made this visit even more uncomfortable.

She fumbled awkwardly for a moment and then plunged into the reason for their coming. "Rex, Doris...Levi and I..." She peeked sidelong at him, and he nodded encouragingly. "I really did intend to talk to you about the store, but there's more to our visit than just a social call."

The Carmichaels looked at one another and then back at Cheryl.

"What is it, Cheryl?" Doris leaned forward in her seat to grip her knees tightly. "Is something wrong with the fund-raiser?"

"Um...I wouldn't say that exactly," Cheryl said, scratching her temple. "It's really more the pie contest where we've had trouble." She drew a deep breath before outlining the details of the disqualifications in the pie contest thus far.

When she finished, Doris pressed her fingers to her forehead. "This is all so odd...almost too strange to be coincidence."

"That's what we thought," Cheryl said. "Which is why we're here."

Rex laced his fingers across his midsection. "You mean you don't think these events were an accident?"

"Not after today." Cheryl went on to explain about the bottle of ipecac discovered in Naomi's things.

Doris looked hesitantly at Levi. "I admit, I don't know your stepmother well, but the few times Rex and I have taken the children to the petting zoo or the corn maze, she has always been so kind and generous. I just don't believe she would ever do something like this, and neither should anyone who has ever met her."

"Danki, Mrs. Carmichael." Levi sat forward, the tension he felt showing in the tight muscles along his jaw. "Forgive me, but I must ask if you can think of anyone who might want to see the fund-raiser fail?"

Confusion crinkled her brow. "I don't understand."

"He means like an enemy of some sort." Rex gripped the arms of his chair tightly.

Levi hesitated. "Perhaps *enemy* is too strong a word. I am inclined more toward someone who might bear a grudge against you perhaps, or someone who might not want to see your family benefit from the work Cheryl is doing with the fund-raiser."

No glance passed between the Carmichaels this time. Instead, Doris lowered her gaze, her clenched fingers white against the fabric of her blue jeans. Rex rose to pace…what little room there was in the cramped RV.

Finally, Cheryl felt compelled to break the sudden silence. She eased to the edge of the couch and gently cleared her throat. "Rex, is there something we need to know?"

He stopped at the window above the sink and raked his fingers through his hair. "I suppose the best way to explain is to say that things aren't so cut-and-dried as a simple grudge."

"What do you mean?" Cheryl asked.

Across from her, Doris nodded encouragingly at her husband. "Tell them, Rex."

Reluctantly, he dragged himself back to his chair and sat. "It started at the brick company where I used to work."

Cheryl read anger, hurt, guilt, and pain in his eyes. This was difficult for him. She lifted him up in a quick prayer.

"I worked there for almost eight years before I got laid off," Rex continued heavily. "The job was hard, but I always tried to do my best, you know? I cared about the company. Not like some of the other guys, who always acted like the job was nothing more than a paycheck. I showed up to work early, and more often than not, I was the last to leave. I'm not trying to boast or make excuses..."

"I can vouch for his work ethic," Doris said, a touch of sorrow and pride in her voice. Her chin rose. "There was many a night Rex's supper got cold waiting for him to get home."

"Anyway, my boss noticed," Rex said. "When it came time to lay people off, I figured I'd be one of the first to go. Instead, I got put on a different job, shuffled around until..." His voice grew pinched.

"There just wasn't anywhere left to move him," Doris finished for him. She rose and went to stand next to him, then laid her hand on his shoulder.

Something about the way they both sounded and the look on their faces was a bit defensive. Like they were trying to excuse what had happened.

Cheryl shook her head, confused. "I'm sorry, but I don't understand. What does any of this have to do with someone holding a grudge?"

"Not everyone was happy about me not being let go," Rex explained. "There were others who had worked there longer who got sent home months before I did."

He dropped his head in his hands, his voice a ragged whisper. "What was I supposed to do?" He looked up, his dark eyes haunted. "Volunteer to get laid off? I had a family to feed, and with my bum hip..."

He trailed off and looked to his wife. Tears shone in Doris's eyes as she continued. "We were both afraid Rex wouldn't be able to find another job if they made him take a physical. The only reason he was able to keep this one was because he was already hired on when his hip started giving him trouble."

"Look, I am not a young man," Rex said. "It's not like there are a lot of jobs out there for me to pick and choose from."

"And the men that got laid off?"

"All of them younger than me. Most of 'em have already found new jobs, I think." He scratched his head. "Leastwise, that's what I heard."

"All except for one." Doris's voice had dropped to a worried whisper. Rex threw a sharp glance at her, but she met his gaze steadily and refused to back down. "Tell them, Rex."

"Tell us what?" Levi eyed them both curiously. "There is something you have left out?"

"Not...exactly." Rex ran his hand wearily over his face. "It's just...there is one person I know about who is still looking for a permanent job, like me. I heard he'd gotten hired somewhere, but it doesn't pay the same and the hours aren't great, so it's just temporary until he can find something better. Anyway, he and I are about the same age."

"Who is it?" Cheryl asked, clasping her hands together tightly while she waited for him to tell.

His eyes narrowed, and his lips thinned. "Understand, we got no proof that this person has done anything wrong. We had words once is all, back when I was still at the company. Could be I done something..."

"It was Harvey Ackerman," Doris blurted. She shot around his chair to stand in front of her husband almost protectively. "Harvey was the one who got sent home before Rex. And he wasn't happy about it. Not one little bit."

Chapter Seventeen

N ow, Doris..." Rex stood and took his wife's elbow.

"It's true, Rex." Her eyes widened to reveal deep hurt as she turned to Cheryl. "He called Rex all kinds of names and said all sorts of bad things about him. He even went so far as to threaten him."

Cheryl's mouth suddenly went dry. She stared at Rex. "He...threatened...you?"

He lifted his hands, palms out. "Now, it's not as bad as it sounds. He was upset, same as me, and worried about his family, that's all. I don't blame him for saying how he felt."

"What exactly *did* he say?" Cheryl asked.

Deep furrows creased Rex's brow. He jammed his hands into his pockets and lowered his gaze. "We were arguing. We both said things we didn't mean."

"He said he hoped we knew what it felt like to worry about losing our home," Doris interrupted. The lines of tension around her mouth and eyes clearly revealed that she was still angered by the things Harvey had said. "He said the company had no right keeping Rex on when others were losing everything. He basically blamed my husband for their troubles and his and vowed to cut him down to size if he ever passed him on the street."

"That's what he said? That he would 'cut him down to size'?" Cheryl held her breath while she waited for their reply.

Doris nodded.

"What do you suppose he meant?" Levi asked. "Did he say?"

Doris faced him, her eyes troubled. "We have no idea. Harvey walked off after that, and he and Rex haven't spoken since."

"But he entered the pie contest," Cheryl said. "I figured he wanted to help."

She gave a derisive snort. "That man would sooner help himself than a member of this community."

"Doris," her husband chided.

"It's true, Rex. When it comes down to it, Harvey was the worst about taking his job for granted. He showed up late, fell asleep on the job..."

"Sweetheart, that's enough." His voice softened as he cupped his wife's face in his hands. "Speaking ill of the man won't help. It'll only keep us bitter."

After a moment, she nodded, and Rex pulled her into a hug.

"Have you thought about going to the police?" Cheryl asked quietly. "I'm not sure there's much they can do about the pie contest, but we should at least let them know about the threats he made to..."

She broke off, struck by a disturbing possibility. Last winter several people fell ill after Bridget Marshall snuck rat poison into a few jars of Naomi's jam because she was desperate to get some of her own jam into a few of the local stores. Harvey certainly would have known, or at least heard, about what happened, and he had motive for using the information against the Carmichaels now. Worse still...

She looked up, her eyes round. "Your house," she whispered.

"Hold on there." Rex released his wife and turned to look at Cheryl. "Harvey may be a lot of things, but he's no arsonist, and he would never do anything that might intentionally harm another person, especially children. A faulty water heater caused that fire, and that's all there is to it."

"There's still the issue of the pie contest," Doris said.

Cheryl nodded. "That's right. Considering everything you've told us, there can only be one reason he'd enter."

"Cheryl, we cannot assume to know his heart," Levi said.

Though he spoke the words quietly, it was enough to make her rein in her escalating emotions.

She blew out a breath. "You're right. We should talk to him, I suppose, and see what he has to say before we jump to any more conclusions."

Her gaze bounced back and forth between the Carmichaels. "I hate to ask, but besides Harvey, is there anyone else you can think of who might have another reason to do this?"

They consulted one another with a shared glance and then shook their heads.

Cheryl rose, as did Levi.

"All right then," Cheryl said, slipping the strap of her purse over her shoulder. "Levi and I will head back into Sugarcreek. First thing tomorrow, I'll see about talking to Harvey."

"*We* will talk to Harvey," Levi said, fixing her under his steady gaze. "That is not something I want you to undertake alone."

So he was worried about Harvey too. Cheryl felt a blush heat her cheeks as he stepped protectively closer.

"All right, we'll talk to him."

"What should we do in the meantime?" Doris asked, pressing closer to her husband's side. "Anything?"

"Probably not. I think the best thing will be to wait and see what he has to say."

"Thank you." Rex stuck out his hand. Cheryl shook it, and then Levi did as well. "We'll wait until we've heard from you."

Cheryl bit the inside of her cheek. "I'm really sorry about this, Rex. I wish we could say it's all an unfortunate accident, but after today..." She shrugged.

"The truth will come to light," he said, squaring his shoulders. "Whoever is doing this won't be able to hide forever."

I hope you're right, Cheryl thought, but kept the words to herself. Instead, she offered an encouraging smile as she and Levi left the RV and headed back down the drive toward her car.

"So? What do you think?" she said once she was buckled inside.

The night air had grown muggy. Cheryl started the car and immediately reached for the AC.

Levi said nothing while he fastened his seat belt. "This is all very odd, for sure and for certain. I would like to think whoever is behind all this did not intend any real harm."

"But after what the Carmichaels just told us?" Cheryl put the car in Reverse and backed down the drive. The headlights made a sweeping arc over the trees as she pointed the car toward Sugarcreek.

Levi gave a low grunt. "After what we just heard, I am beginning to think this mystery may have more twists and turns than this road."

She laughed softly. "You certainly have a way with words, Levi Miller."

In fact, at that moment, she couldn't have said it better herself.

Chapter Eighteen

Friday morning, Cheryl put all the receipts from the previous week's sales into a zippered bag and dropped it inside her purse. She had a couple of errands to run, one of which included picking up Levi so they could speak to Harvey Ackerman. After that she would go by the bank on her way to Village Hall.

She sighed. Thoughts of their conversation with the Carmichaels had troubled her all night, so she woke restless and weary early this morning. She didn't want to believe anyone could be guilty of causing intentional ruin to another human being, but Harvey?

Thinking of his cheerful smile made her stomach hurt. Was it even possible for something so sinister to hide behind that merry chuckle? Granted, he'd been a little ornery on occasion, but nothing that would make her think him devious.

The weather was so pleasant, Cheryl drove all the way to the Millers' farm with her windows down. The soothing wind swept over her skin and went deeper, almost to her core, as though a good stiff breeze could whisk away the shadows of doubt and duplicity so that she, like Naomi, could believe the best of everyone.

She pulled to a stop in front of the farmhouse. From the paddock, Ranger nickered, and Cheryl picked her way across the yard to greet him. He nudged at her shoulder eagerly. He was well accustomed to the treats Cheryl brought, and she plucked a carrot from her pocket and fed it to him in halves.

"Now that is one happy horse." Levi ambled from the barn and joined her at the rail, his forearms braced on top and one booted foot resting on the bottom.

Cheryl reached over the fence to smooth Ranger's inky mane. "So different from when he first came here." She stopped stroking to grin. "I guess the same could be said about me."

"This place is home now."

She slanted a grin at him. They both knew the deeper meaning behind his words.

Levi pointed to the rolling hills opposite the road. "Aaron Lengacher and I have closed on the land. As of today, all of that belongs to me. Soon it will belong to both of us."

Her heart danced a pitter-patter. "I can't wait." Such happiness welled in Cheryl's chest she almost couldn't fathom it. "We'll have to speak to your parents first. Have you thought any more about what we should say?"

He nodded. "There hasn't been a moment when I do not think about it. My heart is telling me to trust in Gott. My head..." He sighed heavily. "My head keeps reminding me of the look on my daed's face the day Sarah left home to marry an Englischer. I have seen that look only one other time—the day my real maam died."

Cheryl allowed her hand to cover his in the briefest of touches. "But Sarah is back now, and things are finally right between her and your father."

He picked at the wooden railing with his fingernail. "Ja, but in between were many sleepless nights…for all of us."

Her heart squeezed inside her chest, but before any doubts could creep in, Levi spoke.

"I am not questioning our decision—just my own wisdom in knowing how to speak to Maam and Daed." His gaze became earnest as he turned to look at her squarely. "You are the only woman for me, Cheryl Cooper. I hope you know this."

She smiled, letting the conviction in his voice and in his eyes drive away her own fears. "I will keep praying that God gives you wisdom. I trust your leadership, Levi, and I believe you will know when the time is right."

She saw him suck in a breath, saw his head lift and a smile ease the lines of tension from his face. What power lay in a few words of encouragement! She tucked the knowledge away for those times when they faced trouble as man and wife.

She gave Ranger one last pat and then drew back from the fence. "Well, I suppose we should head out to see Harvey. Did you tell Naomi where we were going?"

Levi bumped the hat back off his forehead with his knuckle. "Ja. She wanted to come along, but I discouraged her since we are not yet certain that it really was him who tampered with the first few entries." He grinned. "You know my maam though. She gave me stern instructions to let her know exactly what we found out the moment we get back."

Cheryl laughed and glanced at her watch. "That may have to wait. We have about three hours before I need to report to Village

Hall for the final round of judging." She blew out a sigh. "Boy, will I be glad when this pie contest is finally over."

The absurdity of that statement had them both laughing as they walked back to Cheryl's car. All traces of mirth disappeared, however, when they pulled into Harvey Ackerman's yard a few minutes later. A beat-up, blue Chevy pickup took up most of the driveway. A child's tricycle and a battered red wagon hogged the rest. Cheryl wove around the trike and made her way up a set of sagging wood steps to the door and knocked.

Harvey looked surprised to see them as he answered the door. The screen door screeched as he swung it wide and invited them inside.

"Cheryl, this is a surprise. Levi, come on in. What can I do for you folks?"

Dark shag carpeting covered the floor. Cheryl cleaned her shoes on the outdoor mat before stepping into a good-size living room. "Hi, Harvey. Thanks for seeing us. I know we didn't call first."

He shook his head. "No problem. Can I get either of you something to drink?"

Cheryl declined, and so did Levi. The kitchen was open to the living room, and the smell of baking pastry wafted from it, tantalizing the senses.

Cheryl took an appreciative whiff. "That smells wonderful, Harvey. You almost ready for the competition?"

Harvey shoved his hands into his pockets with a grin. "You bet I am. Sure am glad they drew the buttermilk. Don't know what I would have done if I had to come up with one of them fancy French silk pies." He extended his hand toward the living room. "You folks want to sit down?"

"Danki," Levi said.

He and Cheryl followed as Harvey led them into the quaint living room. Though the furnishings were old, everything was well kept and neat. Harvey invited them to take the couch, and he claimed a leather recliner opposite them. As he sat, Cheryl noted his dark blue coveralls with his name stitched on to the pocket.

She pointed toward the patch. "Are you working today, Harvey?"

He nodded. "I'm on the second shift. I have to go in as soon as the pie contest is over."

"That will make for a long day."

He shrugged. "I'm used to it. Besides, gotta provide for my family. Speaking of which, I'm sorry my wife isn't here. She took a job working second shift at the gas station downtown to help offset some of our bills."

Right. Cheryl cast a sidelong glance at Levi. He nodded. Cheryl drew a deep breath. "Actually, that's kind of why we're here, Harvey."

He lifted an eyebrow. "Oh yeah? You going to offer me a job?"

"I wish I could." She laughed nervously and fidgeted with a corner of her shirt. "Harvey, you used to work at the same brick factory as Rex Carmichael, didn't you?"

He nodded and leaned back in his chair. "That's right."

"Do you mind me asking when you got laid off?"

His gaze slid to Levi and back. "About eight months ago. Why?"

"Were you able to find a job pretty quickly?"

His shoulders relaxed, and he nodded. "I was one of the lucky ones, I guess. My brother-in-law owns a towing business in New Philly. It doesn't pay as much as the brick factory, but it puts food on the table. Plus, I make a little extra when I'm on call so I take as many extra shifts as I can get."

Which explained the coveralls. She leaned forward. "I'm glad, Harvey. You heard Rex Carmichael is still looking for a job? He's worried it will be difficult because of the problems with his hip."

He fidgeted uncomfortably. "I know. I heard he was having trouble."

Since she could think of no way of beating around the bush, Cheryl simply plowed forward. "Harvey, is it true that there were a few people who were upset that Rex was left on after guys with more seniority were laid off?"

"More than a few." Harvey sat up straighter. "And I admit, I was one of them." A look of regret crossed his face. "Not because Rex didn't deserve to stay on. He worked harder than any guy there. It was a lot of fear, mostly. People wondering what they were going to do and taking out their frustrations on him."

"Taking out their frustrations... how?"

He grimaced. "Rex didn't tell you?"

"He shared a few things, but I'd rather hear them from you."

Harvey's fingers worked the worn fabric on the arm of his chair. Finally, his lips thinned and he exhaled sharply. "The brick factory isn't union, which means pretty much everyone there is an at-will employee. To be fair, management has always taken seniority into consideration when it came time for layoffs, but with Rex...well...pretty much everyone would agree he was one of the good ones. He worked hard, put in extra time, did all the jobs nobody else wanted, you know?"

Cheryl nodded for him to go on.

"Still, when it comes to a man's livelihood, I guess we all have to be careful not to let the worst in us come out. I knew a few of the men were giving Rex a hard time...leaving threatening notes in his locker, putting things on his windshield, that kind of stuff. It was all harmless, just a way for people to blow off steam. And then..."

He paused to run his hand over his close-cropped hair. "I'm not proud of myself, but I have to admit that when I got my own notice, I took it hard. I confronted my boss about Rex, and word got back to him about it."

"What happened?"

"We had words. Both of us said some pretty ugly things. Nothing came of it. In the end, I found another job and that was that."

Levi sat forward to brace his elbows against his knees. "Harvey, why did you enter the pie contest? If you were angry like the others, why did you bother with the fund-raiser?"

Harvey scrubbed his knuckles across his chin. "The simple reason? I felt bad. I didn't like it, but it wasn't Rex's fault that things happened the way they did. I had no call to go confronting him. I wanted to make it up to him, show him there was no ill will." Shame reddened his cheeks. "And God has kinda taken care of me, you know? I figured it was the least I could do."

Cheryl watched his face as he talked, looking for those tiny telltale signs of discomfort that would indicate half-truths or outright lies. What she saw was chagrin and a bit of self-condemnation, but no arrogance or wounded pride. Could he be telling the truth? Harvey gripped the arms of his chair and pulled himself up straight. "So now would you mind if I asked you a question?"

Cheryl started as she realized that he directed the question to her. She nodded for him to continue. "Sure, Harvey."

"What is this visit really about?" His gaze bounced from her to Levi. "Has something else happened with the fund-raiser?"

The trilling of his phone spared her from a hasty reply. Harvey excused himself to answer.

Cheryl turned to whisper to Levi. "What should we tell him?"

"I think we owe him the truth," he whispered back.

"But what if he's the one behind all the disqualifications? Worse, what if he had something to do with the Carmichaels' house burning down?"

Levi frowned and tilted his head closer. "Do you believe he did?"

She gave a wry grimace. "I hate to admit it, but not really. Besides, wouldn't the fire department have investigated if arson was suspected?"

Harvey's laugh rumbled from the next room. Cheryl threw a quick glance down the hall. When she didn't catch sight of him, she turned to Levi.

"I don't know…something here doesn't feel right—like maybe Harvey hasn't told us everything. But before we draw any conclusions about what that might be, maybe we should talk to the other contestants."

"Ja, I think you are right. Will you have time before you have to start the judging for the final round?"

She checked her watch. "Probably, if we leave right now." She threw another glance down the hall. Harvey was pacing, his footsteps scraping the floor. "Let's just tell him good-bye and get out of here."

Levi rose. Harvey noticed him and stopped pacing to cover the phone with his palm. "Sorry about this. You two heading out?"

Cheryl nodded. "We really need to get going." She patted her purse with one hand. "I've got a couple of errands to run before I head over to Village Hall."

Which, thankfully, was true. She still had the bank bag with her.

Harvey hesitated a moment, then spoke into the phone. "Can you hold on for a minute? Thanks." His gaze swung back to Cheryl as he brought the phone down to his side. "Listen, I realize things must look a little strange from where you stand, but…well…I think you need to know something. It's about Agatha."

Cheryl shot a puzzled glance at Levi and then at Harvey. "Agatha Hilty?"

His feet scuffed the floor. "Uh-huh."

"What about her?"

Indecision warred on his face. He frowned at the phone in his hand then merely shook his head. "All right, I know I just told you I regretted saying stuff about Rex, and I really don't want to make the same mistake again. But if you're worried about the pie contest, I suggest you start with her. She's not everything she seems. Not by a long shot."

CHAPTER NINETEEN

A huge lump formed in Cheryl's throat as she nodded to Harvey and then followed Levi out the door.

Agatha Hilty? What exactly did Harvey mean when he said she wasn't all she seemed? She waited until she and Levi were in the car before pelting him with questions.

"All right, what did you make of that? Do you think he was lying about Agatha to move suspicion away from himself and cast it on to someone else? Maybe we should stick around and ask him what he knows. Do you think we should stay? What if I'm late getting to the contest?"

"Whoa, slow down." Levi held up his hands. "Let us take this one question at a time."

Cheryl jammed the key into the ignition and then swiveled on the seat to face him. "Okay, you're right. So let's start with if you think we should stay and find out what Harvey meant."

He thought a moment and then shook his head. "We are still not sure we can trust him, ain't so? Maybe our time would be better served talking to the other contestants, see how they feel about Agatha... or each other for that matter."

Cheryl frowned and then turned the key. "You're right. Anything Harvey has to say would be suspect since it is his word only."

But wasn't that enough? For the Amish it was. A man's word was better than a guarantee. It reflected his character, his integrity. But Harvey wasn't Amish...and neither was Cheryl. She swallowed hard at the fresh realization of how different her life was from that of Levi's.

She put the car in Reverse and backed out of the driveway. "Anyway, his remark does remind me of something."

Levi looked at her curiously.

"After the first round of judging, when Sandra's entry was eliminated, I am almost positive I saw and heard Agatha react as though she was glad." Her excitement grew as she warmed to her idea. "And then when Tory was disqualified and Sandra was back in, Agatha seemed almost angry."

"That is an odd reaction, unless she has something against Sandra."

"Exactly. I wonder if Harvey knows what that something is but isn't saying."

"*Hmm.*" Finally, he sighed in exasperation. "I am beginning to think I should leave this mystery solving to you and Maam. Apparently, the two of you are better at it."

Cheryl laughed and pointed her car toward town. Before heading to Village Hall, she ducked into the drive-through at her bank to turn in the receipts. She was pulling the bag from her purse when a familiar voice made her raise her head.

"Good morning, Cheryl. Hi, Levi."

She peered through the drive-up window. Sandra Remis waved to her through the glass.

"Hello, Sandra," Levi said, bending low to return her wave.

Cheryl did the same. "Hi, Sandra. I didn't know you worked at the bank."

Her face brightened. "Just started a couple of months ago. I don't usually do the drive-up though. Normally, I work one of the teller stations."

"Oh." And because she felt she should say more, she added, "How do you like it?"

"It's a good job...banker's hours and all that." Sandra laughed.

"Right, banker's hours." Cheryl frowned. "Are you going to get off in time to make it to the pie contest?"

She smiled brightly. "My boss is letting me off a few hours early since it's for a good cause."

"That's good."

Sandra nodded. "I'm so glad the judges drew buttermilk. I have a great recipe I've been dying to try."

"Really?"

"Yep. Buttermilk is pretty straightforward, so it will be hard to make the pies stand out...unless you have a secret ingredient." She chuckled and slid out the drawer for Cheryl. "Anyway, I sure hope the judges like it."

"I'm sure we will," Cheryl said. "Good luck."

She laid the bank bag in the drawer, and Sandra pulled it back.

"Thank you. Just making a deposit today?"

"That's right."

Sandra quickly confirmed Cheryl's total, stamped the receipt, and slid it back to her. "All right then. I'll see you in a couple of hours."

"Yep. See you then."

"Well, that is one person we will need to cross off our list," Levi said, frowning. "I doubt we will have a chance to speak to her before the competition starts."

"True, but hopefully we'll get plenty of answers from the other contestants." Cheryl put the car in Drive. "Plus, we'll know that Sandra has a rock-solid alibi if anything *else* happens between now and then."

Levi's chuckle warmed her through. Oh, but she could get used to that sound. In fact, she looked forward to it.

The drive to Village Hall was quite brief. They still had almost two hours before the competition was scheduled to start. Cheryl held her breath as they pulled in. The parking lot looked suspiciously empty.

"What if no one is here?" She sighed and put the car in Park. "I doubt we'll have time to track everyone down if we have to drive all over Sugarcreek."

"Well, we have already spoken to Harvey and Sandra. That only leaves Agatha, Bella, and Bertie."

"Bertie lives just outside of town." Cheryl reached for the gear lever. "We could head there first."

"Or…" Levi gently laid his hand over hers. "We could wait until they show up. That would give us a little time to talk. Please, Cheryl. There is something I have been meaning to speak with you about."

Something about the tone of his voice raised prickles along her arms. Was he having second thoughts about marrying her?

Had he decided the risk of losing his family was too great? Maybe he realized he couldn't bear the thought of leaving his church. Her throat tightened. "Talk? About what?"

Levi sighed and removed his hand, leaving her skin tingling where he'd touched her. "I have been thinking about what we should say to my family."

"Oh." Cheryl sagged against her seat back. "And?"

His blue eyes shone with intensity. "Maybe we should not hit them with everything all at once. Maybe it would be better if we eased into things a little at a time."

Confusion over where he was leading muddied her thinking. "Okay."

Levi turned slightly to grasp her hand. "I have visited Friendship Mennonite with you several times, ain't so?"

"Yeah, especially after Grace and James invited us to play volleyball that one time."

He nodded quickly. "And neither Daed nor Maam showed any concern about that."

She hesitated and pulled her hand away slowly. "That was different, Levi. You were visiting. Of course they wouldn't be worried."

"Ja, this is true. But here is what I have been thinking... What if I started visiting there more regularly... just to get them used to the idea of me going somewhere else?"

Cheryl reached for the AC control with shaking fingers and then adjusted the vents to blow cool air on to her heated cheeks. "Levi... I know we haven't considered this before, but maybe we should think about... what I mean to say is... what if *I* were to..."

"Cheryl." He waited until she looked at him. "Being Amish is not an easy way of life. It should not be romanticized or coveted or glorified. Being Amish is about desiring to please Gott, to separate oneself for Him. Choosing it because you wanted to make my family happy would be wrong."

"And leaving it because you want to make me happy? Wouldn't that be wrong as well?"

"It would...if that was the reason."

At the first part of his sentence, she'd caught her breath and held it. When he finished, she blew it out on a trembling sigh.

"I am not leaving the church just to make you happy. I am leaving because I know you are the person Gott has chosen for me. And because..."

His throat worked as he swallowed. "I can no longer stay."

Her heart jerked at the look of sorrow that tightened his features. "What do you mean?"

His fingers fiddled with the buttons on his sleeve until finally he lifted his gaze to hers. "I love the Lord, Cheryl, but I do not think I joined the church for exactly the right reasons."

He ran his hand over his face and leaned forward on the seat. "Daed was heartbroken when Sarah left. I thought I could help ease some of his hurt by demonstrating my commitment to stay, to be present for him."

He gestured toward a group of tourists who were happily snapping pictures of an Amish buggy as it rumbled past. "If I could, I would tell those people that everyone who chooses this life does so for their own reasons, but the main reason should always be because they are called to it and not because they have some exaggerated notion of what it means to be Amish."

"You think that's the reason behind the fascination for anything Amish?" she asked hesitantly.

He shrugged. "Maybe. I think people long for innocence and purity. I think they want to remember a simpler time, but that is my point, Cheryl. It is a simpler life, but that does not mean it is an easier life."

As his meaning slowly sank in, Cheryl found herself nodding and falling more in love with the man he was inside. "I think you're right, Levi. I think..."

A knock on her window nearly startled the breath out of her chest. She turned to see Ellen peering expectantly at them. Cheryl pushed the button and rolled the window down.

"Hi, Ellen." She couldn't help the tiny niggle of irritation that seeped into her voice at being interrupted.

"Hello, Cheryl." Ellen bent lower in the window. "Hello, Levi."

"Ellen."

Her gaze swung slowly back to Cheryl. "Um...Cheryl, do you have a moment? I'd like to talk to you about yesterday."

Yesterday? Was she going to offer more protests regarding her disqualification? Cheryl fought to keep her displeasure from manifesting on her face and reached to pull her key from the ignition. "Sure, Ellen. Give me just a minute, and I'll meet you inside."

"Danki. Please excuse the interruption, Levi."

Cheryl put up her window, fuming at the sweet smile Ellen flashed before spinning around and walking away, her plain skirt fluttering. What was it about her that instantly set Cheryl's teeth on edge? Well, aside from the obvious attention she paid to Levi.

"I guess I should go inside."

"I suppose but…" He stopped, and a flash of something warm in his eyes melted Cheryl's irritation in an instant. "I wish you would not. I was enjoying sharing my heart with you."

Her breathing became irregular. "Maybe after the contest…"

"We could get some pizza," he said, their words overlapping.

He laughed and reached for her hand, holding on a second longer when she would have pulled away and sparking a longing deep inside her. Suddenly, she knew he felt it too, for he let go and reached for the door handle in the same moment as she.

"I will keep an eye open for Bertie and the other contestants."

"All right. I shouldn't be long with Ellen."

They exited the car, both pausing to take a deep breath before heading up the sidewalk into Village Hall.

Ellen stood near the entry, admiring the pictures that lined the wall of Sugarcreek's previous mayors. Though she looked up innocently at their appearance, Cheryl couldn't help but wonder if she'd truly been looking at the pictures or observing her and Levi through the window next to the door.

Ellen clasped her hands at her waist, her smile pretty and eyes wide. "I am sorry if I interrupted you and Levi. I did not mean to."

And yet you went ahead and intruded anyway.

Cheryl squelched the uncharitable thought and told herself to smile. "It's all right, Ellen."

She slid a glance over her shoulder at him. "You looked like you were having a pretty serious conversation."

"We were."

"Was it about the pie contest?"

"Among other things." Unwilling to be drawn into sharing the details of her conversation with Levi, Cheryl motioned toward Ellen. "Now, what can I do for you?"

A blush colored Ellen's cheeks. She dropped her gaze and gave a tiny toss of her head. "Well, to be honest, I wanted to apologize... you know... for my behavior yesterday."

"Really." Cheryl gave herself a mental shake and asked again, more brightly, "Really?"

Ellen nodded. When she looked up, her eyes shone with contrition. "I acted a bit like a spoiled *kind*, I am afraid." She put her hand to her mouth. "Oh, I am sorry. Kind means child."

"I know what it means," Cheryl said, exasperation rising in her throat. She crossed her arms but fought the urge to tap her toes. She gentled her tone. "I've learned a lot of Pennsylvania Dutch words hanging around with Naomi and the Millers."

"That is goot!" Her smile was almost too wide as she reached out to pat Cheryl's arm. "So many Englischers do not even bother trying to learn our language or our ways. To them, we are just an oddity to gawk at."

"Well, I suppose I'm not your average Englisher, eh?" Still struggling to remain civil, she ducked out from Ellen's hand and gestured toward the judging tables. "Thank you so much for making time to apologize, Ellen. You didn't need to, but I appreciate the effort. And now I really should..."

"Oh, but that is not all," Ellen said. "I also wanted to ask you about Naomi."

"Naomi?"

"Well, about the bottle we found in her things."

Cheryl narrowed her eyes. "Yes? What about it?"

Ellen had the grace to look flustered. "I heard she decided to withdraw from the contest, and I was just wondering if that was true."

"It's true, Ellen." Cheryl was no longer able to keep her words from sounding clipped. "We'll be making that announcement before the judging begins today."

"I am sorry to hear that." Ellen bit her lip and then pressed on as though something compelled her to speak. "Naomi really is a very nice person, Cheryl."

"Of course she is, Ellen. I've known Naomi a long time, ever since moving to Sugarcreek."

Her chin jutted stubbornly. "I just mean that *I* cannot believe she would be capable of intentionally sabotaging another person's entry." She pressed her hand to her chest, her blue eyes wide and somber.

Cheryl frowned. What on earth was she talking about? "Obviously, anyone who knows her..."

Ellen put up her hand. "But I understand that you did what you felt was necessary. It is just that we Amish tend to look at a person's character before making decisions that could affect their reputation."

"Her reputation?" Cheryl sputtered. Feeling slightly disoriented by the rapid change in conversation, she took a deep breath and blurted, "Amish are not the only people who care about a person's character, Ellen. Englishers are just as concerned with doing what's right, and I don't appreciate the implication…"

To her shock, Ellen sidestepped her and stuck out her hand. "Naomi, I did not see you there."

She rattled something in Pennsylvania Dutch, all the while gesturing to herself and then Cheryl.

Cheryl felt as though a stone had settled in her stomach. Naomi listened to what Ellen said and nodded every so often, but her wide-eyed gaze stayed fixed on Cheryl. To her horror, she read hurt there, and something else… something worse.

Naomi's gaze registered the pain of betrayal.

CHAPTER TWENTY

What exactly had Ellen said to put that look of hurt and betrayal on Naomi's face? She didn't have to understand the words to know that whatever Ellen had said was about her.

Cheryl gulped and stepped toward her friend. "Naomi, we were just talking about you."

"Ja, I heard."

"No, I mean..."

"Cheryl was just telling me you decided to withdraw from the competition," Ellen interrupted. She grasped Naomi's arm and peered at her earnestly. "I am so sorry, Naomi. It is not right, what happened to you, but like I said to Cheryl, I completely understand that she is only trying to be fair."

Why did hearing them from Ellen's lips make the words sound feeble, the action they'd taken slightly unwarranted? Cheryl turned her gaze to Naomi. Had she been wrong to allow her to step down when she knew her to be incapable of intentionally harming anyone?

"Naomi, I..."

What could she say? Both Naomi and Ellen watched her, unspeaking, and then Ellen gestured toward the door.

"Perhaps we should wait outside and give Cheryl time to set up."

No. The last thing Cheryl wanted was for Ellen to spend time with Naomi. Who could tell the kinds of thoughts she'd put into her head?

"There's plenty of time before the contest starts...," Cheryl began.

Levi jogged up, sweat dotting his lip and brow. "Cheryl, Bertie and Bella just arrived."

She craned her neck to see them entering, both bearing a pie and both looking extremely proud of themselves. "Okay. If you would ask them to wait just a moment, I'll be right there."

Levi looked confused by her request. He pointed to the clock above the window. "You see the time? We have less than two hours."

"And we do not want to keep you," Naomi said quietly.

"But I really would like to clear a few things up before you go," Cheryl protested.

Naomi gave a slight shake of her head. "There is no need."

She stuck out her hand and grasped Naomi's arm. "Naomi, really. I don't want you to think that I have any doubt about your innocence."

"Danki," Naomi said, though she sounded a little less certain than she had yesterday.

"I am glad that is behind us," Ellen said. She smiled cheerfully. "Now, how can I help? I know, Levi and I could set up for you," she offered. "I saw how you had everything arranged yesterday. Would you like us to put it all together the same way?"

The only thing worse than putting off explaining to Naomi was having Ellen spend *any* time with Levi. Cheryl gritted her teeth and shook her head.

"Don't bother. I'm sure we'll have plenty of time for all that." She cast one last pleading glance at Naomi. "But we'll talk more after this is all done, all right?"

Naomi nodded her agreement and then turned for the door, Ellen tagging along at her heels.

"Everything all right?" Levi asked, pulling her concentration away from the retreating women's back.

"Fine. At least, it will be once we put this contest behind us," Cheryl growled. And now she was taking her emotions out on Levi. She sighed in exasperation. "Sorry."

He gave an understanding nod and then pointed toward Bertie. "There she is. Go and talk to her. I will track down Bella. She must have set her pie down and gone outside."

He turned for the door, and Cheryl made a beeline for Bertie, who was bent over the table putting the finishing touches on her pie.

"Are those mint leaves?" Cheryl asked.

Bertie smiled and straightened. "A little garnish never hurts."

"Agreed." Cheryl took a deep breath while she willed her swirling thoughts to slow. "Bertie, do you have a moment? I'd like to talk to you about the pie contest."

"Sure." Her eyebrows lifted. "Wait. It's not about another disqualification, I hope."

"No, at least not one that you didn't already know about. Naomi has dropped out."

Bertie braced her hands on her hips. "That's too bad. I mean . . . it's lucky for me, I guess. I hear she's a great cook. But I'm sorry for her. Did she say why?"

Gratitude that she hadn't automatically assumed Naomi guilty filled Cheryl's heart. She felt a tiny bit of tension seep from her shoulders. "She wanted to avoid any controversy. She's hoping that by removing herself from the competition, some of the talk surrounding the ipecac found in her purse will die down."

Her head bobbed. "Probably a good idea. I hope it works."

"Yeah, me too." She bit the inside of her cheek and breathed a silent prayer for the right words to speak. "Bertie, what do you know about the other contestants?"

Confusion furrowed her brow. "Huh?"

"Do you know any of them very well?"

She tugged at her earlobe. "Not all of them, I suppose. I know Sandra Remis from the bank."

"I just found out she worked there."

"Uh-huh. Been there a couple of months, I think. And I know Agatha Hilty pretty well. She and I play Bunco together. Why do you ask?"

She fidgeted nervously with the strap of her purse. "Do any of them have a grudge that you're aware of—against each other, or possibly even the Carmichaels?"

Bertie drew back, her clamped lips pale against her tanned skin. "I see. I take it somebody told you about me and Bella."

Cheryl hid her surprise but only barely. Questioning suspects had taught her one thing—people tended to want to fill silences. They usually talked with very little prompting. She crossed her arms and waited.

"It's not like you heard. All of that happened a long time ago. I've put it well behind me."

"Well, why don't *you* tell me what happened?" Cheryl said carefully.

"I suppose it was Harvey Ackerman that blabbed?" Bertie paced angrily. "He always did have a big mouth. Not that it matters. I'll be glad to tell you all about it. The truth is Bella stole my great-aunt Netty's recipe for mincemeat pie. That's how she won the blue ribbon at the county fair a few years back. I couldn't prove anything, or I'd have stripped ol' Bella of that prize, but she stole it. I know that for a fact, no matter what she or anybody else says."

A bit timid in the face of Bertie's fury, Cheryl phrased her words cautiously. "Do you mind telling me how you knew?"

Bertie stopped pacing to glare. "'Cuz she used homemade brandy, that's why. None of that store-bought stuff. Fermented her own peaches, plums, pears, and apples to create a better-tasting liquor." Indignation swelled her chest. "But the giveaway was in the distilling process. Bella would never have known to put the brandy in a stone crock. That was my great-aunt Netty's secret, one that had been passed down for generations…until Bella happened to stumble upon it while I was preparing my own pie for the fair. Somehow she got a gander at that recipe and made off with Netty's secret."

The muscles in her jaw bunched like marbles the longer she talked. For a woman who claimed to have put the past behind her, Bertie certainly had gotten herself worked into a lather.

Her hands balled into fists. "I'll be honest, I haven't gone out of my way to try and prove Bella cheated, but it wouldn't bother me none if somehow that truth came to be known."

"I understand," Cheryl said. At a loss for anything more to say, she offered a weak smile. "Well, thank you for your help, Bertie."

"No problem." Bending back to her pie, she plucked one of the mint leaves off the top and replaced it with a few fresh raspberries she took from a small grocery bag.

Cheryl blew out a tremulous breath. She certainly hadn't expected so much information, but it would explain why someone might have wanted Bertie disqualified from the competition early. After all, if Bertie held a grudge against Bella all these years, couldn't Bella do the same in reverse? To what length would these women go to see the other disqualified?

A more troubling question...what did any of this have to do with the Carmichaels?

CHAPTER TWENTY-ONE

Now that Cheryl had heard Bertie's side of the story, she felt it only fair that she speak to Bella. Levi had tracked her down as he'd promised, and the two of them...plus Ellen...stood waiting outside the door to Village Hall.

Ellen chatted quietly with Levi. As Cheryl approached, she heard Ellen ask, "It is settled then? You will come by the farm the Tuesday after next?"

Levi looked a bit uncomfortable as he nodded at Ellen but kept his gaze fixed on Cheryl. "Ja, Ellen, I will be there."

Cheryl swallowed a sudden lump in her throat. This jealousy was getting out of hand. She lifted her chin, determined not to let her petty feelings get the best of her. "You're going to the Lengacher farm? I thought you already concluded your business with Mr. Lengacher."

"I have." Levi gave a slight wave of his hand. "This is about one of their mares. She is almost ready to foal, but Ellen is worried she may have trouble with the delivery. I told her I would come by and take a look."

"Ja, and I am very grateful. You are very kind, Levi." Ellen flashed a pretty smile, gave a wave to Bella, and then a nod to Cheryl. "If you would excuse me? I had best look for Naomi."

As she left, Bella gave a nod in her direction. "That sure is one sweet gal, don't you think so, Cheryl? I'm glad I got the chance to know her through this competition."

She had her own opinion, but it wouldn't be fitting to say so. Cheryl smiled politely. "Thank you so much for waiting on me, Bella. Do you have a moment to talk?"

"Of course, though"—her brow furrowed, and her blue eyes lost a bit of their sparkle—"I hope this isn't about another disqualification to the pie contest."

"Not exactly." Cheryl motioned toward the large oak tree under which August had set up his BBQ pit for the past few days. "Mind if we sit?"

"Sounds nice, but don't you have to get inside?" Bella's gaze darted toward Village Hall. "I wouldn't want to hold you up out here."

"We have plenty of time." Cheryl took her by the wrist and gave her hand a pat. Once they were seated on one of the picnic benches, she laid her arms against the table and clasped her fingers. "Bella, I just finished chatting with Bertie."

"Oh?" Her eyebrows rose skeptically. "She been yammering to you about how I stole her great-aunt's recipe again?"

"She did mention it," Cheryl said slowly. Apparently, Bertie wasn't the only one who had yet to let bygones be bygones.

Bella snorted and turned up her nose. "Well, it ain't true. None of it." She jabbed the table with her index finger. "I won that contest fair and square, just like I intend to win this one." She leaned close and gave Cheryl a conspiratorial wink. "I have me a no-fail recipe for buttermilk pie. I call it Miracle Crust Buttermilk Custard because I don't use a typical piecrust." Her voice rose as she pulled away. "Course, Bertie will probably start yapping about how her great-aunt so-and-so used to make a pie just like it."

Cheryl cleared her throat discreetly. "What exactly *did* happen all those years ago, Bella? What made Bertie accuse you of cheating?"

"It was a misunderstanding...simple as that."

Her lips puckered and her expression turned sour so that for a moment, Cheryl thought she might not say more. But then her chin jutted and she said, "I overheard Netty talking about how she used homemade brandy in her mincemeat pie. Course, I had never considered such a thing, so I asked her about it. I *told* her I might try it for my entry," she added defensively. "She encouraged me to give it a whirl and suggested I use a stone crock during the distilling process, but that's the extent of it. I didn't steal her recipe. I made my own brandy by trial and error and finally settled on something I thought tasted good enough to use in a pie."

She scowled and her lip curled in an angry sneer. "I tried to explain that to Bertie, but the woman is stubborner than a deer tick. She wouldn't let loose of the idea that I'd stolen from Netty, even after I showed her my list of ingredients and the adjustments I made after each batch."

A bit of the scowl eased from her face. "A few weeks later, Netty fell ill and passed away. We never did hear the truth from her lips, not that it would have mattered much to Bertie. She'd set her mind to thinking me a thief."

She formed a fist and shook it in Cheryl's face. "I'll tell you what...if I hear about that Bertie telling one more person that I stole that recipe, I'll...I'll..."

Unnerved by the thrust of her chin and the temper sparking in her eyes, Cheryl clasped the edge of the table. "You'll do what, Bella?"

Her anger seemed to whistle out of her like a punctured tire. Bella brushed her hands together in disgust. "There I go again, letting that woman rile me up after I told myself I would leave it all in the past."

Her eyes narrowed as she peered suspiciously at Cheryl. "That ain't why you're talking to me, is it? You don't believe any of what she told you?"

"I wasn't there all those years ago," Cheryl answered in an attempt to be diplomatic. "I couldn't know what happened."

Though it was vague, the answer seemed enough to satisfy Bella. She gave a toss of her graying curls. "Humph. Well, so long as she isn't trying to ruin my chances of winning this here competition, I suppose I'll just have to leave it be."

"I think that would be wise," Cheryl said, hoping once again that a gentle answer truly would turn away wrath. She pushed up from the table. "Well, I probably should go and check on the whereabouts of the other judges."

As she spoke, a familiar silver sedan pulled into the parking lot, and Cheryl gave a cheerful wave to Laura Early, glad that she could extricate herself from Bella without further hurt feelings.

"Good luck today, Bella," she said and then set off at a brisk walk toward Laura.

Laura carried a brown paper grocery bag in each arm. Cheryl took one and walked with her toward the doors.

Eyeing Cheryl critically, she said, "How's it going...or should I be afraid to ask?"

"Ugh. I'll tell you inside." She peeked inside the bag. "What's all this?"

"Plaques for the winners and certificates for everyone else who participated."

"Laura, that's wonderful! I'm so glad you thought of it."

She shrugged. "Eh. I know a guy. He gave me a huge discount. Only charged for the materials since it was for a good cause." She hefted the bag on to her hip and reached into her purse for her cell phone. "I stopped by the hospital to check on Richard."

"Oh? How is he doing?"

"Ornery as ever." Laura chuckled as she pulled up a glowering picture of him on her phone. "He swears he'll never judge another food contest again. On the other hand, who knew the man would enjoy selfies so much?"

Cheryl laughed. When they reached the door, she pulled it open and allowed Laura to walk through first.

"So where do you want these?" Laura asked.

"Let's take them to the smaller meeting room and lay them all out in order. That way they'll be easier to hand out when we announce the winners."

Cheryl paused as they passed the pie table. Silver domes would be placed over each of the pies so that the contestants could present them with a flourish to the judges. It was a bit theatrical, but she hoped it would make for good entertainment.

Behind them, the door banged open and Sandra Remis rushed in carrying her own pie.

"Whew! I made it with plenty of time to spare." Her eyes widened as she looked around the nearly empty room. "Am I the first one here?"

Cheryl shook her head. "No, Bertie is here somewhere, and so is Bella."

"Okay, good." Sandra bit her lip and lowered her gaze to her pie. "Um...what about Agatha? I don't suppose she's arrived yet?"

"Not yet. At least, I don't think so." She cast a glance at Laura. "Have you seen her?"

Laura shrugged. "I just got here myself." She paused and pointed at the pie table. "Wait a minute...it looks like someone *has* been here. There's another pie on the table."

Cheryl turned to look. Sure enough, a fancy card with the words *Brown-Eyed Buttermilk Pie* printed on it had been taped carefully to one of the five silver domes. Cheryl pointed to it and another one labeled Buttermilk Chess Pie. "That one must be Harvey's."

"And Sandra's pie makes five," Laura said, relieving Sandra of her burden and depositing it carefully alongside the other four. She handed Sandra a card. "Go ahead and put the name of your pie on the card and then tape it to one of the silver domes."

Cheryl motioned to the table. "Oh, and did you remember to bring...?"

She cut off when Sandra pulled her recipe card from her pocket and gave it a wave. "Right here."

"Good." Cheryl smiled. "Good luck today, Sandra."

"Thank you." Sandra wrung her hands nervously. "I admit, I'm kinda anxious to get started."

Cheryl smiled and then led the way into the meeting room. While they were laying out the awards, she told Laura all about her visit to the Carmichaels.

Laura gripped one of the plaques tightly in both hands. "Oh, Cheryl...you don't really think someone purposely set fire to the Carmichaels' house, do you?"

"I sure hope not," Cheryl said, "but according to Harvey, there were plenty of people around with a pretty serious grudge."

Laura pondered that a moment and then frowned. "I still can't figure out what any of that has to do with the pie contest."

"Neither can I," Cheryl said, "unless the person behind the sabotaged entries is trying to keep the family from reaping any of the benefits from the fund-raiser."

"Or possibly..." Laura's eyebrows arched.

"What?"

"Maybe the two aren't connected at all."

Cheryl hesitated. That thought had occurred to her, but in the heat of emotion following the discussion with Harvey, she'd allowed her reasoning to become skewed.

Laura set the plaque down carefully. "Do you know if any of the other events have been affected?"

Cheryl folded the bag that the plaques had come in carefully. Wagging her finger at Laura, she said, "That's a very good question. Unfortunately, I'm not sure I'll have enough time to find out before the final round of judging for the pie contest starts."

"Maybe you could ask someone to do it for you."

"Yep. And I know exactly who." She handed the bags to Laura. "Do you think you can finish getting the tables set up while I check?"

"Of course." Laura tucked the bags under her arm and gave Cheryl a gentle push. "Go. And let me know what you find out."

"Will do."

Cheryl rushed outside, eager to find Naomi and Levi. Perhaps they could do some sleuthing into the status of the other fundraising events. Several women in prayer kapps crowded the yard sale tables, their plain dresses fluttering in the warm summer breeze. It took Cheryl much longer than she intended to find Naomi, and when she did at last spot her, she was alone.

Was it her imagination, or did Naomi's smile dim a bit when she spotted her? Cheryl gulped down a bit of apprehension and hurried to her side. "Naomi, have you got a second? I need your help."

Concern immediately replaced every other emotion on her friend's face. "Of course, Cheryl. What can I do?"

Gratitude choked her. Despite whatever doubts Ellen had planted in Naomi's head or whatever careless injury Cheryl might have unintentionally inflicted, Naomi was instantly ready to lay it all aside in the aid of a friend.

Cheryl gestured toward the BBQ pit. "Would you mind checking with August and the other event coordinators to see if they've had anything unusual happen? Laura and I were talking, and she suggested that it might be a good idea to find out. Unfortunately, I don't think I will have time before the judging starts."

"Unusual?"

"As in, similar to the events of the pie contest," Cheryl explained quietly. "Things that could sabotage the fund-raisers."

Naomi's eyes rounded. "What is this about, Cheryl?"

She grimaced, wishing she could explain but knowing there wasn't enough time to do it adequately. She leaned closer and grasped Naomi's arm. "Levi and I paid a visit to the Carmichaels. We have no proof of wrongdoing, but…"

"That is why you need to know of any unusual happenings." Dread sharpened her tone.

"Exactly."

Deep trust shone in Naomi's eyes as she peered at Cheryl. "I will find out. And Cheryl"—she gave her hand a squeeze—"do not fret about what happened earlier. We will clear all this up once the fund-raiser is over, ja?"

Relief flooded Cheryl's heart, and she nodded. "Thank you, Naomi."

Naomi gave her one final pat and then hurried away to do Cheryl's bidding. Thankful to have one task off her plate, Cheryl returned to the judges' table, where Greta and Kathy had joined Laura and waited for their instructions.

Cheryl glanced at her watch. "Thank you for coming early, ladies."

Greta waved dismissively. "No problem. Anything you need us to do?"

"Get the scorecards ready?" Cheryl turned to Laura. "Have you seen Gail?"

"Right here!" Gail hurried over, clipboard in hand.

"Have all the entries been checked in?" Cheryl asked.

Gail nodded. "Yep, all accounted for."

Cheryl blew out a sigh of relief. Maybe they would get lucky and get through this round without any mishaps. She scanned the crowd for the contestants. Harvey stood near the door, and Sandra chatted with some friends nearby. Bella too looked anxious to start, as did Agatha... but where was Bertie?

"Sugar and grits," Cheryl muttered.

Laura's head lifted. "What is it?"

"Bertie still isn't back."

Greta took out her cell phone. "You want me to call her, see where she is?"

"Would you?"

Cheryl blew out a sigh of relief that quickly evaporated when, moments later, Greta turned to her and said, "Sorry, Cheryl. It went straight to voice mail. I left a message for her to call me."

"No problem. Thanks for trying, Greta." She handed Laura the scorecards and several pencils she scooped from her purse. "Here you go. You gals get to work on these and I'll go see if I can track down Bertie. If I'm not back in fifteen minutes, go ahead and draw the names for the order the contestants will be presenting. That way we can jump right into judging at exactly two o'clock."

"You got it."

Laura motioned to Kathy and Greta. Chairs scraped the floor as they gathered around the table. While they got to work, Cheryl set off in search of the missing contestant. Honestly, after the fiasco this contest had become, she doubted she would agree to host another fund-raising event . . . ever.

Chapter Twenty-Two

Smoke from the BBQ pit swirled lazily above the treetops, scenting the air until Cheryl's mouth watered. With everything that happened that morning, she hadn't even had time to think about eating lunch, and her stomach grumbled noisily now.

As she neared the BBQ pit, August saluted with a crisp wave of his tongs. "Howdy there, Cheryl. Can I get you something to eat?"

She stopped alongside the grill and eyed the sizzling hamburgers and roasting chicken longingly. Tempted as she was, she shook her head. "No time, August. Say, you haven't by chance seen Bertie Ford?"

He pointed with the tongs. "Seems like I did see her heading yonder toward the yard sale."

Cheryl gave a wave and turned that way. "Thanks, August. I'll check."

A cursory search yielded no results, but the park surrounding Village Hall was busier than normal since this final day of fundraising had been packed with additional events. For the children, they had added games, face painting, and sack races. For the adults, there were horseshoes, washer boards, and a three-on-three basketball tournament. Cheryl sighed and propped her hands on her hips. At this rate, the pie contest would be over before she bumped into Bertie.

"Cheryl!"

Hearing her name called, she turned to look. A few yards away, Naomi wove through a crowd of people, waving to catch her attention. Cheryl met her near the edge of the parking lot.

"Naomi, I'm glad to see you. Did you find out anything?"

Naomi put her hand to her waist, huffing as she struggled to catch her breath. "I may have." She sucked in another breath and then wiped the sweat from her brow. "Did you know that Sandra Remis and Agatha Hilty used to own a bakery together?"

"What?"

Naomi nodded. "It was called Sweets and Eats, or something like that, but it went out of business not long after it opened."

"Why? Were people just not going in?"

She shook her head. "That is the odd part. Rhoda Hershberger said it was very popular. People used to wait in line to get in."

Cheryl frowned. "So then what happened?"

A stiff wind jerked at the strings of Naomi's prayer kapp. Almost absentmindedly, she caught them in one hand and smoothed them over her shoulder. "According to Rhoda, Sandra and Agatha were once close friends. All of that changed when they opened the bakery. People used to hear them arguing at all times of the day. Rhoda said she even saw Sandra throw a pan of cupcakes to the floor."

"Did she say why?"

"Apparently, it was because Agatha was the better baker. Sandra was envious of her talent, and when she tried to prove she could do as good a job as Agatha, the two got into a terrible row. It was not long after that Sandra left the bakery. Agatha could not run it without her, so she closed the shop. The two have not spoken since."

Cheryl gaped. "You're kidding."

"I wish it was only a joke, but Jacob Hoffman confirmed every word."

"That's terrible." Cheryl thought back over the past couple of days. Indeed, she had never seen the two women speak, but she assumed it was because they didn't know each other. Only today had Sandra asked about Agatha.

Cheryl wagged her finger, thinking. "You know, that would explain Agatha's odd behavior when Tory was disqualified."

Realizing Naomi might not be aware of what had happened, Cheryl quickly filled her in.

"And Sandra did seem a little distant today when she asked if Agatha had arrived with her entry," she continued. "Do you think it was because she wanted a glimpse of her pie?"

"What other reason could there be?" Naomi's eyes widened. "And if that is the case, perhaps we should have someone stationed by the pie tables, just to make sure nothing happens to the entries."

Cheryl gulped nervously. "That's probably a good idea, but first I need to find Bertie."

"What?"

She nodded. "That's what I'm doing out here. I came to look for her. She was working on her pie earlier, but now she's missing."

"Oh no."

Cheryl clasped Naomi's arm. "Can you help me find her? I'm afraid I'll run out of time otherwise."

"Of course," Naomi said. She gestured back toward the yard sale. "I just came from there and did not see her."

"And I was by the BBQ pit. Not there either." She pointed toward the far end of the park, where the squeals of children filled the air. "She has to be there. Let's go look."

Naomi agreed, and the two set off quickly. When they reached the face painting, Cheryl split off one way and Naomi the other. Children and parents wandered among the tables. While Cheryl should have been pleased thinking of the amount of money the generous crowd undoubtedly garnered, all she could think of was what another mysterious disqualification would mean to the contest...and her own credibility.

As the minutes ticked by, Cheryl felt her blood pressure rise. Hot and exasperated, she stopped under a tall tree and pulled out her cell phone. She had Bertie's number too. Maybe if she tried calling her now...

The call went straight to voice mail. She left a brief message and then jammed her phone back into her pocket. She had just enough time for one last sweep of the grounds before she had to return for the judging. Halfway through the children's area, she met up with Naomi, but a quick glance at the disappointment on her face let her know she'd had no more success than Cheryl.

Cheryl told her what she intended, and Naomi half-turned for the yard sale. "Perhaps we should split up again? I can take this side..."

"No need," Cheryl said. "Even if you do find her without me, by the time you caught up with me, it would be too late."

"We will go together then." Naomi hooked her arm through Cheryl's, and Cheryl couldn't help but be thankful that the discomfort from earlier appeared to have passed. Suddenly, Naomi stiffened.

"What is it? Do you see her?"

Naomi pointed. "Ne, but there are Levi and Ellen over by the picnic tables. Perhaps they have seen her."

She dropped her arm and scurried toward them. Cheryl trailed along a bit more reluctantly. What was Levi doing with Ellen? She trusted him. Of course she did. But she couldn't help the almost irrational worry that welled up inside her seeing them together.

Levi was shaking his head as she walked up. "Ne, I am afraid we have not seen her." He rose to his feet. "But we can help you look."

Cheryl checked the time and frowned. "Actually, don't bother. It's almost two. If I don't head back now, I'll be late for the judging."

"Maybe she already went back, and we just missed her," Naomi offered with a hopeful smile.

"I'm sure that's what happened," Cheryl said with more confidence than she actually felt. She met Levi's gaze and avoided Ellen's altogether. "Well, I'd better get inside. I'll see you all later."

To her surprise, and gratitude, Levi separated from Ellen and joined her. "I will walk with you. I want to watch the final round of judging."

"Me too," Ellen said, cutting Cheryl's happiness short when she rose to stand alongside Levi. "It will be interesting to see what happens in this round."

Her teasing made Cheryl bristle. Rather than let her irritation show, she turned and headed for the building. Just before she reached it, Greta rushed outside.

Cheryl's stomach sank. Sugar and grits! What now?

She bit her lip. "Hey, Greta. We looked everywhere, but we couldn't find Bertie."

Greta waved away her explanation. "Never mind that, she's back."

"She is?" Cheryl widened her eyes hopefully. "That's great."

"Not exactly," Greta said, dousing the tiny flicker of relief. "She's back all right, but she's mad as a hornet."

Chapter Twenty-Three

Cheryl jammed her hands into her pockets. Rivers of sweat ran down her back. When did the day get so hot? "I'm almost afraid to ask what happened."

Greta grimaced. "The other judges and I drew the names for the order of presentation like you told us."

"And?"

"Bertie didn't like where she landed in the order."

"But that's why we drew names, to make it fair."

Greta's head bobbed. "She knows that, but she says we should have waited until she got back to draw."

"You mean she wasn't there?"

Greta shrugged and pointed to her watch. "You said fifteen minutes…"

"Did you explain that we tried calling her?"

She nodded. "She says she went outside for a bite to eat. Her phone was dead, which is why she didn't answer."

"I tried too," Cheryl said. Tension seeped into the muscles of her shoulders. She ran her hand over her face. "I'll talk to her."

"Uh…Cheryl?" Greta grimaced dismally. "I'm really sorry, but Bertie got kinda loud and people started grumbling."

"I don't…what do you mean?"

Greta's expression looked pained. "I overheard some people saying the pie contest was a disaster and..."

"And what, Greta?" Cheryl asked, bracing herself.

"That it wasn't being run well. Mostly, they were blaming you." She reached out to touch Cheryl's arm. "I'm really sorry. I just thought I should warn you about what you might be facing when you go in there."

"I appreciate that, Greta," Cheryl said softly.

Though her palms were sweating and her stomach hurt, she forced her shoulders back as she walked back into the building. Indeed, there were many curious stares as she made her way to the front, but at least she was spared from hearing the whispers. She stopped at the table and looked at Bertie head-on.

"Bertie, Greta tells me you're not happy with the way the judges conducted the drawing for the presentations."

Bertie stood with arms crossed and a dark scowl on her face. "That's right. They should have waited until everyone was present."

"Actually, Bertie, the rules state that contestants must be in place and ready fifteen minutes prior to the start of competition," Cheryl said gently. "It's in the copy of the rules you were given before the contest started."

A murmur rose from the crowd.

"I was present," Bertie protested with a stomp of her foot. "I was only gone a few minutes."

"I do understand," Cheryl said, hoping to sound patient but still firm. She turned and stuck out her hand toward Laura. "May I have a copy of the rules please?"

Laura looked flustered as she shuffled several times through her folder. Finally, she located the rules and held them aloft. "Here they are."

"Thank you," Cheryl said. She took the sheet and showed it to Bertie. "It's all right here, Bertie, under rule number seven."

Bertie's frown deepened as she read, and a flush crept up her neck to redden her cheeks. "Fine," she said at last. "We'll proceed, but I still don't think it's right."

Cheryl sagged with relief. Honestly, she didn't know what she would have done had Bertie not given way. She turned to look for Pastor Lory and waved him forward from the back of the room.

"Everything okay now?" he asked.

Cheryl nodded. "I hope so. Let's go ahead and get started. You know who goes first?"

He held up a slip of paper. "Kathy gave me a copy of the list."

"Good. Just call out the contestant's name and let them take it from there. They will be presenting their pie and then sharing their recipe and whatever other information they think will help them win. They each have fifteen minutes, and then the judges will sample their pies."

"Got it." He gave her shoulder a pat. "Cheer up. It'll all be over soon."

"I sure hope so," Cheryl whispered and then gave him two thumbs-up when he failed to hear.

Pastor Lory tapped the microphone. "Is this on?"

When there were several nods around the room, he smiled and began the introduction for the final round of competition. Cheryl and the other judges eased into their chairs while he talked. Agatha Hilty had drawn number one, so she crossed to the pie table and removed the silver dome from over her pie to a chorus of *oohs* and *ahhs*.

Hoisting her pie high, she walked over to the judges and paraded slowly down the table in front of them so that they could all get a good look at her creation.

"My entry is called Brown-Eyed Buttermilk Pie." She twisted and turned her pie to give them the full effect. "The recipe has been in our family for generations, going all the way back to my great-great-grandmother. The story goes that she made it for a young gentleman who had caught her eye in church. She used this pie to win herself a proposal."

There were chuckles from the audience as Agatha went on to explain how she carefully stirred in buttermilk that had been warmed to room temperature before whisking. As she talked, Cheryl felt herself beginning to relax so that by the time Agatha was ready to slice her pie and serve up the samples, she'd forgotten all about the unpleasantness with Bertie. The judges each scribbled notes on their scorecards, and then Cheryl thanked Agatha and signaled to Pastor Lory that they were ready for the next contestant.

Sandra Remis approached nervously. The silver dome covering her pie clattered noisily as she dropped it onto the table. She looked sheepishly over her shoulder at the judges. "Sorry."

"Take your time," Cheryl said encouragingly.

Sandra picked up her pie and brought it to the judges' table. "My pie is called Apple Cider Vinegar and Buttermilk."

Next to her, Cheryl heard Kathy breathe a soft "*Ooh.*"

Sandra seemed to gain confidence as she talked. She lifted her chin higher as she explained the tricky process of mixing the apple cider vinegar with the buttermilk so it wouldn't curdle. The end result was a sweet and savory pie that melted on Cheryl's tongue. She gave it high marks and then signaled to Pastor Lory.

He moved to the next shiny silver dome where Harvey stood looking totally comfortable in his worn coveralls.

"All right, folks, moving right along. Harvey, tell us about your pie."

Harvey grasped the microphone and swung it quickly toward his mouth, making it squeal. "Oops. Sorry about that."

Light laughter followed. Harvey began again.

"All right…so my pie is called Old-Fashioned Buttermilk Chess." He grinned and shot a wink toward Agatha. "Unlike my opponent there, this pie comes from a recipe entirely of my own creation."

His remark invited good-natured hoots and ribbing from the audience. Harvey held up his hand. "Believe it or not, I'm actually a pretty good cook. Ask my wife." He pointed, and she waved to him from the back of the room.

"We'll have to take your word on that, Harvey," Pastor Lory said, chuckling. "So tell us about your pie."

Harvey nodded. "Right. Well, chess pies are not so common here in this corner of Ohio, but when we were growing up in Mississippi, I remember my granny baking one every Sunday."

Pastor Lory eyed Harvey's pie. "What makes it a 'chess' pie as opposed to regular buttermilk?"

"That's easy. Chess pies are sweet. Very sweet." He grinned. "That means lots of sugar. Also, they usually contain a little cornmeal along with the eggs, butter, vanilla, and flour. Oh, and buttermilk, of course."

He'd certainly captured the interest of the judges, Cheryl noted, leaning forward herself for a glimpse of Harvey's chess pie. He didn't parade the pie as his competitors had, but he did display the slices once he'd cut them by holding them high on the pie server for the judges to see.

"You won't notice any difference just by looking," he said, "but you'll certainly be able to tell the difference in the consistency of a chess pie. The custard stands up a little stiffer…holds together a little better."

Each judge took a bite, and several heads bobbed in agreement with Harvey's assessment. Cheryl motioned to Pastor Lory.

"All right. Thank you very much, Harvey."

Harvey returned to stand behind the table, and Pastor Lory moved on down to Bella.

"Bella, what have you got for the judges today?"

Her eyes sparkled as she put her hand on the silver dome, but she did not remove it immediately. "I like to call my pie Miracle Crust Buttermilk."

"Miracle, huh?" Pastor Lory winked at the crowd. "I'm very interested in miracles."

Even Bella snorted.

"So what makes the crust so miraculous?"

"Well…it's because there isn't one." Bella removed the lid with a grand flourish and held her free hand toward her pie like Vanna White.

"No crust?"

Bella's head bobbed like a rooster while Pastor Lory leaned forward for a better look. "How does it hold together?"

"The secret is in the ingredients." Bella held a finger to her lips. "I'll tell you so long as you promise not to share."

There was laughter from everyone but Bertie, who glared, unblinking, at her.

Pastor Lory held up three fingers in imitation of the Boy Scout salute.

"Okay, so I take the ingredients—margarine, eggs, sugar, a pinch of salt, buttermilk, vanilla, a squeeze of lemon, and eggs—and mix them all in a blender."

Kathy looked especially interested as Bella explained, and Cheryl wondered if perhaps she might be adding a miracle crust variation to her menu at the Honey Bee Café.

"After that," Bella continued, "I just pour everything into a buttered pie dish and bake. The flour settles to the bottom and forms its own crust."

"Interesting." Pastor Lory glanced over at the judges. "I wouldn't mind trying this one myself."

Several people in the audience nodded their agreement. Like the other judges, Cheryl slid her fork through the sample Bella provided and had to agree—she was enjoying this part of the competition.

Pastor Lory waited while the judges scribbled notes and then gave a slight nod. "Judges, are you ready for the final contestant?"

Cheryl gave him the okay, and he moved on to Bertie. "Last but not least... Bertie Ford. What do you have for us today?"

"Mine is called Amish Buttermilk Pie," Bertie said.

Naomi quirked an eyebrow, obviously wondering, like Cheryl, what made the pie "Amish."

Bertie lifted her chin proudly. "I use the *freshest* buttermilk and a drop of lemon juice to give it a richer flavor."

"Fresh buttermilk?" Pastor Lory asked.

Bertie gave a quick nod of her head. "We live in the middle of dairy country, so it's pretty easy to find it fresh. It makes a world of difference."

Pastor Lory chuckled then gestured toward the silver dome in front of Bertie. "All right, then let's see your pie."

Bertie's fingers hovered just above the lid. Suddenly, a strange feeling fluttered in Cheryl's stomach... a moment of foreboding that almost made her reach out to stay Bertie's hand.

"Wait...," she said faintly.

Only Greta heard. She turned to look at her curiously a split second before Bertie yanked the lid off and upward.

There was a gasp from the audience and then Pastory Lory moved, blocking Cheryl's view. She hated to look. Had to look.

"What is it? What's wrong?" Cheryl said, glancing side to side at Greta and then Kathy on her right.

"Bertie's pie...," Kathy whispered.

"What? What's wrong with it?" Cheryl demanded.

Kathy turned to look at her, eyes wide with disbelief. "It's gone."

CHAPTER TWENTY-FOUR

Cheryl backed into the small meeting room and quietly closed the door against the uproar that had erupted the moment Bertie—and everyone else—realized that her pie was gone. On the slim chance the pie had somehow ended up back in her car, the judges had asked her to check while Cheryl and the others looked around Village Hall. She wasn't holding out much hope. Bertie's pie was gone, and the odds that they would find it were slim to none.

A knock sounded on the door, and Greta poked her head inside.

Though Cheryl really didn't need to ask, she did anyway. "Bertie doesn't have her pie, does she?"

"No." Greta shook her head miserably and then jabbed her thumb out toward the hall. "But there's someone here who wants to talk to you."

She opened the door wider to let Levi step through. Worry creased his face as he came to stand next to Cheryl, his arm lightly brushing hers. "Are you all right?"

She wrapped her arms tightly around herself, resisting the urge to fall against his chest and weep. "I have no idea what to do . . . what to tell Bertie. What could have possibly happened to her pie?"

He held her gaze steadily. "Perhaps you should go talk to her."

"Someone has to," she muttered, even while wishing with all her might it didn't have to be her. "And I can't hide in here forever."

"Best make it quick," Greta said, pushing her hair behind her ear nervously. "When I left, Bertie was hopping mad and hollering something about Bella making off with her pie." She scratched her head. "Any idea what that is all about?"

"Unfortunately."

Cheryl pressed her hands to her stomach and squared her shoulders, and then both she and Greta headed out the door. The voices spilling from the meeting room were growing louder . . . and angrier.

A crowd of curious onlookers had gathered around the table, drawn by the commotion happening between Bertie and Bella. Cheryl had to weave her way toward the front with several muttered apologies along the way.

Greta was more forceful and simply shouted, "Move please, folks!"

Her method proved effective. The sea of people parted and allowed them to pass. Cheryl's skin burned as all eyes turned in her direction.

"There she is!" Bertie shouted.

Cheryl jumped and then squirmed uncomfortably as Bertie jabbed her finger to point at her. Next to Bertie, Bella stood red-faced and angry, her arms crossed defensively. Off to the side, Harvey watched the proceedings with something akin to amusement on his face. Sandra just looked miserable, and Agatha remained impassive.

"Now we'll get this sorted out." Bertie propped her fists on her hips and waited until Cheryl reached the front. The moment she stopped, Bertie whirled to face Bella. "She saw me putting garnish on my pie less than an hour ago."

"I didn't say you didn't bring a pie," Bella hissed, her eyes narrowed. "I said you took it yourself so you could blame someone else...namely, me."

"Hold on, ladies." Cheryl lifted her hand, halting the flow of words between them. "I'm sure neither of you took that pie. Maybe we can get this sorted out with just a few simple questions."

A rustling sound came from the crowd, and Cheryl risked a peek just long enough to see Naomi push toward the front to stand alongside Levi. She looked worried. Levi wore a frown. Next to him...

Cheryl tore her gaze from Ellen's smug smile. She sucked in a breath and assumed a businesslike pose. "Now, who was the last person to see the missing pie?"

Bertie lifted her hand. "That was probably me. Like I said earlier, I finished with the garnish and then went outside to grab a plate of BBQ from August."

Cheryl glanced at the other contestants. "Did any of you happen to notice if Bertie's pie was on the table when you brought in your entries?"

The four contestants exchanged glances. Sandra and Harvey shook their heads.

Bella glowered. "It wasn't here by the time I came in."

"Me either," Agatha said. "I mean…there *were* pies on the table, but I didn't look to see whose was whose."

Cheryl cast about for a glimpse of Pastor Lory and finally spied him near the entrance. She lifted her hand and beckoned him forward. Sweat dampened his collar and dotted his forehead. He pulled a handkerchief from his pocket to mop his brow.

"Sorry, Cheryl. A few others from the church and I have been out looking for the missing pie."

"No sign of it, huh?"

He shook his head and shoved the handkerchief back into his shirt pocket. "Afraid not."

A murmur rose from the crowd with his words.

"Well then, what are we going to do?" Bertie demanded with a stomp of her foot. Her gaze bounced from Cheryl to Pastor Lory.

Cheryl swallowed the lump in her throat and stepped forward. "We'll have to delay the contest."

The chatter from the audience swelled.

"Now wait just a minute…," Bella began, her head wagging.

"I can't take another day off work," Sandra said in the same moment.

"Neither can I," Agatha said.

"We really don't have any choice." Cheryl lifted both hands in appeal. "It wouldn't be fair to disqualify Bertie when she had nothing to do with her pie's disappearance."

"How do you know she didn't?" Harvey said, chiming in at last.

"Hey! I resent that remark," Bertie protested. She jerked her thumb toward the door. "August Yoder can vouch for where I was. He saw me buy the BBQ. Ask him."

"Now, now…," Pastor Lory said, struggling hard to be heard above the rising din of voices.

Bertie swirled to glare at Bella. "You did this."

"That's a lie."

Bertie's head bobbed like a bull. "You did it all right. You were just mad because I told Cheryl about you stealing my great-aunt Netty's recipe."

A gasp rose from the crowd, and fury stole over Bella's face like a thunderhead.

She shook her finger under Bertie's nose. "What did I tell you about repeating that drivel?"

"Ladies…," Cheryl began, but it was too late. Bella picked up the closest pie and held it aloft.

"I told you if I ever heard you say that again I'd…"

"You'd what?" Bertie challenged. She stood her ground, her brown eyes flashing. She swung one arm wide to encompass the room. "I'm not afraid of you, and it's about time people heard the truth about what you did all those years ago."

"Bella, put down the pie." Cheryl's demand fell on deaf ears.

Her eyes narrowed to slits, Bella marched across the distance separating her from Bertie. "Take it back, Bertie."

Her chin rose. "Why should I? It's the truth, and you know it."

"Hey...that's not...," Harvey said weakly. He stepped forward, his hands outstretched.

"I'm giving you one last chance, Bertie," Bella threatened.

Cheryl watched, transfixed, as she waved the pie back and forth, slowly, like a snake charmer with a flute.

Bertie only snickered. "You wouldn't dare."

"Fine. Don't say I didn't warn you."

With that, Bella hoisted the pie high...and jammed it firmly into Bertie's face.

Chapter Twenty-Five

Buttermilk custard dripped from Bertie's face and eyelashes. After an initial gasp from the crowd, the room fell strangely silent. Cheryl even heard the ticking of the battery-operated clock that hung between the flags at the front of the room.

"Why...you...I can't believe you actually did it," Bertie sputtered.

"Now, Bertie, we all need to calm down," Cheryl warned. She threw a desperate glance at Naomi. "Could you get me a towel?"

Instantly, Naomi disappeared into the crowd. Cheryl turned her gaze back to Bertie. Her breathing had grown heavy, and she snorted. Not a ladylike snort. Like a bull. A really, really angry bull.

"You can't say I didn't warn you." Bella took a timid step back, a tinge of remorse coloring her words.

Harvey stepped forward and plucked the pie tin from Bertie's shoulder. Holding it between thumb and forefinger, he turned it over and examined the bottom.

"That wasn't even your pie." He threw the pie tin to the floor in disgust. "It was mine."

Bella really looked sorry now. Her eyes widened, and her hand rose to cover her mouth. "Oh, Harvey, I'm so sorry."

"You're sorry?" Bertie swiped a glob of custard from her face and watched as it slopped onto the floor. Slowly, she stepped to the table and picked up one of the pies. "Maybe this one's yours. Here, have it back."

"No!" Cheryl cried, but she was too late. Bertie shoved the pie into Bella's face then licked a bit of the custard from her fingers with a smirk.

A split second later, the pie tin clattered onto the floor next to Harvey's.

"No!" Sandra screamed. She slapped both hands to her cheeks in horror. "That was my pie!"

"What?" Bertie stared at Sandra and then at the pie sliding slowly down Bella's face. "Oh no. I'm sorry, Sandra."

Tears burned the back of Cheryl's eyelids. The scene unfolding before her eyes was like something out of a movie—and not a good one. How had things gotten so horribly out of control?

She moved to stand in front of the table and the remaining pies. If anybody else tried to get in on this food fight, they'd have to go through her. Of course, she was only protecting two pies. Of the five original finalists, they were all that remained, and they could hardly count one of those since it belonged to Bella—and she had thrown the first pie.

Pastor Lory blew out a sigh. Had the room not been so quiet, it might not have even been heard. He lifted both hands. "All right, now, ladies. Let's all take a deep breath."

Naomi appeared, a handful of paper towels clutched in each hand. She passed a few to Bertie and gave the rest to Bella.

"Thank you, Mrs. Miller," Pastor Lory said. He cleared his throat. "In light of what has just occurred, I believe it would be best to take a short break so we can collect our thoughts. I'm going to ask that we all please move outside to give the judges time to collaborate."

He turned to the judges, his eyebrows lifted in question. All four heads bobbed in agreement.

"Good." He directed a steady look at Bertie and Bella—one that made even Cheryl duck her head like she'd done as a child when she got into trouble. "Ladies, why don't you both take a moment to get cleaned up and then join us in the meeting room."

Both nodded contritely. Bertie took a hesitant step forward, then stopped to allow Bella to precede her. They both engaged in an odd sort of dance consisting of advance and retreat before finally trudging toward the restrooms.

Cheryl stifled a groan. Why, oh, why had she ever let Pastor Lory talk her into coordinating this event? She'd have been better off serving BBQ or possibly helping Jacob run the silent auction. The Carmichaels might have been better off too, considering the disaster she'd made of things.

Embarrassed and flustered, Cheryl didn't really want to look at anyone but couldn't resist a peek at Levi. He watched her compassionately, his heart in his eyes. Next to him, Ellen half-hid a snicker behind the navy-colored apron she wore from Chester's grocery store.

Ridicule was a hard pill to swallow. Cheryl lifted her chin and did her best to hide her shame behind a confident smile. She trusted Pastor Lory to help sort things out. If not, she would simply step down and let someone else oversee the conclusion of the contest. It was all she could do.

The atmosphere inside the meeting room was somber. It was as though there was a collective releasing of breath as the door clicked shut behind Pastor Lory. Cheryl sank into the nearest chair, unable to even look at the other judges.

"Before we begin..." Pastor Lory directed a sympathetic smile toward Cheryl. "Let's all take a moment and remember why we agreed to this fund-raiser. Our hearts were in the right place. Granted, things have taken a rather odd turn since then, and while that may be a surprise to us, it certainly is no mystery to the Lord."

Cheryl rubbed at her eyes. His words brought only a small measure of comfort, but at least they quelled her tears.

"You've done a great job, Cheryl." This from Laura, whose eyes shone with compassion and encouragement. "I don't think I could have pulled everything together so quickly."

"Me either," Greta said. "You not only organized the pie contest, you helped with *all* the fund-raisers. I sure don't have the skills to administer so many different events at the same time."

"Apparently, neither do I," Cheryl said wryly. She ground her thumb into the arm of her chair. "Look, guys, I'm really grateful for your support, but the truth of the matter is I've let this entire event turn into a fiasco."

"What would you have done differently?" Kathy studied Cheryl with genuine interest. She tucked a strand of blondish hair behind her ear and shrugged. "Seriously…what could you have possibly done that would have made anything that happened turn out any differently?"

"Well…I suppose…" Cheryl frowned as she thought back over the events of the past few days.

"Cheryl, would you mind if we took a moment to pray for you?" Pastor Lory spoke with such gentle concern that Cheryl's eyes instantly burned.

"I…uh…I would really like that."

She closed her eyes before the tears gathering could spill over. Unfortunately, that only made her nose run. Someone pressed a tissue into her hand. She took it and rubbed her nose dry while Pastor Lory prayed. At first her self-recrimination drowned out his words, but then he said something about her being a willing vessel, and Cheryl's spirit quieted.

A willing vessel.

Wasn't that something Aunt Mitzi had written in her last letter? Yes, she had called Cheryl a willing vessel, ready to be filled by God and poured out for His purpose. That much, at least, was true. She was willing and ready. And one other thing Aunt Mitzi had said…that if His people were willing to be pressed into His service, God would equip them for His tasks.

Peace and calm poured over Cheryl like a balm. Suddenly she was no longer worried about what people would think of her. Instead, she focused on letting God show her what she needed to do next.

Open my eyes, Lord. Show me what to do.

The prayer came from deep inside her. Pastor Lory said amen, and Cheryl opened her eyes with renewed confidence. She gulped in a deep breath and stood.

"Thank you, everyone. I know this wasn't what you signed up for, but I can't tell you how much your willingness to help with this event means to me, and to the Carmichaels, I'm sure."

She crossed to the table where someone, probably Gail, had laid the registration clipboard and scorecards.

"We have several choices here." She picked up the clipboard and pulled out the scorecards. "One, we could postpone the final round of judging until tomorrow and allow *all* the contestants to resubmit their entries. Two, we could disqualify the two contestants who were involved in the destruction of two of the entries and allow the three remaining contestants to compete, or three…" She let her gaze rest on each of the judge's faces. "We could simply consider the nature of the contest."

"What do you mean?" Laura asked, her eyes wide behind her glasses.

"Two of the pies survived. Obviously, we couldn't allow Bella's pie to remain in the contest since she was an accessory to the destruction of another contestant's entry. That would only leave Agatha Hilty."

"You mean…just declare her the winner?" Greta said. She craned her neck right and left as she looked at the other judges.

"Does anyone have another suggestion?" Cheryl asked, pausing to give each person a moment to consider. Cheryl looked at Pastor Lory. "We would of course need to discuss this with the contestants."

"Bertie and Bella should be waiting outside. I'll round up the other three."

"Thank you, Pastor."

He slipped out the door, and Laura moved to Cheryl's side. "Are you sure you're okay with all this?"

She nodded. "I am. I only wish I could figure out…"

She broke off as a sudden idea popped into her mind.

"Cheryl?" Concern lined Laura's brow.

"Sorry… I just thought of something." Cheryl crossed back to her purse and rummaged inside until she found what she was looking for. The receipt that had incriminated Tory Landry was still there and…

She flipped it over. It was from Chester's grocery… like the apron Ellen was wearing.

A part of her argued it was too small a connection, too insignificant to mean anything. Another part of her remembered Naomi's bag. It was Ellen who had picked it up and allowed the contents… and the ipecac… to spill out onto the floor. And certainly Ellen remembered the accusations that had been levied against Naomi when Bridget Marshall put rat poison in her jam.

Cheryl shook her head, wishing she could as easily shake all her thoughts into place. But to let herself be disqualified… could Ellen actually have been so devious as to have done it simply to turn suspicion away from herself?

And why? What could her motivation be?

A knock on the door interrupted her thinking. Pastor Lory poked his head in.

"Are you ready for them to come in?"

Cheryl raised her hand, causing the judges' heads to cease bobbing as they turned their eyes toward her in surprise.

"Sorry, Pastor, but could we have just one more moment?"

Her answer seemed to leave him flabbergasted. Finally, he closed his mouth and nodded. "Uh...of course. Just let me know when you're ready."

The door closed with a click, and Cheryl whirled to plead with the other judges. "All right, I know this is a strange request, but I think I have a hunch about what has been going on. I'd like a little time to try to figure it out, if the rest of you wouldn't mind."

"Delay the contest?" Laura asked.

"Just for a little while," Cheryl said. "If I haven't tracked down the truth in say"—she twisted her wrist for a glimpse of her watch—"two hours, we'll proceed with the contest as planned."

Greta frowned. "I don't know, Cheryl. Two hours seems a long time to make these people wait."

"I agree," Kathy said, though she followed it with an apologetic shrug and said, "Sorry, Cheryl."

Cheryl bit her lip, thinking. "All right, then how about one hour? I'm pretty sure I can get the information I need and be back here by then. If not, just go on without me. After all, if we proceed as we'd planned, there won't be any judging involved anyway. I'm sure Pastor Lory can make the announcement without me."

The three women looked at each other and shrugged.

"Should one of us go with you?" Laura suggested timidly. "I mean, I feel kind of strange sending you off alone."

"I appreciate the offer, Laura," Cheryl said, "but if I don't make it back in time, I think it would be better to have you here."

Though she'd offered, Laura seemed a bit relieved by Cheryl's answer.

"All right, then, one hour it is," Cheryl said, reaching for her purse and car keys. "I'll let Pastor Lory know and the rest of you…"

"We'll take care of everything here," Greta assured her. "Don't you worry about a thing. Good luck, Cheryl."

"Yeah, good luck," Laura repeated.

"Anything else we should do while we're waiting?" Kathy asked.

Cheryl quirked an eyebrow. "How good are you at stalling?"

"Uh…"

"We'll think of something," Greta interrupted. "Maybe August can entertain the crowd."

Cheryl managed a laugh. "Now that's something I'd like to see. All right, I'm going. Thank you, ladies. And don't worry. If my hunch is right, there won't be much we'll need to do."

She gave them a thumbs-up before heading out the door. After a hurried explanation to Pastor Lory, she scurried over to Naomi.

"Cheryl, what is going on? What has happened?" Naomi whispered.

"I'll explain in the car." Cheryl pointed toward the exit. "Can you come with me?"

Naomi reached for her purse and squared her shoulders. "Of course."

"Cheryl?" Levi wove through the crowd. Unfortunately, Ellen followed in his wake. "Where are you going?"

She averted her gaze from Ellen, fearful her eyes might give something away. "I...I have to run a quick errand."

He stroked his chin in confusion. "Now?"

"Unfortunately." She leaned toward him and dropped her voice to a whisper. "Can you find Harvey and ask him to have his pliers handy? And one more thing...if you can, put them in a ziplock bag."

He nodded and would have moved had not Cheryl grabbed his arm.

"Go alone."

He met her gaze steadily. In that look, she communicated her concern and Levi nodded in understanding.

"Be careful," he said.

"We will." She whirled without looking at Ellen for fear that her suspicions might cause the young woman to flee. She motioned toward Naomi. "Let's go."

Once in the car, Cheryl quickly explained her theory. "But I think the only way to prove that Ellen is behind the disqualifications will be to actually go to Chester's and see what we can find."

Naomi shook her head sadly. "I cannot believe it. Why would Ellen do such a thing?"

"I haven't figured that part out yet," Cheryl admitted. "But first things first..."

She drove the short distance to Berlin where Chester's Grocery was located and where Cheryl suspected Ellen worked. It was a small store, but it carried a variety of specialty items shoppers couldn't find anywhere else. Cheryl slipped into a parking spot near the door and hurried inside, Naomi at her heels.

At the nearest cash register, Cheryl stopped and pulled Tory's receipt from her purse.

"What are you doing?" Naomi asked quietly.

"Just checking something," Cheryl whispered back. "And if this tells me what I want to know, I want to be sure there is somebody here to witness it."

"Me?" Naomi pointed to her chest.

"You."

A pretty young cashier dressed in a plain dress and wearing a prayer kapp approached. "Good afternoon, ladies. Is there something I can help you find?"

Cheryl held out the receipt. "Actually, I'm wondering if you could help me with this."

The young woman's smile widened, and she pointed toward a broad counter. "Returns are handled through the Customer Service desk."

"This isn't a return." Cheryl turned the receipt so the woman could see it. "Years ago, when I was in high school, I used to work in a grocery store. Each register had a number assigned to it, and it printed on the receipt so that if there was a problem, the store manager could pinpoint the cashier who handled the sale."

The woman nodded. "Yes, we still do that."

"Great," Cheryl said, a tad too enthusiastically. The woman looked at her and frowned. Cheryl softened her tone. "What I mean is, I'm wondering if you can tell me who handled this sale."

The woman looked confused a moment and glanced toward a one-way mirror high on the wall. "Is there a problem?" she asked, her gaze returning to Cheryl.

"Not really," Cheryl said, trying to reassure her with a smile. "But it is important that I figure out who handled this particular transaction." She held the receipt a little higher. "Do you mind?"

After a moment, the woman took the receipt, looked it over, and then handed it back. "That was cashier number one hundred twenty-four."

Cheryl found the number near the bottom of the receipt. "Here?"

The woman nodded. "That is right."

"One hundred twenty-four…" Cheryl pinched her bottom lip between thumb and forefinger. "That would be Ellen Lengacher, right?"

The woman's brows rose in surprise. Even had she not nodded, Cheryl would have known the answer.

"That is right," she said, "but Ellen is not working today. Is there someone else who can help you? I can call the manager if you would like."

"That's all right." Cheryl slipped the receipt back into her purse. "Thank you for your help."

Though she still looked confused, the woman nodded and turned to go.

"Oh, and one more thing, if you don't mind," Cheryl called, stopping her before she could disappear down one of the grocery aisles.

The woman turned back and eyed her curiously. "Yes?"

"Can you tell me if you sell syrup of ipecac?"

She nodded and pointed toward her left. "As a matter of fact, we do. It is in aisle four, about halfway down. You will see it. It is next to the stomach remedies."

"Thank you." Cheryl grabbed Naomi's arm and dragged her in the direction the woman pointed. "Wanna guess what brand they carry?"

They came to a stop about halfway down the aisle. After a bit of searching, Cheryl found the ipecac, just as the woman had said. Cheryl picked up a bottle and held the label out for Naomi to read.

Naomi put her hand to her mouth. "That is...that is exactly like the bottle that..."

Cheryl nodded. "It's just as I suspected. This is exactly the same brand that fell out of your purse." She pulled her wallet from her purse and turned for the cash registers.

"I'm pretty sure I know who bought it."

"Ne, Cheryl. You do not mean Ellen?"

"I do. And you want to know something else? I'm betting this is the same stuff that landed Richard in the hospital."

Naomi hurried her steps to match Cheryl's. "If that is true, then what are we going to do?"

"I know what I'm going to do." Cheryl slapped a five-dollar bill onto the counter and waited while the cashier rang up her purchase. "First, I'm going to buy myself a bottle of ipecac. And then...I'm going to find Ellen."

CHAPTER TWENTY-SIX

Cheryl clutched the bag containing the ipecac tightly to her side as she made her way up the sidewalk toward Village Hall. Naomi huffed alongside her, her rubber-soled shoes making a soft swishing sound against the hot pavement.

"I do not know, Cheryl. Something about this feels wrong… like maybe we have not stopped to consider all the possibilities." She wiped the sweat from her forehead and then scuffled to a halt. "Cheryl, did you hear me?"

Cheryl blew out a frustrated sigh. "I heard you, but I can't take time to go through all this again, Naomi. I only have half an hour before I need to get back to the judges, or they will go on with the contest without me." She checked her watch. "Less than that, actually. I need to hurry."

Naomi grabbed her arm and gave a stubborn shake of her head. "Ne, Cheryl, I do not think we should rush into a hasty decision simply because we are short on time. It would not be right."

The bag rustled as Cheryl threw her hands high. "Then what should I do? Just let Ellen get away with sabotaging the fund-raiser and casting suspicion on you while she was doing it?"

Naomi stared at her, unflinching.

Cheryl dropped her arms to her sides and let her shoulders slump. "All right...it's true we don't have a motive, but all the clues point toward Ellen. Why don't we just confront her with the facts and then let her tell us why she did it?"

Naomi frowned. "That sounds very much like saying someone is guilty and then asking them to prove they are not."

Before Cheryl could answer, the door to Village Hall swung open and Harvey stepped out, his jacket slung over his shoulder. Catching sight of his coveralls reminded Cheryl that he'd told them earlier he had to work that night. She hurried over to him.

"Harvey, are you leaving?"

He shrugged and pointed at his watch. "'Fraid so. Gotta catch my shift. I'll be late if I don't leave now, and I really need the hours."

The weight on Cheryl's shoulders grew. "I'm so sorry, Harvey. I wish we'd had a better ending to this whole mess."

"Don't worry about it. It's all for a good cause, right?" He turned for the parking lot, stopped, and looked back at her. "Hey...I don't suppose you had a chance to talk to Agatha Hilty, huh?"

She swallowed hard. "Agatha?"

"Yeah." He cast a quick glance toward Village Hall. "You remember I said she isn't all she seems?"

"I remember." Cheryl gave a slight nod. "And yes, I spoke with her. She told me she and Sandra Remis used to own a bakery together."

"And? Is that all she told you?" Harvey hooked his thumb into the pocket of his coveralls and waited.

"Well, yes... that's all." Cheryl felt a peculiar itching start at the base of her neck—a prickling of sorts, as though Harvey knew something she didn't, and whatever it was... it was important.

"She didn't say anything about her husband?"

Harvey stopped short and looked at Naomi, who stood next to Cheryl.

"It's all right," Cheryl said, casting a glance sidelong at her friend. "She's helping me."

Harvey eyed Naomi suspiciously, but he gave a grudging nod. "All right then, I suppose it will be okay. Anyway, I thought you should know I wasn't the only one who used to work at the brick factory." He lowered his head as though telling a secret. "Norman Hilty does too. That's Agatha's husband."

"*Does* work at the factory? As in, he still works there?"

He nodded. "Norman didn't get laid off like the rest of us. I sure would be interested in knowing why."

"Was he in a management position?"

Harvey snorted. "Norman? No, he's just a regular Joe, like the rest of us. 'Cept he spent a lot of time in the boss's office when it came time to handing out pink slips, if you know what I mean. Anyway, I just thought maybe you would want to know that. Whether it helps?"

He shrugged, then took a couple of steps and stopped. "One last thing. While I'm thinking about it... you did know that Sandra Remis used to have a thing for old Norman, right? Before he and Agatha married, I mean."

Cheryl's heart had begun to beat double-time in her chest. "No...I...wasn't aware." She shuffled her feet. "Was this before or after they opened the bakery together?"

He tilted his head, thinking. "Right after, I suppose. Folks said Agatha used her cooking skills to win him away from Sandra." He grinned and patted his belly. "I guess the saying is true, eh? The way to a man's heart?"

Every word Harvey spoke cast more and more doubt in Cheryl's mind. She nodded lamely. "Thank you for the information, Harvey. Have a good night."

He swung his jacket off his shoulder and laid it over his arm. "Hey, uh, let me know what happens, huh? With the pie contest, I mean. Not that I figured I'd win or anything like that, but I'm still curious about what you all decide."

"Will do." She sucked in a breath and waved good-bye when he turned for the parking lot once more.

"So?" Naomi said gently.

Cheryl rolled her shoulders, easing the tension that had been building there. "So...you were right, and I may be wrong in my assumptions about Ellen," she said grudgingly.

"What do you want to do now?"

Cheryl slapped the bag containing the ipecac against her leg. "We could talk to Agatha again, I suppose, or try and contact her husband's boss at the brick factory."

"And Sandra?"

Cheryl nodded. "Her too, I guess."

Naomi narrowed her eyes to peer at Cheryl. "But you are not convinced either one of them has anything to do with the disqualifications."

"Not really," she said. "If I'm honest..."

She paused midsentence, struck by a sudden sense that they were being watched. Stepping closer to Naomi, she reached for her arm and lowered her voice. "Naomi, do you remember when I told you I'd had a funny feeling the last few days?"

Naomi's eyes widened. "Of someone watching you?"

"Uh-huh. Well it's back." Cheryl squeezed her arm. "Look carefully... do you see anyone behind me?"

Naomi eased her head sideways. A second later, Cheryl felt the muscles in her arm relax and Naomi's lips spread in a smile. "It is all right, Cheryl. It is just Levi."

Levi.

Cheryl let out her breath in a whoosh. Of course... she'd asked him to locate Harvey's pliers. He had probably seen the man leaving and was either coming out to check or...

She turned to greet him and stopped, frozen by the sight that met her eyes. Strolling alongside Levi, hanging on his every word and looking up at him with something akin to adoration in her eyes... was Ellen Lengacher.

Chapter Twenty-Seven

Every bit of suspicion Cheryl had against Ellen came charging back...only it had nothing to do with the contest. Ellen was trying to steal Levi away from her...except...she couldn't know she was doing it. No one knew about their engagement so, in reality, Ellen was innocent.

Cheryl gritted her teeth and realized in almost the same instant that she was clutching the bag so tightly her hand hurt. She forced herself to relax.

Levi hastened to her side. "Cheryl, I am glad you are back. Everyone is getting a little restless. Did you find what you were looking for?"

"Sort of," she said, training her eyes on Levi and away from Ellen. "But I still have one more person I'd like to talk to. Do you know where Agatha Hilty is?"

Levi shook his head and looked at Ellen. "Have you seen her?"

"Ne. I was inside...with you."

Dangerously close to pulling her own hair out, Cheryl turned to Naomi. "I'm going to go look for her, and maybe Sandra too."

"I will help you."

Ellen's lips parted slowly. "Should Levi and I...?"

"It would be best if you waited inside with the others," Naomi interrupted firmly. "Levi, perhaps you could help us look?"

"Of course."

Ellen looked genuinely taken aback. She ducked her head obediently before turning and going inside.

"Thank you," Cheryl breathed, only loud enough for Naomi. Whatever her friend had sensed, she knew Ellen was the cause and she'd chosen to side with Cheryl. She turned to Levi. "I wish I could explain everything that's happened..."

He shook his head. "No time. Maybe we should split up?"

First Naomi, and now Levi? Neither one demanded an explanation. They cared about her and wanted to help. Better yet, they believed in her, no questions asked.

Embarrassment washed over Cheryl like the tide. She wasn't in competition with Ellen for either Naomi's or Levi's affections, yet she'd allowed herself to behave like she was. It was childish and it was unfair since neither of them deserved to be treated like a prize to be won.

Levi's strong hand closed around her forearm. "Are you all right?"

Cheryl startled at the warm touch. Levi was always so careful, so vigilant regarding any sort of public display, especially in front of his family, and yet in this case, his concern for her overruled his caution.

"I'm fine," she whispered.

Though she longed to prolong the innocent contact with him, she eased out from under his grasp before it drew Naomi's attention. Levi had demonstrated nothing but honor and chivalry toward her. She would not allow her behavior to be any less.

"We'd better not waste any more time."

He nodded his understanding. "We will cover more ground if we split up."

"I can search near the silent auction tables." Naomi gestured in that direction and set off when Cheryl gave her agreement.

"I will check the children's area and anywhere else I can think of," Levi said, but instead of moving away, he stepped closer and lowered his head. "I am sorry about Ellen. Her actions have hurt you, and mine too I think."

"My hurt feelings have more to do with my own insecurities than your actions or Ellen's," she replied quietly. "But I'm grateful for your thoughtfulness."

Longing for the comfort of his arms speared her heart. He felt the same way, if his clenched fists were any indication of his inner turmoil. She stepped away before either of them could be tempted.

"Let me know if you find them. I'll be by the picnic tables."

He blew out a breath and turned, his broad back a welcome barrier since she feared her emotions might not be as hidden as she hoped.

Soon, she reminded herself. They would find a way to tell his family, and then it wouldn't matter if her love for him shone on her face. In fact, she'd be free to tell the entire world.

The thought made her smile, and then remembering the bag still clutched in her hand, she veered toward the BBQ and the trash cans. She was wrong about Ellen. She'd been wrong to blame her without proof and wrong to purchase the ipecac simply because it was the same brand from the same store where she worked. Anyone could have purchased it, and once this mess was cleared up, she'd find her and apologize for...

"Edgar, you've had enough. Put it down before you make yourself sick."

The childish male voice pulled her up short.

"You're just saying that because you want the rest," was the petulant reply.

"I am not. You've eaten more than I have."

"Have not!"

The boy's voice lowered. "Quit your yelling. You want Ma to hear?"

"I don't have to quit. You're not my boss, Ethan."

"Am too. Momma said so. She told me to keep an eye on you. You heard her."

What in the world...?

Cheryl rounded the large rubber trash cans lined up against the back wall of Village Hall. It was shaded here and actually quite cool away from the bustle of the crowd. She could understand why two boys might choose this spot to sit, but with the trash cans full to almost overflowing, it was smelly and probably not very sanitary.

She peeked over the top of one of the trash cans. "Hello?"

Two blond heads tipped back, and two pairs of wide brown eyes stared up at her.

She smiled. "Hi, guys. What are you boys doing back here?"

The younger one, probably Edgar, swiped his arm across his face and stared at his brother, who stood.

"We...uh...we were just..."

Cheryl's gaze fell to the item on the ground that they'd been haggling over. Her eyes bulged. "Is that a pie?"

The older boy nodded and shoved both hands behind his back. "Yes, ma'am."

She tried hard to remain calm. "Do...uh...do you mind if I ask where you got it?"

Ethan glanced down at his brother. "We didn't take it. Someone left it here, and we...um...we just figured..."

"Wait." Cheryl bent toward the pie tin. The boys had picked off the raspberries and mint leaves and shoved them to one side, but what was left of the pie looked very familiar. She turned to the older boy...Ethan. "You *found* this? Would you mind telling me where?"

He nodded and pointed to the stack of crates. "It was just sittin' there. We didn't take it."

Edgar finally spoke up. "Why would anyone throw away a whole pie? Especially one as yummy as this one?"

His grin was cut short by a rather loud burp. Slapping his hand over his mouth, he looked at Cheryl and mumbled, "Sorry."

She waved away his apology and bent at the waist, her hands propped upon her knees. "Listen, boys, this is really important. Did either of you see who left this pie here?"

Edgar's smile faded at her somber tone, and he looked to his older brother.

"Yeah," the boy said, the toe of his tennis shoe scuffing the ground. "I saw her."

Cheryl's heart rate sped. "And . . . do you know her name?"

Doubt crept over his freckled cheeks, but he nodded. "Yes, I know her name. That's why we weren't afraid to eat it. I knew it would be good."

She could hardly keep the tremble out of her voice. "Who was it? Who left the pie?"

The boys exchanged a glance, and then the younger one lifted his chin. "It was an Amish lady."

"Ellen," the older boy added.

Edgar dragged his gaze from his brother's face to stare at Cheryl. "Yeah, Ellen. She left the pie."

CHAPTER TWENTY-EIGHT

*I*t was Ellen. Ellen left the pie.

The words rattled round and round in Cheryl's head until she felt dizzy. She'd been right about Ellen all along. It *had* been Ellen who'd tried sabotaging the fund-raiser. Ellen who'd stolen Bertie's pie. Unless…

She bent toward the boys again, her hands braced against her knees. "You're certain it was Ellen? Ellen *Lengacher* left this pie?"

The older boy poked out his chest, and his lips turned in a pout. "We ain't lying, if that's what you're asking."

"No, no, I don't think that at all. I just want to be sure of what you saw. Would you mind telling me?"

He hesitated, and his blond head bobbed. "Edgar and I were playing over by that big tree when we saw her come around the building."

"We know her from Chester's," Edgar said, his smile tinged with pride that he could add something his brother hadn't.

"Yeah, from Chester's. She checks out our groceries sometimes."

"She's nice!"

Ethan gave his brother's shoulder a shove. "Quiet, Edgar. Let me finish."

A pout formed on Edgar's lips, but he sat quietly and let his brother speak.

"Anyway, we saw her come around the corner with a box in her hands."

"What kind of box?" Cheryl asked.

"White, like the kind you get when you buy donuts." He looked toward his brother. "Show her, Edgar."

He reached behind the stack of crates and pulled out the pastry box.

"Okay," Cheryl said. "What else did you see?"

The boy pointed. "I thought she was looking for somebody at first, but then she just set the box down there and walked off."

"Why did you think she was looking for someone?"

"She did this." Edgar hopped to his feet and turned his head from side to side.

"Yeah, kind of like that," his brother grudgingly agreed. He peered up at Cheryl, his brow furrowed with concern. "Are we in trouble?"

She smiled in an attempt to soothe away some of his worry. "Not trouble, exactly, but I would like for you to tell someone else the same story you just told me. Would you do that?"

His gaze remained uncertain. "Who?"

"A friend of mine. Her name is Naomi. She's Amish, like Ellen."

"Will she be mad about the pie?"

"I don't think so," Cheryl said. "I think she'll probably be sorry to hear about it because Ellen is a friend, but she won't be mad at you."

"Me either?" Edgar piped.

"You either," Cheryl said. "So? What do you say? Will you talk to her?"

The boy shuffled from foot to foot and finally let his shoulders slump. "I guess so, if you promise not to let our mom know. She won't like that we ate a whole pie before supper."

She probably wouldn't like that the pie had been left near the trash either, but Cheryl kept that thought to herself as she led the boys back toward the silent auction area where Naomi said she would be. Cheryl found her easily and offered only a brief explanation before letting the boys repeat the information they had given to her. When they finished, Cheryl sent them off to find their mother.

Naomi blew out a long sigh. "So it *was* Ellen who took Bertie's pie. But why would she do such a thing? It makes no sense."

"Maybe we should ask her," Cheryl said softly.

Naomi laid her hand on Cheryl's arm. "I will fetch her so we can speak to her in private, ja?"

Cheryl understood what Naomi was asking. The Amish were a close-knit community. When possible, they preferred to resolve their differences privately. She squeezed Naomi's fingers. "That's probably a good idea. If she is behind all these strange disqualifications, I would at least like to give her a chance to explain."

"Danki, Cheryl."

"But, Naomi..." She forced the unpleasant words past the knot in her throat. "You understand that if she did something to put Richard in the hospital, we will have to inform the police?"

"Ja. I understand." Naomi shook her head sadly but said nothing more before setting off toward Village Hall.

While she waited for Naomi, Cheryl paced the narrow strip of grass between the silent auction tables and the parking lot. Whatever explanation Ellen gave, would it be enough to justify the damage she'd caused?

"Cheryl, there you are." Levi hurried toward her. Sweat formed a dark ring around the collar of his shirt. He took off his hat, ran a handkerchief over his brow, and then shoved it back into his pocket. "Did you find her?"

Cheryl stared at him. "Who?"

"Agatha. Do you not remember? That is what we were doing out here in the first place."

"Oh." She smacked her palm against her forehead. "No, sorry. We didn't find her... or I should say we stopped looking. We got distracted."

He blinked in confusion then reached up to scratch his temple. "Cheryl, is everything all right?"

She spread her hands wide. "Not exactly. You'll never believe what has happened."

Before she could explain, Naomi returned, a sullen Ellen in tow. Tilting her head, Naomi said something in a stern Pennsylvania Dutch then thrust her chin in Cheryl and Levi's direction.

Upon catching sight of Levi, Ellen's gaze fell. She clasped her hands behind her back—a move that made her look much younger than her years.

Suddenly, Cheryl felt a bit sorry for her. She pulled the receipt from Chester's from her purse and took a step forward. "Ellen, is this your handwriting?"

Color suffused Ellen's cheeks as Cheryl extended the receipt toward her.

"We could always compare it to something of yours, but it might be best to tell the truth now," Cheryl said gently.

The warning did not seem to affect her. Ellen lifted her chin defiantly. "I heard about the receipt Bella found, but I have never seen it before."

"What about the ipecac? If I was to ask at the store, I'm guessing someone there will remember you purchasing a bottle."

The tips of her ears glowed bright red, and when she looked up, her eyes were troubled, but she clenched her lips and said nothing.

"We have the pliers, Ellen." Levi pulled the ziplock bag from his pocket and held the pliers out on his palm.

Cheryl picked up the ziplock by one of the corners then held it to eye level. "I'd be willing to guess that if Chief Twitchell were to dust them for fingerprints..." She lifted her eyebrows, questioning.

A trembling started around Ellen's lips. It spread down to her chin.

"Ellen, do you have something you need to tell us?" Levi demanded. He motioned toward the bag. "Did you use these pliers to loosen the bolts on the pie table?"

Her answer, when it came, was as weak as a kitten's first mewl. "Ja."

"But why would you do such a thing? You had to know when we found them that they would cast suspicion on to Harvey."

Cheryl handed the bag back to Levi. With a look, she implored him to be gentle. He clamped his lips shut and turned his back. Cheryl turned to Ellen.

"The ipecac? It was you who placed the bottle in Naomi's bag?"

She nodded but refused to look at them. "I remembered what happened last winter...how that woman put something into Naomi's jam to cast suspicion on her. But I did not mean for that man to end up in the hospital. I did not know he would eat so much."

Levi whirled and threw both his hands into the air in exasperation. "Do you understand the danger you placed that man in? What if his health were not good? Why would you take the chance?"

"I think I know." Cheryl closed her hand around Levi's. His muscles quivered under her fingertips. She waited until she was certain he had calmed enough to listen. "The swing...remember? I told you I felt like someone was watching us. I felt the same way later, at the restaurant, only I didn't say anything because it seemed so foolishly paranoid." She swung her gaze to rest on Ellen. "But someone *was* watching, weren't they, Ellen?"

A flush fell over Ellen's features, and instead of looking remorseful, she looked angry. Her mouth puckered, and the skin around her lips turned white.

"You are an Englischer." She turned to Levi and said something forceful and clipped in Pennsylvania Dutch.

Naomi stepped forward. "Ellen, ne. That is enough."

"It is not enough, Naomi. Perhaps they have managed to hide the truth from you, but I have seen what is going on between them with my own two eyes."

"Whatever you think you have seen," Cheryl began, her heart pounding, "I doubt that it is…"

"You deny it then?" Ellen spun toward Cheryl, her gaze as sharp as razors. "You deny there is anything between you and Levi?"

She did not pause long enough for Cheryl to reply. She leaned in to point her long narrow finger at Cheryl's nose.

"How could you?" she accused. "Knowing what this family has been through, how could you put them through it all again? You claim to care for them, to be their friend, and yet you would inflict the same grief and pain that Sarah caused?"

"Whatever rift was caused has been healed," Levi interrupted firmly. He stepped between Ellen and Cheryl, shielding her from the brunt of Ellen's fury with his body. "And even if it were not, that would not give you the right to hurt others as you have done. Do not attempt to justify your actions by using my family's past pain." When Ellen remained silent, Levi shifted a bit to the side.

Though it took almost a full minute, Ellen's anger finally seeped out of her, and her shoulders slumped. "I was not…I did not mean to hurt anyone. I only wanted…"

"What did you want, Ellen? Were you trying to drive a wedge between me and the Millers? Was that the point of *all* this?" The words were sharper than Cheryl intended, but once she started, she couldn't seem to stop. "And what about the Carmichaels? Did you stop to consider what effect your actions would have on them? They've been through so much...suffered so much. All we were trying to do was give them a little bit of hope. But your actions even had us wondering if someone in Sugarcreek was holding a grudge."

She shot a glance toward Village Hall, and the motion of her hand followed. "And the contestants themselves...granted, you couldn't have known about the secrets some of them were keeping, but do you even realize the pain you have caused by opening up some of those old wounds?"

Each word seemed to strike Ellen like the blow of a hammer. Her face crumpled with misery, and tears soaked her eyes.

"Ja...I do realize it now, and I am sorry...very sorry...for the damage I have done. If I could go back and undo it, I would."

Something about the whispered words rang genuinely. Angry as she was for the trouble Ellen had caused, Cheryl couldn't help but feel sorry for her. Ellen had brought shame on herself and her family, and it would be difficult to overcome, even if she had yet to realize it.

Cheryl turned to Naomi. "I think it would be best if you went with Ellen to speak to her parents first. Let them decide how they want to handle telling Richard, but make it clear that at some point she will need to do so—and it'll probably be better if it's sooner rather than later. Also, she will need to speak to the bishop. I'm sure there will be consequences that will have to be dealt with, but that's farther down the road."

She spared Ellen a quick glance. Surprise registered on her face for one brief moment, as though she had not expected Cheryl to understand the workings of their faith. The look just as quickly disappeared, and Ellen cast her gaze down to her shoes.

"As for me," Cheryl continued, "I'll take care of wrapping up the contest, but you should know, Ellen, that I will have to let other contestants and judges know what has happened. I will do my best to stick to the facts and let you tackle telling people what you will about your motives."

"Thank you, Cheryl. I know you will do what you can to be discreet, but it is perhaps more than Ellen deserves." Naomi eyed Ellen sternly before laying her hand over Cheryl's wrist. "We will talk tonight, ja? After the contest is done." Her gaze swung from Cheryl to Levi. "Come out to the farm. I think we have much to discuss."

Cheryl agreed with a nod. This was certainly not how she and Levi had intended the truth of their relationship to come out, but now that the moment had arrived, she felt oddly at peace.

She watched as Naomi led Ellen away from Village Hall—her back straight and stiff, Ellen's back bent and her head bowed. The weight of sin was heavy indeed.

Levi's warm hand closed on Cheryl's shoulder. She didn't even have to look up to sense his gaze on her—troubled, loving, curious.

"Are you all right?"

She smiled and reached up to cover his hand with hers. "Surprisingly, yes. You?"

She let her gaze travel up to settle on his beloved face. He sighed and dropped his hand. "I am angry with myself for not recognizing Ellen's destructive deeds sooner. If I had, maybe you would not have had to endure such criticism…"

"Ellen's choices were her own," Cheryl interrupted firmly. She crossed her arms over her chest. "No one made her do the things she did. Besides, I'm fairly certain no one could have stopped her once she set her mind to a course of action. Only *she* had the power to control her choices or determine her direction and I..." She paused as she considered the truth of her own words. "I'm learning to realize that for myself," she finished softly.

Levi's eyes shone with renewed appreciation... something that made Cheryl feel stronger, braver even, and gave her a fresh burst of confidence.

His smile changed as he squared his shoulders. It offered a knowledge and intimacy that only two people destined to be together could know. "You are an amazing woman, Cheryl Cooper. I have never been more proud of you."

His words filled her heart near to bursting. After a moment, she tipped her head toward him to whisper, "Danki, Levi Miller, but I think you are pretty amazing yourself."

He froze, and Cheryl feared he might have misunderstood the intent behind her use of the Amish word.

Instead, he captured her hand and brought it up to his chest. "It does my heart goot to hear the use of our language on your lips."

Her breath caught as she met his gaze. "Well then I will need to use it more often."

He shook his head. "You do not understand. It makes me..." His eyes grew earnest. "Cheryl, whatever happens with my family, whatever they may say, I want you to know I have never been more certain that you are the woman I want to spend the rest of my life with. You believe this, ja?"

"I believe it, Levi," she said in a voice as earnest as his. "And whatever happens later, I know we *will* work it out...together."

He released her hand slowly, almost reluctantly.

"I need to go back inside." She would have stepped back, but weakened by his touch, her knees had begun to tremble.

"I will go with you," he said.

His words, and the promise of him by her side, conveyed a strength Cheryl would not have thought possible. She smiled and turned for Village Hall, suddenly more aware than ever what her future held. Though there would be uncertainties, she would always have a strong shoulder to lean on and a godly man by her side.

She would never want for more.

CHAPTER TWENTY-NINE

Aloud clamor erupted when Cheryl and the other judges announced their decision not to prolong the contest and simply award the honor of first place to the only remaining contestant.

"You mean...I won?" Agatha Hilty lifted her chin and puffed out her chest. "I mean...I won!"

Laughter followed her remark, and even Cheryl couldn't help but smile. The other contestants had been quite understanding after she'd explained about Ellen, and not wanting to delay in getting the money from the fund-raiser to the Carmichaels, they had all agreed to forego another round of competition in favor of declaring Agatha the winner. Even Richard was there and slightly less grumpy than normal as he caught Cheryl in a quiet corner once the prizes had been handed out.

"You did a good job," he muttered.

"Thank you, Richard," she said once she'd recovered from her shock. She cleared her throat and offered a small smile. "I'm glad you're feeling better."

"Me too. Who'd have thought that sweet woman could...?" He shrugged. "Anyway, it's all over now."

"So you won't be pressing charges then?" Cheryl asked hopefully.

He rolled his shoulders. "What would be the point? It could just as easily have been food poisoning that landed me in the hospital and not the ipecac. Anyway, no harm done." He rubbed his hands together briskly. "And now…I think I'll get a plate of that BBQ I've been hearing so much about."

He winked and gave her a grudging tip of his hat before ambling off toward the food tent.

"Now that is something I did not think I would see," Levi said, coming to a halt at Cheryl's side.

"Me either." She laughed. "Maybe that stay in the hospital did him good."

"Maybe."

She peeked up at him impishly. "I wonder what they gave him? You think if I ask nicely, they'll give him a year's supply of it and just have it shipped to his house?"

Levi laughed and shoved his hands into his pockets. Slowly, his smile faded. "So we should head out to the farm. Maam and Daed will be waiting. Are you ready?"

"I suppose so." Cheryl swallowed hard and wiped her suddenly sweaty palms down her pant legs. "Am I odd for suddenly feeling like I'm back in grade school?"

Levi chuckled softly. "If you are, then we are both odd because I feel the same way."

She blew out a breath as she walked with him toward the door. "I just don't want to hurt them, Levi. Your parents have come to mean as much to me as my own family."

"I am sure they know how you feel. And they feel the same way. That is why I am certain that they will be as inclined as we are to find a solution." He smiled encouragingly as he pushed the door open to let her pass. "What about your own parents? We will have to speak to them soon too."

Cheryl nodded. "You're right. I've just been so focused on what we would say to Seth and Naomi that I haven't had time to think about it." She gave a wry grin. "Of course, you know my parents will love you."

He lowered his gaze humbly. "I hope so. Most of all, I hope they realize how much I love their daughter."

Cheryl clung tightly to his words some time later as they crossed the covered bridge leading to the Millers' farm. It was only dusk, but the row of solar lamps lighting the driveway had already begun to glow. Inside the house, the cheery flicker of lamplight beckoned, and Cheryl breathed a silent prayer for courage as she stepped from the car to follow Levi up the steps.

He paused with his hand on the doorknob. "Ready?"

"It's now or . . . " She broke off and nodded. The words sounded too flippant for the occasion they faced. "I'm ready."

His smile offered silent encouragement before he opened the door and invited her in. Inside, the ticking of the hall clock greeted them . . . and only the clock. Except for the quiet murmur of Seth's and Naomi's voices, the house was unusually quiet.

"Where is everyone?" Cheryl whispered.

"Maam and Daed will have asked them to leave us alone so we can talk," Levi informed her steadily. "Come, they will be waiting for us in the living room."

Thankfully, he extended one hand in an invitation for her to precede him, for at that moment Cheryl truly might have behaved like a grade-school child and hung back.

"It will be all right, Cheryl," Levi whispered gently, dipping his head to her ear. "Trust me."

Indeed, she would be learning to trust him for the rest of her life. Cheryl lifted her chin and walked slowly into the living room. Seth occupied one of the beautifully carved rocking chairs near the brick fireplace, and Naomi the one next to him. Seth's expression, what she could see of it behind his full beard, was hidden in the dim light of the room, but Naomi's smile was gentle, and Cheryl fixed on it.

"Come in," Naomi said quietly.

She motioned toward the blue cloth couch against one wall, and Levi led Cheryl to it. She sank onto the cushions, then grasped one of the dark blue and white quilted pillows and held it tightly on her lap. How different this moment felt than when she had gone before her father with Lance at her side! It was more somber somehow, and more important that she say the right things.

She took a deep breath, the words she'd prepared rolling across her tongue in a jumbled mess.

"Daed, you are aware of my feelings for Cheryl."

Levi spoke before she could. Her gaze flew from him to his father. He studied his son quietly, his eyes unreadable in the low light.

Levi continued, his voice low. "You should know that Cheryl, too, cares deeply for me."

Heat flooded her face. This was not going at all how she'd thought it would. She studied the braided rug, the tips of her shoes, everything but Seth's face for fear of what she would see written there.

Levi took her hand, and his jaw firmed as he drew his shoulders back. "We have spoken. It is our desire to be married. We have come tonight seeking not only your blessing but your wisdom." His voice broke on the last. He let go of her hand and leaned forward, his arms braced against his knees. "It is not my wish to hurt you or Maam, but I love Cheryl, Daed. She is the wife Gott has prepared for me. I know this to be true in my heart."

Seth held up his hand, and Levi fell into respectful silence. "You have considered the differences in your faith?"

"Ja. We have."

"And what have you decided?"

At this, Cheryl's heart began to pound so hard she was certain it could be felt outside her skin. Levi's hand closed over hers, and she clung to him as tightly as she had the pillow.

Levi took a deep breath and let it out slowly. "Es dutt mir leed."

Cheryl felt his apology as sharply as any knife. She wanted to blurt out her own apology, to tell Seth and Naomi of the weeks and months of struggle that had led to this moment. She wanted to plead their forgiveness and promise them...

Seth cut into her thoughts quietly. "I wondered how long it would take before the two of you were compelled to speak." He smiled sadly and steepled his fingers beneath his chin. "Naomi and I have seen the love growing between you for some time. I must tell you that though we have been troubled, we were confident you would seek the Lord's wisdom before making a rash decision. I am honored that you have also chosen to seek mine."

Tears sparkled in his eyes. Cheryl held her breath while he continued.

"I confess, Levi, since you were a *boppli*, I had hoped to see my oldest son married to an upstanding Amish woman. Gott has dealt with me and shown me the error of my thinking." His gaze swung to rest on Cheryl. "Better that I should desire that my son share his life with a godly woman...and I think he has found that in you, Cheryl."

Tears rushed to her eyes at the tender way Seth spoke the words.

"Thank you," she whispered.

"Our family has come to love you," Naomi said softly, drawing their attention from Seth. "You have long felt like one of our own. I hope you know this."

Cheryl could only nod.

Again, Seth spoke. "My wife and I think that perhaps Gott, in His wisdom, brought you to us first as a friend to the entire family so that when your relationship with Levi became something more, we could accept. You understand my meaning?"

"I do." Of course she did. It was a momentous thing she and Levi were asking, especially considering the family's history.

Seth's gaze returned to Levi. "I would ask that you consider something before you make up your mind about leaving the church."

Levi glanced sidelong at Cheryl and then nodded for his father to continue.

"It used to be one was either Amish or Englisch. There was no in between, ain't so?"

Levi nodded.

"I used to think the divide between them was too great a span to cross. Now I think perhaps the rift has grown smaller." He looked at Cheryl. "You have attended a Mennonite church?"

She agreed with a nod.

His gaze swung to Levi. "And you still believe there is wisdom in the Amish ways?"

Cheryl felt Levi's fingers stiffen. "I do, Daed."

"So then I am correct in assuming your desire is not to turn your back on the church but to find a solution that allows you to be with the woman you love...a woman who is not Amish and has not chosen to become so?"

Her heart hitched in her chest. Where was Seth going with his questions?

Levi's chin rose. "You should know that Cheryl was willing to consider it. It was I who dissuaded her because I did not want her to make such an important decision based on her feelings for me."

"And yet...this is what *you* have done."

"No," Levi replied, shaking his head. "No, I made this decision based on what I think is right for me." Cheryl felt a tremor on his hands, belying the calm expression on his face.

Seth leaned forward, his rocking chair creaking with the shift of his weight. "Son, perhaps the answer is not that you should leave, but that you should find a place that suits you both."

"There is an Amish-Mennonite church not far from here." Both Cheryl's and Levi's gazes swung to Naomi as she began speaking. "Seth found it not long after we realized there was something between the two of you."

"It is a goot church," Seth said. "I have spoken with the preacher there at length, and I am confident that this way might provide the means of being together you both seek."

He rose and paced, his boots scraping the smooth wooden floor. Finally, he came to a stop near the window. "You would not be shunned, my son, but there will be some who say you got your hair cut. You have considered this?"

"Um...sorry?" Cheryl's gaze bounced from Seth to Levi.

"It is a saying we have for a man who joins a church less exacting than his own," Levi explained.

"And I'm guessing it's bad?"

"Not too bad," Levi said with a smile.

"Better than if he went Englisch," Seth said, "but make no mistake, some remarks will not be kind."

Levi gave Cheryl's fingers a squeeze before he rose and went to join his father at the window. "I can bear the remarks of others, Daed."

He met Levi's gaze steadily. "What of your wife? There will be some who will always consider her an outsider. While that will not be true in our home, she may see it at weddings or gatherings of the brethren. Have you prepared her for this?"

"Cheryl understands the trials we may face."

Indeed she did. Cheryl shuddered thinking of Ellen and the things she had said and done.

"Daed, I will protect Cheryl when I can," Levi continued softly. "What concerns me is what you and Maam have to say."

Seth took a deep breath and then laid his hand on his son's shoulder. "I think…"

At his look, Naomi crossed to stand next to her husband.

Seth's grip tightened on Levi's shoulder, and then he let go to run his finger beneath his eyes. "We have raised a wise and honorable man."

"And he has chosen a wise and honorable wife," Naomi continued, stretching out her hand to Cheryl.

Cheryl could no longer keep the tears from rolling down her cheeks. She took Naomi's hand and let the tears fall, grateful for the strength and comfort she had found with this family and for the acceptance and love she knew would be hers by their side.

Naomi sniffed and wiped a few tears from her cheeks as well. "So, Cheryl, have you spoken with your parents yet?"

Cheryl gazed up into her fiancé's eyes, loving the promise she read there. "Not yet, but we will. For now we're going to take things one step at a time, right, Levi?"

Levi nodded his agreement, and Cheryl looked back at Seth and Naomi. "What do you think?"

"I think that is a goot plan," Seth said, his chuckle a hearty rumble deep inside his chest. "A very goot plan, indeed."

Author Letter

Dear Reader,

So many of my favorite memories are tied to food. As a child, I can remember waking up to the inviting scent of fried eggs, warm tortillas, and frying bacon. Later, as an adult, I recall fondly the many countless hours spent icing Christmas cookies with my kids or laughing with friends over potluck meals. In fact, I have an entire book of recipes exchanged or passed down from these many get-togethers. The loving pages, many of them handwritten, are among my greatest treasures.

Sorting through those old recipes made this book so much fun to write! Baking has long been one of my hobbies, so it truly was a pleasure to combine two of my loves into one "tempting taste of mystery."

I hope you enjoy this story as well.

God bless you,
Elizabeth Ludwig

ABOUT THE AUTHOR

Elizabeth Ludwig is an award-winning author whose work has been featured on *Novel Rocket, More to Life Magazine*, and *Christian Fiction Online Magazine*. Her first novel, *Where the Truth Lies* (coauthored with Janelle Mowery), earned her the 2008 IWA Writer of the Year Award. This book was followed in 2009 by "I'll Be Home for Christmas," part of the Christmas anthology collection *Christmas Homecoming*.

In 2011, her second mystery, *Died in the Wool* (coauthored with Janelle Mowery), was nominated for a Carol Award. In 2012, the Edge of Freedom series released from Bethany House Publishers. Books one and two, *No Safe Harbor* and *Dark Road Home*, respectively, earned four stars from the RT Book Reviews. Book three in the series, *Tide and Tempest*, received top honors with four-and-one-half stars and was recently named a finalist for the Gayle Wilson Award of Excellence. Elizabeth was also named a finalist in the 2015 Selah Awards for her novella "One Holy Night," part of the best-selling anthology collection *Christmas Comes to Bethlehem, Maine*.

Elizabeth is an accomplished speaker and teacher, often attending conferences and seminars where she lectures on editing for fiction writers, crafting effective novel proposals, and conducting successful editor/agent interviews. Along with her husband and children, she makes her home in the great state of Texas. To learn more, check out ElizabethLudwig.com or visit her on Facebook.

Fun Fact about
the Amish or Sugarcreek, Ohio

As you know, I recently made a trip to Sugarcreek, Ohio. One of the things I loved about the experience was sampling the authentic Amish cooking. I even found several Amish cookbooks to add to my treasure trove of books. Unfortunately, if you've ever used one of these cookbooks, you know that many of the recipes can be very vague—a "pinch" of this, a "smidge" of that. Oh my! Apparently, the authors of these recipes assume you know what temperature to bake a pie or exactly how much of each ingredient to add. That's because many of these dishes have been passed down for generations, and the cooks in the family know exactly how something should taste.

The problem is I don't always know exactly how long a pie should bake or what the finished product should look like. That's why I'm so glad I have a loving family to experiment on! My growing collection of Amish cookbooks will make a fun addition to the family table—one I'm glad to be able to share with you.

Something Delicious from Our Sugarcreek Friends

Miracle Crust Buttermilk Pie

1½ cups sugar	⅓ cup butter, melted
1 cup buttermilk	1 teaspoon vanilla extract
½ cup all-purpose baking mix	3 eggs

Heat oven to 350 degrees. Grease a nine-inch pie plate. Beat together sugar, buttermilk, baking mix, melted butter, vanilla, and eggs until smooth. Pour filling into pie plate. Bake until knife inserted in center comes out clean, about thirty minutes. Cool five minutes.

Read on for a sneak peek of another exciting book
in the series Sugarcreek Amish Mysteries!

To Have and To Hold
by Tricia Goyer & Cara Putman

Cheryl Cooper entered the office of the Swiss Miss, flipped on the light, and then closed the door behind her. The garment bag hung heavy from her hand. She placed it over the coat hook on the back of the door and blew out a breath. This was really happening. After months of wondering, wishing, and hoping, in a little more than a week she would be a bride, a wife...Levi's wife. The wedding dress inside the garment bag was confirmation that her dreams were coming true.

Tingles danced up and down her arms as her fingers moved to the zipper. She unzipped the bag enough to peek at the dress inside. The white fabric and simple lace caused her heart to double its beat. She imagined the day she would wear the gown and walk down the grassy path to Levi. The Millers' farm would be groomed to perfection, and as she closed her eyes, a chuckle burbled inside. He wasn't the groom she'd pictured as a young woman, but neither was this dress.

In junior high, her friend Heidi's older sister, Monica, had gotten married, and Monica had given the two junior highers her well-worn bridal magazines when she was through. Cheryl and Heidi had spent hours flipping through the pages and picking out every detail of their someday weddings. Heidi had always selected ball gowns that hit below her knees with layers of ruffles, but Cheryl had loved the dresses with long lace trains covered in glimmering sequins. A slight smile touched Cheryl's lips at the memory.

Her real wedding dress couldn't be more different with a high collar and cap sleeves. The dress barely touched the tops of her shoes, and there wasn't a sequin in sight. At least she'd gotten lace.

Cheryl zipped it back up and released a heavy sigh, thankful for Levi. He was kind and gentle, hard-working and honest. She couldn't imagine wanting to give her life, her heart to anyone else. *Thank you, Lord.* In just eight days…

Eight days. The reality caused Cheryl to straighten her shoulders. Eight days to get everything in the store in shape before she left for a week-long honeymoon. Eight days to finish her wedding to-do list too. She'd made a new list last night, trying to capture on paper each detail swirling around her mind. Cheryl thought it would help to see it all written out, but it did the opposite. All the small tasks added up to two pages. Picking up her clipboard she opened the door, stepped out of the office, flipped off the light, and shut the door behind her. She didn't have time to daydream or dawdle, not if she wanted this wedding to go off without a hitch.

Walking to the front of the store, Cheryl unlocked the front door and flipped the sign to Open. She then moved to the counter, placed her clipboard on it, and then lit a candle. Peppermint lemongrass. Its fresh, clean scent was becoming her favorite. She'd just returned the lighter to the drawer when the front door opened.

A deliveryman walked in wearing a brown uniform and a wide smile. A large satchel filled with packages was slung over his shoulder, and his nametag read Brad. Cheryl didn't remember seeing him before, but he looked official. Even though it was still morning, a line of sweat glistened on his forehead brought by the July heat. He paused just inside the door and wiped it away. "It's already hot as blazes out there. At least you have it nice and cool in the shop." He approached the counter.

"It's supposed to cool off by next week. I'm stalking the local weather page." Cheryl prayed the forecast didn't change, or her outdoor wedding could be miserable as the gorgeous dress wilted in the sun.

He wiped his brow with his sleeve. "Let's hope it does."

"Would you like a bottle of cold water? I have some in the back."

"I thought about stopping by for something to drink at the Honey Bee, but if you don't mind..." He smacked his dry lips.

"Not at all."

He pulled out two packages and placed them on the counter as Cheryl hurried to the back. She opened the door to the small refrigerator and took out a bottle of water. When she returned, the man was still searching through the satchel. "I could have sworn it was right here...," he mumbled and then shook his head.

"Lose something?"

"Oh, I didn't lose anything. That's not the way this company operates." He knocked on the counter. "But I thought I had three packages for you. Must have been mistaken."

"Is one from Oregon?" She reached for the two packages he'd set on the counter. "My grandmother's wedding ring should be arriving any day. My mother promised she'd send it, and I really need it this week." If it arrived by then, she'd have just enough time to get it sized if needed. But when she looked at the return addresses, both were from friends who lived in Columbus—gifts from friends at her old church who couldn't attend the wedding.

"From the look on your face, neither is from Oregon."

"Sadly, no." She sighed. "I told my mom to bring the ring with her when she came, but she insisted it needed to arrive early." She wrinkled her nose. "At this rate she'll arrive before the ring does." And time was running out for the ring to arrive before the wedding.

He readjusted his satchel. "Maybe it'll arrive tomorrow. I'll most likely see you then." He wiped his brow again.

"I hope so. See you..."

He rushed out the door, and Cheryl watched him go, wondering if she should have asked him to look through his satchel one more time. "If he does find it in there, I'm sure he'll be back," she mumbled to herself. "Or—like he said—tomorrow."

She was turning back to her list when her gaze was drawn to a young woman walking by the window of the Swiss Miss. At first Cheryl thought she was looking at the display because she walked with slow, deliberate steps. But she wasn't. Cheryl was almost certain the young woman was looking deeper into the store. The woman couldn't be more then twenty-five years old. She was tall with a narrow face and light brown hair pulled back into a low ponytail. Her complexion was milky smooth, and her large blue eyes were inquisitive.

What in the world is she looking at?

A camera hung around her neck, and she looked like a tourist, although something about the young woman's face looked vaguely familiar but Cheryl couldn't place why.

Cheryl moved toward the door. *Should I invite her inside?* Obviously the woman was looking for something. She got halfway to the door when the young woman spotted her and jumped. Her eyes widened, and she tucked something inside her camera case before hurrying away. Cheryl's brow furrowed, and she continued to the door, opening it and stepping out on to the sidewalk.

The hot sun beat down, and Cheryl shielded her eyes. Her gaze followed the woman's quickened steps. Who in the world was the young woman? Why did she seem so startled to see Cheryl, and what had she so quickly tucked into her camera bag? Surely she couldn't have swiped the box from the deliveryman's bulging satchel. *No, I just need to stop worrying. The ring must be en route. It has to be.*

Cheryl was about to step back inside the store when she heard the familiar clopping of a horse's steps and the rumble of buggy wheels. Cheryl looked over her shoulder, and her heart leaped to see Levi pulling up. Thankfully there was an open parking spot in front of the store, and he parked the buggy and jumped down. His smile was wide, and seeing it pushed the worries from her mind.

"Well, hello there. It's a surprise to see you," she called to him. She opened the door and walked inside. He quickly followed her. The door barely shut when he pulled her into a hug. She lifted her face to him.

"How's the future Mrs. Miller?" he said in a husky whisper. His blue eyes were filled with so much tenderness, so much love. Cheryl was sure she was the luckiest woman in the world.

"*Goot* now that you're here," she stated, practicing her Pennsylvania Dutch.

"Oh *ja*. I like to hear that. But things weren't goot before I arrived? Surely you are relishing every moment of your last days as a single woman." His eyebrows rose with the question.

"Do you really want to see my list?" Over his shoulder she noticed tourists walking down the sidewalk, gazing in through the window. She pulled back from his embrace and rubbed her forehead. "I didn't sleep well last night thinking about it all. There are so many things to do between now and our day."

He reached over, caressed her cheek, and tipped up her chin until her eyes met his. "Now, Cheryl. Wipe away that frown. You will complete what needs to be done."

"I hope so."

"And if you do not, we will still get married...even if you marry me in the dress you wear now. In fact, we should run to the church now and forget all the fuss. Why do women need elaborate plans anyway?"

"Oh, Levi." She chuckled. "Don't I wish? I'd never hear the end of it from my mother...or your mother for that matter. I'm not sure whether Mom or Naomi is more excited. I think it might be a tie."

"That is good. It will be a wonderful day—the best of my life—but before then I have a few more things for you to do." Her eyes widened, and her shoulders drooped. Seeing that, Levi chuckled. "Oh, do not worry. It is not hard, I promise. I need your opinion on some flooring samples for the house." The excitement on his face was clear.

This wonderful man really loves me. How can I be so blessed?

"Flooring samples, *uh-hum*." She tapped her lower lip. "I think I can handle that."

"Goot." He hurried to the counter and reached deep into the pocket of his overalls. "I know you said you like the lighter wood for the floors, but I was not sure if you liked the honey color or the one that is more white. Both are nice."

She looked at the two colors. He was right. Either would look great. The bell on the front door rang as she picked up the two samples. "Welcome to the Swiss Miss!" she called over her shoulder.

"Thank you!" a familiar voice called back. It was Levi's younger sister, Esther.

The young woman hurried forward. "I have never felt so welcome." Then she looked closer at the wood in Cheryl's hand. "Oh, are those the flooring samples that you were telling *Maam* about?"

"They are."

"Which do you like, Cheryl?" Esther asked, leaning in. "I think I like the more golden one."

Cheryl lifted that one up closer, noticing how the light gleamed off it. "Levi called it honey. I think I like it best too."

"Are you sure?" Levi leaned close. "I do not want you to pick because Esther likes it."

"No, this is my favorite, the one I like best. Don't you think it'll make the house warm and inviting?"

"I think *you* will make our home warm and inviting...but the floors will look nice too."

Esther chuckled. "Oh bother, listen to you two. I am ready for that wedding already. In fact..."

The ring of the telephone interrupted Esther's words. "I will get that." She moved to the phone.

Levi tucked the samples back into his pocket. "Honey it is...and it will look lovely. Just like you."

Cheryl soaked in the words. Soaked in the tenderness in his gaze. Esther talked on the phone in the background, but at that moment all Cheryl wanted to think about was Levi.

Too soon Esther hung up the phone and turned to her. "Cheryl, that was the florist, and she sounded upset." Esther moved to where Cheryl and Levi stood. "She says you are needed at the shop as soon as possible. A large delivery has arrived in your name."

"A large delivery? I don't understand. I thought we were using flowers from around the farm with just a few things from the florist?"

"Yes, well, you better talk to her. She asked that you come to the shop right away. She seemed miffed that you did not let her know you completely changed the floral designs."

"Completely changed the designs?" Cheryl scratched her head. "I haven't confirmed anything yet. How can I change something I didn't finalize in the first place?"

Esther shrugged. "I am not sure, but I will cover the store while you figure it out."

"Thank you, Esther. I'm afraid I'll be asking you to do that a lot this week." Frustration built with Cheryl's every word—of all the times to have an unexpected complication arise. Her to-do list was already a page too long to get everything accomplished in time. Then she felt Levi slide his hand into hers.

"It is worth it, right?" There was softness in Levi's voice and a twinkle in his eyes that immediately reminded her what all this preparation was really about.

She squeezed his hand. "Of course, Levi. All the busyness. All the craziness will be worth it when I'm walking down that aisle and you're waiting at the end."

If I can just survive until then, she wanted to add. *Dear Lord, help me survive until then.*

A Note from the Editors

We hope you enjoyed Sugarcreek Amish Mysteries, published by the Books and Inspirational Media Division of Guideposts, a nonprofit organization that touches millions of lives every day through products and services that inspire, encourage, help you grow in your faith, and celebrate God's love.

Thank you for making a difference with your purchase of this book, which helps fund our many outreach programs to military personnel, prisons, hospitals, nursing homes, and educational institutions.

We also create many useful and uplifting online resources. Visit Guideposts.org to read true stories of hope and inspiration, access OurPrayer network, sign up for free newsletters, download free e-books, join our Facebook community, and follow our stimulating blogs.

To learn about other Guideposts publications, including the best-selling devotional *Daily Guideposts*, go to Guideposts.org/Shop, call (800) 932-2145, or write to Guideposts, PO Box 5815, Harlan, Iowa 51593.

Sign up for the
Guideposts Fiction Newsletter
and stay up-to-date on the books you love!

You'll get sneak peeks of new releases, recommendations from other Guideposts readers, and special offers just for you . . .

and it's FREE!

Just go to Guideposts.org/Newsletters today to sign up.

Find more inspiring fiction in these best-loved Guideposts series!

Mysteries of Martha's Vineyard

Come to the shores of this quaint and historic island and dig into a cozy mystery. When a recent widow inherits a lighthouse just off the coast of Massachusetts, she finds exciting adventures, new friends, and renewed hope.

Tearoom Mysteries

Mix one stately Victorian home, a charming lakeside town in Maine, and two adventurous cousins with a passion for tea and hospitality. Add a large scoop of intriguing mystery and sprinkle generously with faith, family, and friends, and you have the recipe for Tearoom Mysteries.

Sugarcreek Amish Mysteries

Be intrigued by the suspense and joyful "aha!" moments in these delightful stories. Each book in the series brings together two women of vastly different backgrounds and traditions, who realize there's much more to the "simple life" than meets the eye.

Mysteries of Silver Peak

Escape to the historic mining town of Silver Peak, Colorado, and discover how one woman's love of antiques helps her solve mysteries buried deep in the town's checkered past.

Patchwork Mysteries

Discover that life's little mysteries often have a common thread in a series where every novel contains an intriguing whodunit centered around a quilt located in a beautiful New England town.

To learn more about these books, visit Guideposts.org/Shop